Acclaim for Steve Yarbrough's

Prisoners of War

"Yarbrough . . . is a sophisticated, gentle writer with a
gift for subtlety. The latent heat of a Delta autumn
wafts through his Southern memories. . . . His characters are superbly fleshed out, and his setting so
richly drawn that when the action crosses the
county line late in the book, the reader might feel as
if he is leaving his own hometown."

—*The Denver Post*

"We can't help but see ourselves in [these characters],
feeling the shackles of our own time and circumstances around our own ankles and wrists. . . . A
compelling story [that] provides a mirror for us to
look back at ourselves, at our own worlds and lives,
more carefully." —*Richmond Times-Dispatch*

"The rural South of Steve Yarbrough's hypnotic third
novel, *Prisoners of War*, is like nothing you've ever
seen in Southern letters. . . . Yarbrough weaves a
page-turner." —*Ft. Myers News-Press*

"Animated by superbly fleshed-out characters and
richly drawn settings." —*San Jose Mercury News*

STEVE YARBROUGH

Prisoners of War

Steve Yarbrough's honors include the Mississippi Authors Award, the California Book Award, and a third from the Mississippi Institute of Arts and Letters. The author of two previous novels and three collections of stories, he is a native of the Delta town of Indianola and now lives in Fresno, California.

Prisoners of War

WAR
Prisoners of

A   N O V E L

To Brown—

STEVE YARBROUGH

Wishing you much success and happiness—

VINTAGE CONTEMPORARIES
Vintage Books
A Division of Random House, Inc.
New York

FIRST VINTAGE CONTEMPORARIES EDITION, MARCH 2005

Copyright © 2004 by Steve Yarbrough

The Library of Congress has cataloged the Knopf edition as follows:
Yarbrough, Steve, [date]
Prisoners of war / Steve Yarbrough.
p. cm.
1. World War, 1939–1945—Prisoners and prisons, American—Fiction.
2. World War, 1939–1945—Mississippi—Fiction. 3. Delta (Miss.: Region)—
Fiction. 4. Germans—Mississippi—Fiction. 5. Prisoners of War—Fiction.
6. Race relations—Fiction. 7. Teenage boys—Fiction.
8. Mississippi—Fiction. 9. Soldiers—Fiction. 10. Escapes—Fiction.
I. Title.
PS3575 A717P75 2003
813'.54.—dc21   2003040071

Vintage ISBN: 1-4000-3062-5

Book design by Robert C. Olsson

www.vintagebooks.com

Printed in the United States of America
10 9 8 7 6 5 4 3 2 1

For my father

Doubt is a noble thing . . . . The most fervent people are doubters.

—Czeslaw Milosz

Prisoners of War

ONE

THE ROLLING STORE was one of two old school buses his uncle Alvin had bought after they were deemed unsafe to haul children. The one Dan drove in the summer of 1943 had a couple holes in the floorboard. Half the time the starter wouldn't work, and then he'd have to put the transmission in neutral, get out and turn the hand crank. The rear wheels, which had been pulled off a cotton trailer, were bigger than the ones in front, so the bus always looked like it was headed downhill.

His uncle had outfitted each bus with display cases, candy counters, a soft-drink box and a Deepfreeze. Dan and the other driver, L.C., sold farmers and hoe hands everything from chocolate bars and Nehi sodas to coal-oil lamps and radios. Gas rationing had made the routes more successful than they otherwise might have been, since a lot of folks couldn't get into town very often.

Alvin never had any trouble getting gas, because he never had any trouble getting sugar, something the bootleggers couldn't do without. He traded them hundred-pound sacks of it for cases of bootleg whiskey, which in turn he passed on to the members of the local rationing board. "Seem like making tough decisions gives a fellow a case of cotton mouth," Dan had heard him say. "That's the thirstiest bunch of doctors and lawyers and bankers I ever saw."

His uncle had a special knack for handling people, which usually involved satisfying their appetites. You could tell a lot about a man, he always said, by watching what he put in his mouth.

Dan drove into the lot behind Alvin's country store and parked next to the other bus. L.C. finished first every day. His route was shorter, his bus drove a little better and he generally ignored the thirty-five-mile-an-hour speed limit.

Dan had asked him once if he didn't feel bad about breaking the law when everybody else was trying to conserve gas for the troops, and L.C. had wrinkled his nose, as he was apt to whenever something amused him. "Let me ask you, Dan," he said. "Do your uncle feel bad about breaking the law?"

"He don't break it. He just bends it a little."

L.C. laughed. "For him, it bends. But for a nigger, it just too stiff. We working with a lot less flexibility than y'all are."

L.C. said *y'all* a lot, and *we,* constantly calling attention to the differences between them. He also liked to employ a phrase he'd heard last Easter, when his momma made him go to church: *parallel universes.* "That's what the preacher say we living in, Dan. You got your universe, I got mine. I see you spinning by, you see me, time to time we both wave, say hey. But never the twain shall meet—and that last part come straight from the Bible." When Dan protested that he couldn't see what the parallel-universe theory had to do with Easter, L.C. said, "Course not.

Over there in y'all's universe, Easter mean colored eggs. But we ain't got no eggs to color. Sure enough interested in that rising part, though."

Today, as always, L.C. was waiting for him, sitting atop the propane tank, his dusty work shoes lying on the ground and his big toe protruding from a hole in one sock. "How much you sold, Dan?"

"Took in close to thirty dollars."

L.C. whistled. "That's the profitable route. I had me that route, I'd be tempted to steal your old uncle blind."

"You could steal from him anyway, if you got a mind to."

"Naw. I take from him, he might take from me."

"What could he take? You ain't got nothing anyway, far as I can tell."

"Got myself. He could take and give it to the army."

"Army don't want it. They got all the bus drivers they need. Army wants fighting men."

"Army'll make the niggers fight, before it's all said and done. You know old Jeff Davis wanted the same thing in the Civil War, make the niggers march with Robert Lee?"

"Who told you that?"

L.C. looked at him. "Just imagine my granddaddy covering your granddaddy's ass while he go crawling out the bushes toward them Yankees."

"You ain't got a granddaddy."

"Everybody got a granddaddy," L.C. said. You could almost see the curtain falling over his face. Sooner or later, the banter always turned serious, and Dan could never quite figure out when it was going to happen in time to shut his mouth.

L.C. jumped down, all business now, and slipped on his shoes. Together, they carried the small Deepfreezes off the buses and balanced them, one at a time, on a handcart, then rolled them over to the tractor shed that served as his uncle's warehouse and plugged them in. Next day they'd restock them with ice-cream sandwiches, fruit Popsicles, pig tails and neck bones.

After they washed up at the sink, L.C. said he was going home, and he set off down the road. Dan walked around to the front of the store and saw his father's old pickup parked near the porch. He opened the screen door and stepped inside.

The place smelled of molasses, salt meat, leather and patent medicine. Horse collars, trace chains and hame straps hung on the walls, and the shelves were filled with canned goods and hardware. Toward the rear, stacked almost to the ceiling, were several hundred cases of sanitary napkins—all the sanitary napkins, his uncle said, in the Delta. He'd concocted some deal with a distributor over in Greenville that allowed him, at least briefly, to corner the market, and women had been streaming into the store for days, coming in groups of four and five from as far away as Clarksdale and Yazoo City, buying in bulk.

The store was empty except for L.C.'s momma, Rosetta, who sat behind the cash register, fanning herself with a copy of *Negro Digest*. "Where L.C. go off to?" she asked.

"Went on home."

"Now that ain't nothing but a bald-face lie." Her eyes followed a fly that buzzed back and forth above the till. "Question is, L.C. lie to you or get you to lie to me?"

Dan walked over to the counter, lifted the top off a big jar and grabbed a handful of oatmeal cookies. "I don't believe L.C. lies to me," he said.

"Course he do. And lying within limits is all right."

"That ain't what it says in the Bible."

"Colored folks' Bible or white folks'?"

"I thought we was all using the same one."

The fly made the mistake of lighting on the counter. Rosetta reached over with her magazine and swatted it. "Y'all's Bible may be the same book," she said, flicking the body off the cover, "but the words got a whole different meaning."

"You saying it's all right for L.C. to lie to white folks but not colored?"

"There's niggers I've knowed forty years and ain't yet spoke a word of truth to. I'm saying it's not all right to lie to his *momma*."

"Our Bible don't make them kinds of distinctions," Dan said. "I reckon the Lord was scared we'd get confused." Stuffing a cookie into his mouth, he walked over to the back of the store and opened the door to his uncle's office.

His mother was sitting on the edge of his desk, her long, smooth legs hanging off the far side, and his uncle was in the coaster chair. It looked like maybe they'd been disagreeing about something, because his mother's face was flushed. She had the milky white complexion that often accompanies red hair, and if she got agitated, you could always tell.

His uncle, though, seemed perfectly calm, maybe even a little amused. His hands were locked behind his head, and he'd rocked back in the coaster chair and crossed his legs. One end of his mustache was arched just a little, like he was doing his best not to grin. "How'd it go today, partner?" he said.

"Not too bad. I'm starting to have a problem with that Deepfreeze, though."

"What kind of problem?"

"Had to throw out a few Popsicles and some of the ice cream—the stuff thawed out and started running. That freezer may have a bad seal on it."

"Naw, there ain't nothing wrong with that freezer. It's just too damn hot. Thermometer on the wall outside hit a hundred by three o'clock." Alvin's eyes had that little gleam that appeared whenever he'd figured out a way to get something for nothing. "Tell you what you do, Daniel. You know the old gin up there at Fairway Crossroads?"

"The one that went out of business?"

"Yep. You probably get to Fairway along about eating time. Well, I happen to know the power's still on at the gin. So tomorrow, carry you an extension cord and pull up there to the loading dock. The outlet's right there beside the door to the press room. Plug that Deepfreeze in and set back and eat you a good long lunch, and when you're through, that freezer'll be nice and cold again."

His mother looked over at him. "You may have to run me up to Memphis the beginning of next week, Dan. I was trying to get your uncle to do it, but he claims he doesn't have time."

"No," Alvin said, "I didn't say I don't have time. I said I *may* not have time. I said just wait a little while and we'll see."

"I don't know that I can wait. That ad in the *Commercial* said they'd be getting the fabric on Monday. It'll go in no time." She got down off the desk and picked up her purse. "I guess pretty soon, the direction things are headed, we'll all be naked."

The springs in Alvin's chair squeaked as he rocked forward and stood up. Taking his cup, giving it a quick sniff, he walked over to the metal urn, drew himself some coffee and took a long swallow. "I seriously doubt," he said, "that anybody's going naked."

TWO

BEHIND THE WHEEL, his mother posed a threat to herself as well as everybody else, so he drove home. When they pulled into the yard, he cut the motor, and for a minute or two they just sat there. More often than not, neither one of them wanted to go inside the house, preferring instead to postpone walking through the door into all that silence.

He thought of that instant as one of confrontation and imagined she did, too, though what she confronted, he suspected, was a lot different from what he had to face. He believed, too, that she could name her problem and could've recited in her mind a whole set of specific actions or nonactions that had brought it to pass. Whereas his problems were vague, ill-defined. He didn't like where he was, and he didn't like what he'd most likely become if he managed to survive the war that was waiting for him a few months down the road. But he didn't know where else, or what else, he'd rather be. His imagination, he guessed, was a lot like an acre of buckshot. Nothing much grew there.

He opened his door and got out, as did his mother. Brushing a loose strand from her eyes, she looked at him across the hood of the truck. "I thawed out a couple pork chops," she said. "How does that sound?"

"All right."

"Just all right?"

"It sounds good," he said.

"Good," she said. "I'm glad you think so."

Inside, she stepped quickly into the kitchen. He kicked off his shoes and set them on a few sheets of old newspaper in the corner of the living room. His father had always done that when he came in from the field, and Dan wanted everything left just the way it had been when his father was alive.

The one time he and his mother had fought was the day he saw her boxing up a bunch of his father's pants and shirts, getting ready to carry them to the church for the clothing drive. He'd pulled the box from her hands, dumped the clothes on the bed, thrown the box on the floor and stomped it flat. She slapped his face that day, then burst into tears and locked herself in the bathroom. She didn't come out for hours, no matter how hard he begged. When she finally did emerge, her eyes were dry and her voice steady. "Okay, have it your way," she said. "But if you mean to be treated like the man of the house, you need to go ahead and be one."

She'd opened a bottle of his uncle's whiskey, and Dan had sat beside her on the couch, sipping at his drink while she poured herself one after another. He'd drunk beer a couple times but had never tasted whiskey and didn't know how it burned in your nose; his mother laughed every time he took a swallow.

She told a lot of stories that night about folks he'd never heard of, people she'd known growing up down in Jackson or met at dances she'd been to. Some colored musicians from

New Orleans, she said, used to come through once a year, and she and a few of her friends would slip off to a roadhouse just outside Raymond and watch them play instruments she'd never seen before. One of them had some kind of long silver pipe that made the eeriest sounds you'd ever heard; he'd get down on his knees while he played, blowing sound right into the floor.

She talked until she began to slur her words, then yawned and tried to stand. After helping her to bed, he walked out back and made himself throw up, just to get the taste out of his mouth.

Tonight they ate without saying much, and while he was clearing the dishes, she went into the living room and stuck a Roy Acuff record on the phonograph. "Come on in here," she called. "Let's listen to some music."

He figured she'd have the whiskey out again, and he was right. A bottle and a pair of glasses stood on the coffee table, next to the illustrated Bible that had belonged to his grandmother. He walked over, picked the bottle up and set it on an end table.

She watched him the whole time. "Jesus turned the water into wine," she said.

"He didn't turn it into moonshine."

"This is *not* moonshine." She examined the label on the bottle. "This is bonded whiskey, a hundred and one proof, made legally in Claremont, Kentucky."

"Maybe it's legal to make it there, but it ain't to drink it here."

She poured some into one of the glasses. "Well, then go

ahead and turn me in." She lifted the glass and took a swallow, then coughed and held a hand to her mouth, her eyes watering.

He realized she didn't like the taste of it, either, and sat down on the couch. "Rosetta's worried about L.C."

"How come?"

"I believe she thinks he's getting ready to run off."

"Where would he run to?"

"I don't know. He talks a good bit about Chicago and Detroit, places like that."

"Well, if he leaves here, it won't be any time till he gets picked up." She took another swallow. "He hasn't got a selective service card, and he's eighteen."

"He didn't register?"

"Of course not. Your uncle cut a deal for him."

"Who with?"

Instead of answering, she said, "He could do the same thing for you, and it'd be a whole lot easier. He might not even have to make a deal at all. Because you're the only man in the—"

"The day I turn eighteen," he said, "I'm gone."

"Well, I believe you've said as much before."

The needle on the record player reached the end of the song, so she got up and flipped the record over and Acuff started singing "The Great Speckled Bird," with a weeping steel guitar in the background.

When she bent over to pick up her glass, he could see down the front of her dress. She had small breasts, and there was a bunch of freckles near the top of her brassiere. As a boy, he'd often tried to get a glimpse of her naked. Now the sight of her secrets just embarrassed him, as if he'd walked into the bathroom and found her sitting on the toilet.

She took another sip, then set the glass back on the table. "Get up and dance with me," she said.

"It's not the kind of music you dance to."

"You can dance to anything," she said, "as long as you've got a partner."

She took his hand. At first he resisted, but she wouldn't let go, so he finally stood, and she pulled one of his arms around her waist. He didn't know a thing about dancing, but he let her push him gently around the room while she hummed along with the music. Her breath smelled sweet, like her mouth was full of sugar. The top of her head grazed his chin, and her hair was damp. Once or twice he felt her heart beat.

"Lord," she said, "I'd forgotten what it's like to be with a boy your age. You always shut your eyes and make believe he's older."

That night, he dreamed of his father.

They were riding in the pickup, as they often were in dreams, and his father was looking out the window he'd rolled halfway down. He was saying something about rain, how there'd been too much or too little—Dan couldn't be sure which, because the wind was whipping in and his father's voice was muffled. He sat staring at the back of his father's head, his neck burned bronze by the hot Delta sun.

He was young in the dream, maybe only eight or nine, and he'd decided that when his father turned around, he'd ask if they could drive all the way to the Western Auto and get a new baseball bat, since his old one was a piece of junk. He wouldn't sound too insistent about it, wouldn't act like it meant the world to him or anything. He'd just raise the topic and see what his father said; and if he said no, or said nothing, as he sometimes did, that would be all right, too.

Finally, his father turned around. But it would not be accurate to say that he faced him, because his father's face was gone.

THREE

THE NEXT AFTERNOON, just east of town, he saw a man in uniform walking along the side of the road. The soldier's back was to him, but as Dan got closer, something about the man began to seem familiar. He was tall, and he walked with his right fist propped on his rib cage, so his arm stuck out like the handle on a coffee cup. He had a duffel bag slung over his left shoulder. Once or twice, he moved his head in a circle, as if trying to work a kink out of his neck.

When the rolling store stopped and the door swung open, Marty Stark looked up. His eyes were bloodshot, and a front tooth had been chipped. He'd lost a lot of weight. Dan hadn't heard anything about him getting wounded, and couldn't imagine why in the world he'd been shipped home. A little over two months ago, at the hardware store, Mr. Stark had told him that Marty had gone ashore in Sicily with Patton's Seventh Army.

"What the hell are you doing here?" Dan blurted.

"Just walking down the road."

"You must've dropped thirty pounds. Army wouldn't feed you?"

"*Au contraire*, son. Army's fed me plenty." He let the duffel bag slide off his shoulder, then heaved it up into the bus. "Been feeding me a mouthful of chickenshit every day for fifteen months, but that won't keep the weight up." He stepped back and glanced at the black clouds billowing from the tailpipe. "Engine sounds like a dog trying to puke," he said. "What're you doing driving this high-tailed heap?"

"Just helping out."

"Helping who out?"

"Uncle Alvin."

"How come you ain't in the cotton patch? Your old lady sell the farm?"

It was hard for Dan to think of his mother as anybody's old lady, and even harder to believe Marty thought of her that way. He'd once told Dan he considered her the nicest-looking woman in Loring, Mississippi, and didn't care if she was nearly forty, that he still wouldn't mind running off with her somewhere. Dan had come within an inch of saying he wasn't the only one to harbor that ambition.

"Can't sell what you don't own," he said. "Bank owns the place now. But me and Uncle Alvin'll get the picking done this year. He's already made arrangements for a POW detail from Camp Loring."

Quietly, Marty said, "I heard about your daddy."

"Yeah, I figured."

"I sure am sorry."

"Yeah, me too."

Marty pointed at the silver insignia on Dan's shirt pocket. "You in the State Guard?"

"For now. I'll be eligible to join up in December."

"Ain't no reason to rush it."

That was easy enough to say as long as you weren't driving a rolling store all day, then going home every night to the house Dan lived in. "Your daddy said you'd been in heavy combat," he said. "What's it like?"

"Plain *combat* wasn't strong enough—he had to stick something else in front of it?" Marty planted a boot on the bottom step. "Let's put it this way, pal. It didn't have much in common with an opening kickoff."

"I didn't figure it would have."

"You didn't? I sure did. And boy, was I one dumb monkey. Too stupid for the circus but just right for the zoo." He jammed his hands in his pockets, then pulled them out and looked down at them—first at the left one, then at the right, as if he didn't know why they weren't in his pockets—before putting them back in again. "I come off that LST, and you know what I asked myself? 'Where are the fucking cheerleaders?' Can you believe it? 'Where's the band, and the water boy? And how come the other team can see me when I can't see hide nor hair of them? Where are the goddamn referees, huh?' And you know what? Ain't one of them questions been answered yet. Not a damn one." The engine idled, burning gas, but he made no move to climb the steps. Again he worked his head around in a circle, then moved it up and down a couple times. "Man, I been on that train all the way from New Jersey. Every tooth in my head's about to come loose."

"You get a medical discharge?"

"Naw, no such luck." Grabbing the handrail, he finally climbed up inside. "I'm traveling under delayed orders. Got till Friday morning before I report to my next posting."

"So where's that at?"

Marty slid the lid of the drink box open, reached in, sloshed some bottles around and pulled out an RC, stuck the neck in the opener and popped off the cap. Turning the bottle up, he started swigging, stopping only when the drink was all gone.

He set the bottle down and wiped his mouth on his shirt-sleeve. "I'll be out at the Fritz Ritz," he said, "guarding the fucking Krauts."

Dan pulled over at the end of the Starks' driveway. Mr. Stark's white Cadillac stood parked near the house, and his pickup truck was there, too. Their black lab, Lucy, lay on the veranda, her head lifted now as she watched the rolling store.

Marty shouldered his duffel bag and told Dan he'd be in touch in a few days, once he got squared away, that when he had liberty they'd go over to Greenville to drink some beer and shoot pool. Then he stood there at the top of the steps, looking out over the yard where he'd played as a boy, as if unwilling now to set foot in it.

FOUR

A T FIRST GLANCE, the camp didn't amount to much more than three or four rows of tents and five or six buildings, surrounded by a double barbed-wire fence. At the MP training center, he'd been told that all camps had to be situated at least five hundred feet from any road, but only a shallow ditch separated this one from Highway 47. The fences, which were supposed to be at least eight feet high, might've been six and a half feet but were probably less; a bad pole-vaulter could have made it over with no trouble, and a good high jumper would have had a decent chance.

Guard towers stood on the north and south sides of the camp, both of them empty that morning. Anybody caught in there during a thunderstorm was in for an exciting time, since somebody, probably an army engineer, had put on tin roofs.

His father parked a short distance from the gates. "Well, Martin," he said, "you got everything you need?"

His mother had asked him the same thing his first night back, posing her question while he stood before the mirror in his old bedroom, getting ready to go down to the colored part of town and find himself a whore. He'd always heard they were down there, standing on the street corners, their dark legs exposed. He wanted to take his clothes off in a hot, dirty room with a woman he didn't know, especially one who had all the reason in the world to hold a thousand things against him. A woman whose sinew would ripple beneath his body with disgust.

That night, he'd told his mother that no, he didn't have everything he needed. When she asked him what was missing, he meant to make a joke and say he needed to rent Clark Gable's face. But after remembering how Raymond Sample's had just disappeared, his features dissolving into a scarlet mass of meat, he couldn't keep his lips from quivering like they had on the Niscemi road, and he said he was missing himself. That much he could say to his mother, though he wished he hadn't, because it made her cry. But he couldn't say it to his father, however much he wished he could.

"No, sir," he said. "Don't have my discharge papers, and I sure do need 'em."

His father stared hard into the distance. "The army can't discharge you from responsibility, Martin. You got to face that for the rest of your life, whether you wear a uniform or not."

The only uniform his father had ever worn was the dark suit he put on every Sunday morning, when he went to church and listened to the preacher condemn folks for drinking liquor, or lying, or coveting their neighbors' wives; then he went back home and took it off, and felt free to get drunk, screw Mrs. Bivens from down the street and lie about it all day long.

But some uniforms were not shed so easily. Some uniforms stuck to you.

Marty reached under the seat for the pint bottle he'd left there last night. He drank the last inch or so, then put the bottle back. Now his father was looking at him, and that was all he'd really wanted.

"Showing up with whiskey on your breath's not likely to stand you in good stead with your commanding officer. For your information, he's a graduate of the United States Military Academy."

"Yeah, but he's stateside."

"*You're* stateside."

"But I want to be, and he doesn't."

"How do you know where he wants to be?"

"I know *exactly*. He wants to be about a hundred yards beyond the last rung of a ladder barrage, where he can feel the ground shaking under his feet when them eighty-eights hit. Maybe even a little closer, so he can dodge some nonlethal debris while he barks orders into a field telephone. He wants to wave his arms around and point at a little rise in the distance with a machine-gun barrel poking up over it, then watch his boys run right at it. And when the two or three of 'em that don't have their guts falling out their shirtfronts get close enough to pitch a few grenades and cause a little weeping and moaning someplace like Hamburg, he wants to run forward his own self. That's where he wants to be. Not in Loring, Mississippi, commanding what looks like a run-down church camp."

His father was thumping the wheel with an index finger.

"I was hoping for bedpan duty," Marty said. "Could've got it, too, if the division psychiatrist hadn't worried about me running loose in a base hospital, drinking all that rubbing alcohol. I figure if you can handle Mississippi 'shine, anything else ought to slide right down."

"Martin," his father said, "I don't know what to say to you."

"Well, to start with, you might tell me about how my great-granddaddy helped roll up Howard's flank at Chancellorsville. You could put him on a big white stallion, with a bunch of gold braid on his uniform and a cavalry saber that's got engraving on the hilt, and he's right there beside Stonewall Jackson and Little Sorrell when them Tarheels get all confused in the darkness and bring old Stonewall down. Hell, you could let Stonewall speak his dying words to *him*. What was it, now? 'Let us cross over the river and rest in the shade of the trees'? Nobody I ever saw die said anything like that."

"Go on and get out, Martin," his father said, then glanced over his shoulder to see if the lane behind him was clear. "I need to get down to the headquarters. Picking season's coming, like it or not."

Marty climbed out, shut his door, then walked around and opened the trunk. Reaching for his duffel bag, he noticed the corner of a red foil wrapper sticking out from under the mat next to one of the wheel wells, and he pulled it loose. A Trojan, designed for both comfort and protection.

Lifting the mat, he discovered four more, all of which he stuffed into his pocket. Then he hoisted the duffel bag onto his shoulder, slammed the trunk shut and snapped off a salute while staring at the rearview mirror.

If his father noticed, he didn't let on. He put the car in gear, made a U-turn and drove back toward town, quite possibly to visit Mrs. Bivens.

THE COMMANDING officer—Captain Munson—appeared to be about thirty, a short sandy-haired man decked out in class A's, his tie tucked in between the second and third buttons.

Two color photographs in easel frames occupied a corner of his desk, positioned at an angle, so you could see the faces while awaiting your orders. One picture showed an attractive young woman whose chin was propped against her fist, the other a little red-haired girl with an enormous smile that revealed she was missing all but one of her front teeth. Just a few inches from the second photo lay a bone-handled .45, snug in its canvas holster.

Munson made a point of staring at the file open before him. He paged backwards through it a couple times, as if he couldn't quite believe something he'd read and was looking to correct his misunderstanding. Finally, he raised his head. "This is a little bit unusual."

"What is, sir?"

"Sending a man to pull MP duty in his hometown. Especially one with your particular . . . experiences."

"Yes sir."

"Though I'm sure Fourth Service has good reasons."

"Yes sir."

"Any idea what those reasons might be?"

"No sir."

Munson frowned. "Your father owns that big plantation out on Choctaw Creek?"

"Yes sir."

"I believe I know him by sight. Drives a white Cadillac, if he's the man I'm thinking of. I believe I've seen him at—" Munson never finished his sentence, interrupted by a burst of guttural syllables.

The captain gazed at him as if wondering whether he would piss or shit himself, weep or foam at the mouth. If the son of a bitch actually knew how it felt when piss ran down your leg—how you initially assumed it couldn't be what it was, that surely somebody had stolen up behind you and poured warm water under your waistband—he might have had the good grace to keep his eyes averted.

You never got so scared you couldn't be embarrassed, but he wouldn't know that. He'd assume that if a shell burst nearby, the stain on the seat of your pants would cease to matter once you discovered you were still alive. He probably even figured that later you and your pals would float a few jokes about Hershey bars and hip pockets.

Munson watched him for another moment or two, then rose and stepped over to the window. Three shirtless POWs who'd been painting the quarters next door were laughing, horsing around, one of them cocking a dripping brush as if intending to fling a few gobs on his buddy. The skin stretched tautly over their bodies, revealing bone and muscle.

Munson rapped his knuckles on the windowpane. The prisoner brandishing the brush whispered something, and one of the others laughed; then they all bent over and went back to work.

Satisfied, the captain turned and leaned against his desk. "All right, Private," he said. "There's not likely to be much around here that'll surprise you. Reveille's at oh-five-thirty. Breakfast at oh-six hundred. Prisoners return to their tents after breakfast. They shave and use the latrine, police the grounds, and at oh-seven-thirty they go to their work assignments.

"Once the farmers begin picking cotton, we'll need every available man in the fields. The contractors provide the prisoners' lunches, which they'll eat wherever they're hired out. They leave work locations at sixteen hundred, get back here, shower and put on their German uniforms, then eat dinner at eighteen hundred. After dinner, they're free till lights-out.

"As of today, we have three hundred and four prisoners. Most of these fellows were captured in North Africa, though a few trickled in last week from Sicily. My own opinion is that the vast majority are probably neither strongly anti-Nazi nor strongly pro-Nazi, but most of them *were* in the Afrika Korps, so officially we assume they're all Nazis.

"We've had one or two instances in which a group of prisoners administered beatings that may have been ideologically motivated, but various factors indicate to me that they weren't much more than pranks. We found one guy who'd been whipped pretty good and then shackled to a toilet seat with his pants down around his ankles—that kind of thing. Whoever tied him up had enough rope to hang him twice if they'd wanted to, but clearly they didn't. Of course, we never found out who was responsible. The man who'd been beaten wouldn't talk.

"At the training center, they probably told you the prisoner-to-guard ratio's never supposed to be worse than ten to one. Well, right at this minute, we've got eighteen MPs here, nineteen counting you. That's about sixteen to one. It's not going to get any better—and, in fact, it's going to get worse. Soon. They also probably told you that the War Manpower Commission says contract labor goes out in groups of twenty men. But they didn't have the Mississippi Delta in mind. Most of the contracts we've made are with these small farmers, and eighty cents a day per man is pushing them to the limit. For the most part, we've got the prisoners set to go out in groups of eight or ten.

"All the groups are going to be unguarded at least part of the time, and Sergeant Case has worked out a rotation. We'll have single guards accompanying some detachments, whereas other groups will leave in the morning with the contractors, unguarded, and a roving pair of MPs will be checking on them throughout the day. We'll vary the arrangements from one day to the next, so the prisoners themselves never know in advance if they'll be on their own or not.

"Mostly, it's public perception we're worried about—that and the actual welfare of the prisoners. We don't want folks to think we're coddling the enemy, because we're not. But we also don't want to have to report any acts of violence *against* POWs to the Swiss, because they're bound by the Geneva Convention to pass those on to Berlin. And we're worried about the safety of our guys in the German camps.

"The truth is, there's nowhere for these fellows here to go if they do manage to run off. We don't want them walking into a train station in their prison uniforms and getting everybody worked up, but we'd rather not have to report that we shot them while trying to foil an escape. So what I'm saying to you, Private Stark—and I'm going to say it loud and clear, and I want you to tell me if you've got any questions about it in your own mind—is that Fourth Service Command has chosen, for whatever reason, to take a lot of responsibility and place it squarely on your young shoulders. If you think you can't handle it, then you'd better say so right now."

"I don't think I can handle it, sir," Marty said. "In fact, I know I can't."

"I see," Munson said. He moved over to a bookshelf mounted on the wall and stood there examining—or pretending to examine—the titles arrayed before him. Hardy's *Light Infantry Tactics*, Fuller's *Generalship: Its Diseases and Their Cure*, Sandusky's *A Company Leader's Guide to Decisions in the Field*. Plenty of theory for a man spared practice.

"I appreciate your honesty, Private," he said. "But if there's anything good about war, it's this: it gives each of us a chance to overcome our limitations."

"Hilfe! Ich hab mich verfangen!"

On his way to Supply to draw arms, Marty halted and looked in the direction the shout had come from. Off to his right, at the corner of the latrine, a prisoner had gotten the back of his shirt caught on a jagged piece of tin siding. Unable to free himself, he stood there, hollering for somebody to come let him loose. Which apparently nobody had any intention of doing. The three men painting the barracks near the CO's quarters glanced his way but kept right on working, as did the two guys repairing a busted sewer pipe.

In an effort to free his shirt, the prisoner had turned his back to Marty, who walked over, reached out and grasped the fabric. Surprised, the man jumped and looked around, the shirt tearing loose.

The POW was tall and blond, with thick wavy hair. His glasses, which he'd knocked askew in his agitation, sat on his nose at an angle. An angry purple stain, either a birthmark or a rash, covered the right side of his neck and part of his jaw, a single streak flaring up toward his eye. For an instant, the two men stood there, their faces inches apart, and Marty was suddenly far away, on his knees in a ditch where the red water smelled like fish, and this man was standing over him, pointing a rifle at him and screaming, and Marty was begging and pleading. *Don't shoot! Dear God, please!*

"*Danke schön,*" the POW mumbled, straightening his glasses, starting to walk away.

"Wait," Marty said.

The man kept going, his footsteps stirring dust.

"Hey, wait!"

The prisoner stopped, and when he turned around, a glow—almost like a halo, except that it surrounded his whole body—began to emanate from him. Marty felt as if the ground beneath his feet had suddenly tilted, that he was standing at the bottom of an incline, with the other man on top. "Sicily?" he said, the word emerging as little more than a whisper.

For a moment or two, the prisoner just stared, then he said, "*Ich verstehe Sie nicht.*"

"Sicily." Louder this time.

The man held his hands out, palms-up, as if for some reason he believed it was important to show they were empty.

"Sicily. Was that where you got captured?"

"Ich kann nichts verstehen."

"Were you *captured* in *Sicily*?" Marty moved a step closer, and the aura surrounding the other man's body seemed to dissipate. "You were, weren't you?"

The prisoner glanced over at the men painting the barracks, who'd put down their brushes and were watching.

"Nein," he said. *"Nein. Nicht in Sizilien. . . . In Nord-Afrika."*

His eyes never straying from the prisoner's face, Marty Stark slowly dropped to his knees.

SIX

FRANK HOLDER had lost a lot in the last year, and one of the things he didn't have any longer was the radio aerial on his pickup truck. The spindly little thing had gotten bent, and then it had rusted, and one day while he was driving into town to buy some cottonseed, it broke off and flew past his window, and he didn't bother to stop and retrieve it. But he wished he had it, not because he liked listening to the radio—he found the uppity way announcers talked annoying, and considered listening to music a waste of time—but because the aerial would've been the perfect place to attach the flag he now had to drape from his side planks.

His sense of himself as an American was all of six months old. Before that, if you'd asked him what he was, he might have given any number of answers, depending on who was asking, and none of them would've been "American." If it was the preacher from Arva's church, he'd say, "Nothing," because he knew the fellow was trying to trick him into admitting he was a Christian. If it was somebody from Memphis or Jackson, he'd say, "I'm a redneck." And if somebody from New York was fool enough to walk up and ask, he'd say, "I'm a Southerner, and you're not, so why don't you get on back where you come from?"

He now would say he was an American because he wanted to find common ground with his son, and that's how Biggie had always referred to himself in the letters he sent home before getting killed back in February at the Kasserine Pass. He'd said he was proud to serve with the boys in his company, who came from all over, and he never would have known them if they hadn't all come together as Americans, to do what was right for their country. *Some's from Michigan, some's from New York, there's fellows here from Indiana and California and a lot of what you hear about folks from them places is not so. They sound different than us but they're not. It's hard to think your granddaddy fought a war against these people, but I'm glad they're on my side now and me on theirs.*

That Biggie had felt the need to explain why he'd ignored his father's wishes and enlisted was to Frank's great shame. He'd told his own son that he was a goddamn fool and an ingrate, too. "Me and your momma," he'd said, "what did this country ever do for us? We durn near starved to death back in '33 and '34, and ain't nobody got a answer but to wear the Blue Eagle. You know folks was coming down here offering to buy babies if we'd rut one up? That's right. Folks in big long cars, people that couldn't have babies and wasn't meant to, and they wouldn't come inside, they'd stand out there in that goddamn yard and make a offer while they smoked a big old smelly cigar. Happened not once, but twice. Second time, the fellow's wife was in the car herself, and when I told him to get his ass out of my yard and get it out fast, he shakes his head and says folks like us deserve to starve, that we're too ignorant and backward to survive. And you mean to go die for that kind of bastard? You was sitting on the porch at the time, and he didn't want *you,* boy," he'd said, jabbing Biggie so hard in the chest that he almost lost his balance, "because you already had the look of a poor man in your eyes. He wanted him a nice fresh *baby*."

There was scarcely a day, hardly an hour even, when Frank failed to recall that conversation. Every time it came surging back in on him, he wanted to fall to his knees, and if he was where nobody could see him, he did exactly that. He'd knelt down in the cotton patch and in the outhouse; he'd even climbed out of his pickup to kneel in the middle of the road. He wasn't praying when he dropped down, just assuming what he saw as the proper posture for a man who'd called the son he loved names.

He'd been thinking about that conversation shortly before the colored boy who worked for Alvin Timms stopped the bus near his barn. Holder and three of his hands were in the lot, all of them hot and sweaty, trying to shore up sagging joists in the feed shed. Termites had eaten a good bit of the floor, and as he lay on his back looking up through the rotten boards, sweat stinging his eyes, he found himself thinking that the world, when you got right down to it, was just crawling with vermin. If you added up the creatures that served some purpose, like building something or growing food, then added up the ones that were only here to eat and shit, to hurt and kill, you'd see how far out of balance things really were. He was getting to the point where he didn't give a damn at all and would just as soon knock the shed down as shore it up. It could cave in while he was under it, for all he cared.

Then the colored boy parked Alvin's bus on the side of the road and honked the horn—not once, but twice.

His son was dead, the termites were eating his feed shed, his cotton crop was so scrawny that he hated for anybody to see it and a nigger felt like he could pull up to his barn and make a ruckus. "Now if that don't beat the blue-butted devil," he said. "He think he's in Chicago?"

If he'd been the kind of man who reasoned things through, he might have realized that L.C. couldn't see him because he was under the shed, that he could only see three colored men standing in the yard, that if he'd known a white man was within range of that horn, he would never, under any circumstances, have blown it. But Frank Holder applied reason to hard objects only, to a pump that wouldn't prime or a hoe that needed filing.

He pressed his palms against the ground and shoved himself backwards; then, as soon as he'd cleared the shed, he rolled over and bounced up. He was a big man—huge, most folks would've said—and when he began to move in a particular direction, people got out of the way. His hired help scattered fast.

The boy sat at the wheel, fingertips drumming his kneecap, his eyes clamped shut. He was humming.

Frank smacked the side of the bus with an open hand. He figured that would make the boy's eyes pop open like those doors on cuckoo clocks, but for some reason they stayed shut. So he slammed the bus again, setting it rocking on its axles. Then the boy took notice.

"You think that horn's a trumpet, or *what*?"

"No sir," the boy said.

"Think you one of them nigger bandleaders?"

"No sir."

"I like to rose up and hit my head when that damn thing went off. What you in such a goddamn hurry about?"

"Mr. Alvin say tend to business and then get on home."

"Mr. Alvin does, does he?"

"Yes sir."

"Mr. Alvin know you're sitting on the bus with your eyes shut and chanting mumbo jumbo?" The boy just looked at him, and his silence was enraging. "Mr. Alvin tell you that when a white person asks you a question, you supply an answer and make it fast?"

"Yes sir."

"So let's try again, just like before. Because some folks seem like they need to practice. Ready? One, two, three. Mr. Alvin know you're sitting on the bus with your eyes shut and chanting mumbo jumbo?"

"No sir."

"That's better. You been to school, ain't you?"

"Yes sir."

"How much?"

"Seven or eight years' worth."

"Sir."

"Seven or eight years' worth. Sir."

"So you familiar with the concept of being sent home with an assignment?"

"Yes sir. Sir."

Frank considered the possibility that he was being made fun of, then rejected it. The boy was so scared now that he'd probably developed a stutter.

"I'm gone give you an assignment," he said. "Call it a chance to further your education. What I want you to do, when you get through with your route, is to tell Mr. Alvin Timms, 'Sir, I been sitting on that big yellow bus chanting mumbo jumbo. And a gentleman by the name of Mr. Frank Holder done seen it and corrected me.' Think you can do that?"

For just an instant, the boy looked away. Then, as if he realized his answer would be disallowed unless he was staring at an appropriate spot, he aimed his gaze below the man's eyes but above his waist. "Yes sir," he said.

"That's good," Frank said. "Keep improving that comportment and you can't never tell, maybe one day you'll make janitor at the Piggly Wiggly. Ever nigger loves the city."

To send the boy on his way, he slapped the fender again and kicked one of the tires, but even that brought him no pleasure.

SEVEN

SATURDAY NIGHT. There had been a time—not so long ago, either—when those two words, linked together, had possessed magical qualities. Shirley remembered one time in particular. It must have been 1936, because by then they'd quit renting from the Stancills and were living on their own place. Jimmy Del had gone into town that morning to see old man Gaither for the purpose of requesting that year's furnish, but the banker came very close to saying no. As it was, Jimmy Del told her, he'd loaned them enough to get the crop in the ground, but not nearly enough to buy any of the new fertilizers that might actually have made cotton grow on land as poor as theirs. When she asked him what they were going to do now, he tipped his hat back and grinned at her. "Why don't we invite some folks over and build us a big old bonfire?"

They came from all over the community—the Youngs with their hand-cranked Victrola and a bunch of hard-pressed 78s, Luke and Noonie Baker, the Washington brothers and their wives, the Blanchards, Alvin and the store clerk he was seeing. They ate molasses candy with parched peanuts, the kids used a tin can to play stickball and later on, when the young ones had been put to bed, those not opposed to drinking sipped wine made from possum grapes. She got drunk and danced with every man she knew, and Jimmy Del sat there on the porch steps, master of the ball, grinning and cranking that Victrola.

Then the war started—"Yet another of those bastards" was the way he once put it—and he turned morose and brooding and couldn't get along with her or Dan or Alvin or anybody else, either. He'd sit on the back steps for hours at a time, whittling a piece of wood, watching the shavings pile up around his shoes.

And Saturday night came to mean no more than any other.

"You mark my words," Alvin said. "When they look back on this year, they'll say there wasn't a single good movie made. Not a one."

This Saturday night, they were walking down the street past the darkened Western Auto, where several lawn mowers stood on display behind the window. She'd been seeing the same stuff in all the store windows for the longest time, and knew the lack of variety wasn't due solely to a shortage of new products. Most folks had stood all the change they could take and weren't looking for anything new, whereas Shirley had weathered so much change that she wanted a lot more of it. If she'd had her way, she would've torn down every building in town, replacing all of them with bigger, modern-looking structures made of glass and steel. She would've lined the windows with bright lights and filled the shelves with wondrous junk.

She walked as close to Alvin as she dared. Not just because she was on the side nearest the street and a light rain had begun to fall, dripping on her whenever she stepped out from under the awnings, but also because she wanted him to offer his arm. And he wouldn't.

"I liked *Road to Morocco*," she said.

"That was last year."

"Well, then, what about *Mrs. Miniver?*"

"That was last year, too. See, you've proved my point. This is a year to forget."

They passed the dime store and turned the corner onto Loring Avenue. A group of girls came toward them, talking loud and acting silly. As they got closer, a chubby redhead blew a huge bubble, which another girl promptly punctured. Bubble gum clung to the plump girl's face, sending the rest of them into rollicking hysterics. The little redhead peeled some of the gum free and stuck it in the other girl's hair; then all of them took off running, shrieking their lungs out.

"You remember what that felt like, I reckon?" Alvin said as they walked on down the block.

"What?"

"Being the age of them kids."

"More or less."

"I don't. Seem like I've always been forty-two years old."

"Last year, you said it seemed like you'd always been forty-one."

"Well, last year it did. I've always thought it was a shame I wasn't born in 1900, since my body seems to keep such perfect time. If I had've been, everybody could just look at me and tell how old the century was. Then we wouldn't need no calendars."

"I don't need a calendar to tell how old this one is. It's older than any century's got a right to be."

"You saying not all centuries was created equal?"

"They may have been created equal. They just don't stay that way."

The rain fell harder, and by the time they got to the parking lot, it was coming down in sheets. He told her to wait under the awning while he got the truck. She watched him pull his collar up, then hunch over and dart across the pavement, water splashing as he ran.

When he reached the truck, he stood there in the rain with his back to her—probably fishing for his key. Then he turned around and, instead of opening the door, pulled his hat off and threw it straight up, the waterlogged fedora spinning in the air like a yo-yo.

"Recess!" he hollered while the rain pelted down. "Ain't it time for recess?"

Turning up her collar, Shirley stepped into the downpour, grateful at least for the chance to get soaked.

They sat in the porch swing at his place, listening to the Opry and watching the rain. He produced a bottle and poured her a drink, but since he didn't pour himself one, she left hers untouched. She'd gotten sloppy the last time she'd been over here, and he'd left the next morning to spend a week in St. Louis, not even letting her know where he'd gone. He came back with a story about meeting Stan Musial that she felt sure he'd made up.

"It keeps raining like this," she said, "I guess all the cotton'll just float away."

"It won't float away. Weather Bureau says the front'll pass

through tonight, and then we're looking at sunshine. We'll get Dan in the field with them Germans by the middle of next week."

"If he doesn't take a notion to hit the road."

"He ain't the road-hitting type. Not as long as he's got some responsibility to shoulder."

He leaned back in the porch swing and crossed his arms behind his head—a frequent gesture on his part, and one she'd always hated. She believed that if you'd sat him down in a chair against a brick wall, facing a firing squad, he'd rear back like that right before they shot him. Just to keep anybody from suspecting he might value his life.

"But he'll make a perfect soldier," he said. "They ask for volunteers, his hand'll go up every damn time."

"Somebody's hand's got to go up sometime, I guess."

"If a war's to be fought, it sure as hell does. That's exactly what Jimmy Del thought."

"But not you."

"No," he said, "not me. I was always the worthless one. And I'm worth a lot less now than I was back then."

She felt herself starting to melt. She added up to so much less than she used to. The years were slipping away, just as people had, and more of both would be gone in no time. She rarely let herself wonder what would happen when Dan enlisted. Being in that house alone was something she couldn't imagine doing. There were no bars on the windows, but there might just as well have been.

"I think I want to look for a job," she said.

"What for? You know I'll help y'all make it."

"I have to help myself make it."

"Well, if that's what you want."

"Did you think any more about driving me up to Memphis? Before I look for work, I ought to do something about my clothes."

"I don't believe us taking trips together'd be a real good idea."

"You used to think it was a great idea."

"Well, things used to be different. You know that as well as I do."

"Yes," she said, "and when they were, it made a lot less sense for us to go to Memphis or anywhere else. But we went all the same, didn't we? My God, how far we went."

She picked the glass up and took a big swallow of whiskey, then rose and walked over to the edge of the porch. Rivulets ran down the screen, which sagged wherever several drops clung together. The air smelled of ozone, and a cool breeze was starting to blow.

When she turned around again, she'd made up her mind to hurt him, if only she could find the right words. Then she saw the way he was looking at her, his eyes starting at the floor and traveling up her body, moving slowly, lingering over this detail and the next, caressing every inch of her before coming to rest, finally, on her face.

Whistling, he shook his head. "Shirley, if I had a million dollars, I still don't think I could afford you. Just flat couldn't meet the asking price."

EIGHT

A HUNDRED and ten bolls for every ten feet of row—that's what we're looking for," Dan's father had always told him. If you got that yield throughout the field, the land could be counted on to produce a bale an acre. They never quite managed it, but a few times they'd come close.

One year—their best year, he'd heard his father say—they had as pretty a stand as anyone had ever seen. Dan remembered climbing into the trailer and packing the cotton down, tromping it with gusto and then, after he grew tired, falling asleep and lying there while his daddy towed it in. But once they reached the gin, it stood out in the yard, alongside his daddy's other trailer, while cotton belonging to the Starks and the Stancills went onto the scales. A big front was sweeping down from the Great Plains, and his daddy pleaded with the gin operator, who said only that he'd get around to them when he could.

But Dan had defied local logic by becoming friends with Marty Stark. "My dad says we could go under," he told him the next morning on the playground, where they were tossing a football back and forth. "Both our trailers are standing out in the yard over at the Choctaw Creek Gin, full of cotton, and if we don't empty 'em before the rain hits, what's left'll mildew and sell below grade."

"How come they don't pull 'em in there and gin it?"

"Mr. Crider told Daddy we don't give him that much business. Says he's got to get y'all's ginned, and the Stancills', and I don't know who all else's."

"Buford Crider? My daddy says he ain't got no more spine than a clothesline. And I reckon Daddy ought to know, because he don't have much spine neither." Marty drop-kicked the ball straight into the air, ran under it and caught it, then drew his arm back and fired Dan a perfect spiral. "I'll tell my grandpa what's happening," he said. "I guarantee you *he* can speed old Crider up."

The trailers were empty by five that afternoon, and his daddy had them back in the field by five-thirty. They picked most of the remaining cotton before the storm hit, and his father received an abject apology from Buford Crider, though he never figured out what had prompted either the action or the apology, and Dan never told him. He was only twelve years old at the time, but he already knew a thing or two about dignity.

He thought about that episode, and about being dependent on somebody else's good intentions, as he walked through the field that Monday afternoon with his uncle. Alvin's good intentions, assuming he had any, mattered a lot right now, starting with footing the bill for the POW labor. But the way Dan figured it, his uncle owed somebody something, though he'd never been sure who the somebody was or how great the sum might be.

"Problem you'll have with them Germans," Alvin said, pulling his hat off and mopping sweat from his forehead, "is they don't know a cotton boll from a butter bean. You'll have to show 'em how to pull the cotton loose—and if you don't watch 'em, I bet they'll drop the whole boll in the sack. Another thing: when their sacks get full and they haul 'em in to weigh up, make sure they go back to the same spot, or you'll end up with a lot of piece rows. I'll get you a package of white handkerchiefs from the store. Give one to each of them Krauts and make 'em tie it to the top of a stalk before they head for the turnrow. Tell 'em you ain't trying to make 'em surrender again, you just don't want nobody getting lost."

They counted the bolls at the ends of several rows, using his daddy's method, then headed for the low spots in the center of the field. While they walked along through the hot, dusty middles, Alvin speculated about how the Germans might fare when they found themselves out there."They ain't got no place in their own country that gets this hot," he said. "On the other hand, I was talking to that Captain Munson the other day, and he said most of 'em was over in Africa, right smack in the middle of the desert, so I reckon they had ample opportunity to sample warm weather. He claims they're good workers. Says there ain't a chance in hell they'll run off."

"You know the army shipped Marty Stark home and made him a guard out there?"

"Yeah. I heard it the other day."

"Why you reckon they sent him back? He ain't been wounded."

"He didn't say why?"

"Not a word."

"His daddy's a big wheel. Maybe he just don't feature his son dodging bullets."

"Mr. Stark ain't that big a wheel."

"Big enough to share a drink with Jim Eastland."

"Where'd you hear that?"

Alvin squatted down and began to count the bolls on a cotton stalk, actually touching each one, as if he couldn't believe it was open until he'd felt the fiber. "Friend of mine told me she saw him up at Eastland's place one time."

Dan wondered which friend this had been. The dime-store clerk who'd finally figured out Alvin cared less about her than he did about his boots, or the rich redheaded widow from over in Greenville? The friend could've been any one of several women. Or it could've been someone he didn't even know about, or no one at all.

"I don't imagine Mr. Stark cares that much, one way or the other, about Marty dodging bullets," Dan said. "If you ask me, he never was much of a father." He squatted down himself, intending to count the bolls on his row.

"You'll make a hell of a rifleman, Daniel," his uncle said. "You see stuff other folks don't."

NINE

ROSETTA'S HOUSE stood in the middle of a cotton field Alvin rented out, where the tractors plowed right up to her windows. L.C. had told Dan that sometimes, in June and July, she'd nail cardboard over them to keep from choking on the dust.

Wednesday morning, when Dan turned his pickup into the yard, L.C. was waiting, lunch bucket in hand. "You got a gun?" he asked.

"What the hell for?"

L.C. walked around to the passenger side, opened the door and got in. "Case any of them Nazis takes a notion to run off."

"They ain't going nowhere. Most of 'em ain't Nazis anyway."

"What make you say that?"

"They just ain't."

"They wore the uniform, didn't they?"

"Wearing a German uniform don't make you a Nazi."

L.C. held his forearms up and examined them, rotating them one way and then the other. "I got nigger skin," he said. "Reckon that mean I'm white?"

"Sometimes," Dan said, "I think that's all y'all study."

L.C. laughed. "Sometimes that's what we want y'all to think."

Dan turned the pickup around and headed back toward the highway. L.C. always made him feel like he was the butt of a joke without ever saying anything you could call a real punch line. Once or twice, he'd been tempted to ask if there was such a thing as black math. Two and two would always be four, as far as he was concerned, but he doubted L.C. would see it that way. He'd think there was something funny, maybe even simple-minded, about wanting two numbers to add up the same from one day to the next.

L.C. was thumping his foot against the floorboard, humming a weird-sounding melody that didn't seem to have any real words, just an *uuh-huh* from time to time, or an occasional *I mean*. He fancied himself a guitar player and was pretty good, to hear Alvin tell it.

"What you call that music?"

"Don't call it nothing."

"Sounds a little bit like them colored spirituals to me."

"Yeah, well, it's got some spirit to it. Maybe not the good kind, though."

"What other kind is there?"

"Evil spirits."

"You mean to tell me you believe in all that trash?"

"Ever know a nigger that didn't?"

Dan had half a mind to tell him he'd never known a nigger, because it was impossible to know one if you yourself were white, though it went without saying that they all knew you. "You wouldn't like it," he said, "if I was to call you what you just called yourself, would you?"

L.C. rolled his eyes, as if this was complete nonsense. "You call me that all the time."

"I ain't *never* called you that."

"Naw? In your mind, what you think of me as?"

He had him there.

"See?" L.C. said. "You know it as well as I does." Shutting his eyes, he started thumping the floorboard again and singing about somebody named Holloway, who seemed to be some kind of colored Jesus, because fallen women adored him and—unless Dan had misunderstood something—he died every Saturday night and rose again on Sunday morning.

Through the wire mesh you could see the prisoners milling around in small groups, wearing what looked like washed-out army fatigues with the letters *PW* stenciled on the backs of their shirts. There were guards inside as well, but Dan didn't see Marty.

He saw somebody else he knew, though. Frank Holder sat on the tailgate of his truck, drawing lines in the dirt with the toe of his shoe. Dan had played football with Biggie, but he'd never found the father very easy to talk to. He was the kind of man who never seemed to smile, never told a story or even drove into town to watch his son play ball.

Still, Dan hated to see him sitting there alone. When they held the memorial service for Biggie, Mrs. Holder had clawed the varnish off a church pew and Holder himself had buried his face in a handkerchief.

Leaving L.C. in the pickup, he walked over. "Hey, Mr. Holder."

"How you doing, Danny?"

"Not too bad. You waiting for a labor detachment?"

"Yeah. Supposed to get me eight of 'em."

"Me, too. You reckon Germans can learn to pick cotton?"

"They're pretty sharp folks," Holder said. "I imagine they'll do all right." He gazed at Dan's pickup. "Ain't that the nigger that drives Alvin's rolling store?"

"Yes sir."

"What's he doing here?"

"He'll help me get 'em started this morning."

"I been watching that boy. He come by my place one day and laid down on that damn horn, and when I walked over and asked him what the hell he was doing, he didn't show too much respect. Since then, I seen him tearing up and down the roads, throwing up rocks and dust, just batting it to beat all. Like to run me in the ditch one day. I got a good mind to report him to the Civil Defense." He shook his head. "These Germans is the enemy all right, and if the army asked me to, I'd stand ten or twelve of 'em up against the barn and cut loose. But if they could speak English, I bet you wouldn't have no trouble understanding what they was saying. Not like the niggers. Maybe they know what they mean when they open their mouth, but can't nobody else figure it out."

One of the guards unlocked the gates, and a sergeant Dan had seen downtown, eating a burger and reading the funny papers, stepped out holding a clipboard. "All right now," he said, his voice loud and unmistakably northern. "We'll be following the same procedure every morning. What I got here's a list of all the contractors and the men assigned to each one. When I call off a contractor's name, I'll ask him to hold his hand up to identify himself. And don't none of you local gentlemen worry, you're not volunteering for hazardous duty or nothing like that." He paused in case the line drew a laugh.

It didn't. Dan had heard more than a few folks say they didn't like having so many outsiders around—and it was clear they weren't referring to the Germans.

"All right, then. Ain't nobody got a sense of humor here this morning. But hell, this is serious business, right? Right. We got to get these Jerries out there picking old king cotton. And so we will, so we will. My first name on the list this fine morning's Mr. Robert L. Brown, and I bet I know what the *L* stands for. Probably had an ancestor fit for the greatest in gray. Where's Farmer Brown?"

Raising his hand, Bob Brown stepped forward.

In a low voice, Holder said, "Lock that damn Yankee in a room with one of them Krauts and his breakfast'd run the hundred down his leg."

The sergeant pointed at Brown, then turned to the prisoners and began shouting names. "Abeken, J. . . . Daim, R. . . . Detten, A. . . . Lasker, G. . . ."

Dan watched the Germans stream through the gates. He'd always heard they were usually blond, but a lot of them had dark hair, and there were even a couple redheads. Few exhibited any memorable physical traits, and they were mostly of average height and average weight. Standing there, he had a hard time believing any of them would've been willing, much less eager, to kill him. It seemed impossible that he couldn't have convinced them to let him live, if only because he was every bit as ordinary as they were.

Two men in each group carried five-gallon water cans,

which they hoisted into the backs of the pickups. The other prisoners stood by silently while the farmers signed for them; then they climbed into the trucks and rode off. Most detachments were unaccompanied by guards.

"Daniel Timms," the sergeant finally called. "Where's Mr. Daniel J. Timms?"

Dan stepped forward, his hand in the air.

The sergeant looked him over. "Your father send you?"

Right then, for the first time that morning, Dan saw Marty. He was standing inside the fence, a rifle slung from his shoulder. The MP armband had slid down close to his elbow. Raising his right hand, he pointed an imaginary pistol at the sergeant's back.

"My father's dead," Dan said. "I'll be in charge of the group, but my uncle'll be looking in on 'em, too."

"How old are you, son?"

"Almost eighteen."

"Seventeen, in other words."

"Yes sir."

"Yes sir." The sergeant shook his head. "Well, I guess that's between you and the army." He checked Dan's name off. "Best, T. . . . Feder, D. . . . Fentzel, W. . . ."

L.C. pulled the sacks down off the trailer, which was standing on the turnrow. The Germans waited together in a loose group, not saying a word. Every now and then they'd glance at the far end of the field, as if trying to estimate the distance from turnrow to turnrow.

One of them was taller than all the rest by several inches,

but his ears were so tiny, they looked like they belonged on a six-year-old. His hollowed-out cheeks might've made him appear haunted if he hadn't been teetering on the verge of laughter since the moment he walked through the gates. The only other one who stood out in any way was a blond guy who would've been handsome but for the deep purple stain covering the right side of his neck and most of his cheek.

"You wear the sack like this," Dan said, feeling foolish because the sergeant had told him that no one in the detachment spoke English. He looped the strap over his head, allowing it to rest on his shoulder. "The sack drags along behind you." He took a few steps to demonstrate, then turned and nodded at L.C., who began distributing the sacks.

All of the prisoners put them on correctly except the tall one with little ears, who worked the loop down around his waist.

Dan tapped himself on the shoulder. "Like this."

Chuckling silently, the tall prisoner just shook his head.

"All right," Dan said, "suit yourself."

He gripped a lock of cotton, pulled it loose, transferred it to his left hand and dropped it in his sack even as his right hand reached for another boll. "You use both hands, like that," he said. "You need to drop the cotton in the sack without looking back. Otherwise, it'll take you all day to pick a row, and you'll get a bad crick in your neck, too." He held his right hand up so they could see he'd bound his fingertips with white adhesive tape. "The burrs'll tear your fingers and make 'em bleed unless you tape 'em. I got a roll here y'all can use. And one other thing: your back'll hurt like the devil from all the stooping."

L.C. laughed. "Shit, Dan," he said. "If it was me, I believe I'd try to tell 'em something positive."

"Yeah?" Dan said. He looked at the Germans, then gestured at the sky. "Well, sometimes it rains. And when it does, y'all can stay at the prison."

They set out into the field, Dan and L.C. flanked on either side by four of the POWs. The guy with the stain on his face was trying to pull the bolls off and then separate the cotton from them, and he kept getting stuck. Once, when he pricked himself badly, he put his finger in his mouth to suck it, and the prisoner with the funny ears laughed and said something in German that made a couple of the others laugh, too.

"That cat back yonder looks like he's having a hard time," L.C. said.

Dropping his sack, Dan stepped across a couple rows and walked back to where the man'd fallen behind. "Look," he said. He pulled a boll loose and showed it to the German. "This part of it, the stem? It's still green. That's why it's sticking you. See? *Green.* I don't know what that word is in your language."

The German shaded his eyes and looked ahead toward the others; then he stepped closer. *"Grün,"* he whispered.

Taken aback, Dan said, "What?"

The prisoner smiled. Sweat was streaming down his discolored face and onto his neck, soaking the front of his shirt. Though Dan knew it was silly, he looked a little more closely, to see if the liquid produced by the man's pores might not be purple, too.

"Grün," the prisoner whispered again. "Almost same word in your language and their."

TEN

KIMBALL HAD drawn his first breath somewhere in California, and he seemed to believe this conferred a mark of distinction—for which, from time to time, he felt the need to offer an apology. "Dad and I were down in L.A. that weekend," he was saying while he drove. "L.A., by the way, isn't as you probably imagine it. Hollywood's Hollywood, and Beverly's Beverly, but Pasadena's Pasadena and no rose at all. What I'm saying is this shit about California being the Golden State's only partly true. It's a little bit golden—I'd be the last to deny it—but don't kid yourself: it's mostly made of copper." Sometimes he sounded as though he feared that once the war ended, Marty and his relatives would load up the jalopy and head for the Imperial Valley, in which case he didn't want their disillusionment on his conscience.

There were days when Marty felt like leveling the Lee-Enfield and spraying his brains all over whatever field they were driving past at that moment. What prevented him was the realization that Kimball would never see the results, whereas he would have to.

While Kimball ran his mouth as if it were an entry in the

Belmont Stakes, Marty stared at the countryside. Tin cans, most of them bereft of their labels, littered the ditches, and the road signs were rusted and full of bullet holes. Some of the tenant shacks that'd had folks in them two years ago were abandoned now, their roofs falling in, floor joists collapsed. You could drive for miles without seeing a single windowpane intact.

Ever since he'd gotten home, he'd been feeling like the whole world was in a state of rot and decay, and he kept smelling odors that reminded him of rancid meat. He'd lie on his cot every night, doing his best not to think about smells, or trying to think of nice ones—the scent of honeysuckle, say, or perfume. But when he finally got all the stink out of his nostrils and fell asleep, the dreams would start. They always involved naked bodies, or at least parts of naked bodies. Sometimes the parts looked as if they'd come off not a person but a statue, because they were hard and smooth and white as chalk. Once, he'd dreamed that he saw his buddy Raymond's head and torso protruding from a pile of pale arms, legs, buttocks and shoulders. None of the other parts looked like they belonged to Raymond, but in that kind of jumble, you couldn't say for sure.

Last night in his dream, he'd reached out to fondle a woman's breast, but the second he touched her flesh, his hand went right through it, into her heart and out her shoulder blade, and then her body caved in beneath his weight, both of them dissolving into white dust. He woke up soaking wet, and his sweat stank like death.

Up ahead, near a bend in the road, seven or eight prisoners were in the field, their cotton sacks dragging along behind them. The land was worked by a man named Ed Mitchell, who farmed on the Sixteenth Section and still plowed with mules.

Kimball pulled the scout car to the shoulder. Mitchell was out in the field himself, dragging a sack, followed by his wife and three black kids with their mother. He looked up, saw the car and dropped his sack.

Marty climbed out, but Kimball said, "All this dust has got my hay fever in overdrive." He withdrew a handkerchief from his pocket and polished his nose. "I'll just wait right here."

Marty jumped the ditch and walked over to Mitchell, who grinned shyly, displaying two rows of grayish teeth as oddly canted as old gravestones. "Boy," he said, "I don't know whether to shake your hand or salute you."

"A handshake'll do," Marty said, and they shook. "Them Jerries been behaving?"

"They ain't bad. Not atall." Mitchell pulled out a tin of Blood Hound snuff. "Want some?"

"Believe I'll pass, but much obliged."

Mitchell took a pinch, put it in his mouth and stuck the tin back in his pocket. "I been listening, trying to see if I can understand anything they say, but I can't puzzle it out. Don't sound like nothing I ever heard."

"Any of 'em pick a hundred pounds yet?"

"That'n over yonder." He pointed a long, skinny finger at a chunky young man with rosy cheeks, who, Marty had noticed, was surprisingly agile in the soccer matches they sometimes played after supper. "That little devil weighed up nearly two eighty yesterday," Mitchell said. "And hadn't never seen a cotton stalk till this time last week." He shook his head. "It's a damn shame to be so far from home, no older'n he is. He's a good-natured boy, too."

The sensation Marty had been experiencing lately—that something in his chest was dissolving, moving from one state to another, from solid to viscous liquid—came on strongly. When would it stop? When he turned into a puddle on the side of the road? "It probably ain't all that long," he said, "since he was pumping bullets into some other good-natured boys."

"Yeah, but if he done that, I bet it was because they made him."

"Mr. Mitchell, can't nobody make somebody kill somebody else. If you do it, you do it. If you don't, you don't. Two fingers can't pull the same trigger."

For a moment or two, a wall of woods on the horizon absorbed Mitchell's attention. He studied it with wonder, as if the trees had sprung up recently and caught him unawares. "You ain't seen old Danny boy, have you?" he finally asked.

"Yes sir. Saw him the day I got back."

"Reckon you heard about his daddy."

"Yes sir."

Mitchell pursed his lips. "Sad story."

"Why you reckon he did it?"

"Well, there's them that says this—and there's them that says that."

"What do you say?"

"I don't say nothing, because it ain't nothing I know a thing about."

"If you knew anything, would you say it?"

"Well," Mitchell said, "I can't say as I would."

Understanding that for the time being he'd just heard Ed Mitchell's last word on that or any other subject, Marty asked him to let them know if any problems developed, told him good-bye, then went back and climbed into the scout car.

As he and Kimball drove past Dan's house later that afternoon, he checked to see if Shirley Timms might be in the yard or on the porch, but she wasn't.

He'd spotted her downtown the day after he got back. He'd been standing before the magazine rack in the Piggly Wiggly, staring down at the very spot where he used to sit chewing bubble gum and reading *Marvel Comics,* and when he finally looked up, she was just going by on the other side of the plate-glass window. She'd aged, he could tell, but was still a pretty woman.

One day when he was twelve or thirteen, he'd been out in the pasture behind the Timms house with Dan, hitting fly balls, and his friend had jammed a pitch in on his knuckles, the seams tearing the skin off in three or four places. Mrs. Timms bathed his knuckles in some kind of salty solution, then held a cold cloth pressed against them for several minutes, and while doing that she said he had nice hands. "Some folks would say too nice for a young man. But if you ask me, every man ought to have hands like these."

If she noticed the flame that lit his cheeks, she never let on. She waited till he quit bleeding; then she painted the skinned areas with Methylate, applied a bandage and suggested he run along. For a good while afterwards, he kept wishing he could call her by her first name, rather than having to say *Mrs. Timms.* And he couldn't be around Dan's father, whom he'd always liked, without feeling vaguely resentful.

Mr. Timms never picked up on the resentment. He grinned at Marty when they met on the street, slapping his back and asking how football practice was coming, wondering if Loring would ever figure out how to beat Indianola. Folks considered Jimmy Del Timms a little unusual, mostly because it didn't seem to worry him that he'd never made much money, but everybody respected him. He'd won the Distinguished Service Cross during the First War, been wounded twice and cooped up for six weeks in some underground prison.

He always had a smile ready up until a couple years ago. He certainly hadn't been smiling the last time they'd crossed paths, one Saturday in the Piggly Wiggly parking lot. His shirtfront was unevenly buttoned, his hair uncombed, and his khaki pants had dirt caked on both knees, as if he'd lately been kneeling in a mud hole. "Let me have a word with you," he said.

It occurred to Marty that he might want him to talk to his father or grandfather and help secure a loan. By then, the Timms place was failing, and everybody knew it.

But Jimmy Del Timms didn't want to borrow anything. Instead, he wanted to give something—namely, advice—and as they sat in the cab of his pickup that morning, two days before Marty was to leave for the induction center, he offered it, staring through the windshield the entire time at the redbrick wall of the grocery store.

"Don't never volunteer for nothing, Marty. There's two other words mean the same thing as *volunteer*. One word's *fool*. The other one's *corpse*. You'll know I'm wrong the day you see a general officer volunteer—volunteer himself, I mean. Then you can say Jimmy Del Timms was a lying son of a bitch. Send me a postcard from wherever you're at, and I'll gladly write back and own up.

"Probably there ain't no way to get around fighting it. Never is. There's better and worse in the world—I ain't one to deny it—but a bullet can't tell the difference and a shell don't give a shit. Somewhere in Berlin, there's a gold-hearted German, but to me right now, he ain't fit to piss on. That's a goddamn shame, or call it whatever you take a notion to.

"So where can you run to, where can you hide? A boy like you ain't no cotton-eyed joe that can skulk around the rear and clean latrines. You're tall, you got a military chin and you'll look good when they line you up and point you toward the Krauts and kick you in the ass. Just make sure when they put their boot up your butt, it comes out with shit on the toe."

Marty had a lot to do before he went to Jackson, was already scared to death and didn't want to hear any more. Telling Mr. Timms he needed to go, he climbed out of the truck and started to walk away. But unlike Billy Barsotti—who'd swaggered around town the week after he enlisted, running his mouth about the horrors he'd wreak on the Japs or the Germans just as soon as he got a chance—he knew perfectly well there was a possibility he'd never return, just as Billy Barsotti would not return, having died on the *Yorktown* at Midway. And if he failed to come back, Jimmy Del Timms might not remember much about him except that he hadn't felt like listening the last time they met.

He turned and walked back to the truck. Dan's father was still sitting there staring at the wall, but at least he'd quit talking.

"Mr. Timms? If I write to you, will you write me back?"

"You won't write, Marty."

"Yes sir, I will. I promise."

"Naw, son." He stuck his hand out the window, and Marty took it, careful not to look him in the eye, because he knew that whatever he saw there would only scare him worse. "You may send me a card with your name on it, and it may be in your handwriting," Jimmy Del Timms said. "But it won't be you that wrote it."

The same pickup truck they'd sat in that morning—a couple years older, with a few more nicks on its fenders—was parked on the turnrow near a green cotton trailer. The yellow rolling store stood on the side of the road, and Marty could see Dan moving around inside, straightening up.

"You aim to get out here?" he asked Kimball.

He laughed. "That's funny. Where I come from, you don't *aim* anything but a gun."

"Yeah? You ever aimed one?"

"What?"

"You ever aimed a gun?"

"During basic, I—"

"I ain't talking about basic. I'm talking about aiming a gun at somebody with an intent to squeeze the trigger."

"I told you, my dad pulled strings. Yours must've, too, or else you wouldn't be here right now."

"My daddy didn't pull shit." He hopped out of the scout car, jerked the rifle from its boot and experienced a moment of intense satisfaction when Kimball's eyes doubled in size and his mouth dropped open in the shape of an egg. "Tell you what— I'll just stay out here and pick cotton and let one of them Afrika Korps fuckers ride back to town with you. How's that sound?" Slinging the rifle onto his shoulder, he started for the school bus.

Dan stepped out, wiping his nose on the back of his hand. "Man, I took a sneezing fit about the time I crossed that little bridge over Choctaw Creek this morning and like to run right in the water."

"Has everybody in the world but me got trouble with their nose?"

"I sure do."

"You reckon Choctaw Creek's deep enough to drown in?"

"Could be. Why?"

Marty turned and nodded back at the scout car, where Kimball was climbing out, stepping carefully to avoid stirring up dust.

"He in charge of you, or you in charge of him?"

"Ain't neither one of us in charge of nobody, including ourselves. You got a lesson or two to learn, pal."

"You in charge of them Germans, ain't you?"

"Nominally."

"What the hell does that mean?"

"I don't know, but the fellow I heard say it was always getting laid."

Kimball straggled up, then reached out to shake hands with Dan. "Name's Kimball," he said. "I'm from California."

While he explained what Dan could expect in basic training, Marty let his eyes scan the field. One of the prisoners, the tallest, had pulled his sack off, and it was lying on the ground at his feet. He did a rapid set of knee bends, then began bobbing up and down in a series of toe touches.

"What's that lanky bastard up to?" Marty asked.

"He'll do it every once in a while," Dan said. "Keeps at it for a few minutes, then puts the sack on and goes back to work."

The prisoner with the disfigured face was picking toward them, not far away, and he looked determined to avoid breaking a sweat. He'd study a boll for a moment or two before reaching for it, and after pulling the fiber free, he'd hold it to his nose and sniff it. "Him over there," Marty said, pointing, "the one with the fucked-up face, he ever give you a hard time?"

"No. He's actually the only one you can talk to."

"How's that? You been studying German?"

"I reckon I picked up a few words in the last week," Dan said. "But you don't have to know German to talk to him."

Kimball raised his forearm, holding his wrist much too close to Marty's face. "Almost sixteen hundred, Stark. We better get our asses back."

Marty shoved his hand aside. "What the hell you mean, you don't have to know German?"

The force of the question seemed to take Dan by surprise, and for an instant Marty wondered what his friend might've heard. He wouldn't put it past his father to get in touch with Eastland, to see what he could find out, and the senator would get answers. And while his dad would hardly broadcast the results of that inquiry, Mrs. Bivens might—if it came up in a tender, postcoital moment.

"Well," Dan said, "that fellow with the purple face can speak English."

On the twelfth of July, just east of Gela, someone spoke English well enough to lure Raymond Sample and two lost paratroopers from the Eighty-second into a grove of olive trees. Whoever it was had cried *Jesus* and *Sweet Mary, mother of God,* without the trace of an accent, calling for Berea, Ohio, to open its arms and welcome him home. Then he fired a burst from a Schmeisser that sounded like an outboard motor starting up. And for a moment, lying there spread-eagled, Marty convinced himself he was back on the lake near Loring with Dan and his daddy and the no-good uncle, who carried whiskey in a quart jar and caught nothing but a gar, which Jimmy Del Timms insisted a true sportsman would just knock in the head.

ELEVEN

THIS'LL BE your jack panel," Miss Edna Boudreau said, "and it's brand-new. You won't have any problem with the plugs getting stuck like they do in the older ones." She glanced over her shoulder at Cassie Pickett, who sat in a tall swivel chair, wearing a pair of headphones. "Cassie, will you kindly move over so I can get close enough to show Shirley the procedures?"

Cassie, who looked like she'd eaten her last full meal back in the Roaring Twenties, cast an appraisive glance at Miss Edna's hips, as if to suggest that they, not the position of her chair, were the problem. She rose, though, and pulled the chair over a few inches.

"When a call comes in," Miss Edna told Shirley, "you'll see a blinking light beside the number. At that point, what you do is plug your headset into the jack and then you just say 'Operator' . . . pause . . . 'May I help you?' Got it?"

"I believe so."

"Let me hear you say it."

Shirley felt like a first grader. Indeed, the building housing the telephone company had served as Loring's first school-house, back in the 1880s. It had heavy oak floors and low water-

65

stained ceilings; it was as if the odor of anxious little bodies still hung in the air. "This is the operator," she said. "May I help you?"

"Not 'This is the operator.' Just 'Operator' . . . pause . . . 'May I help you?' Would you like to know why?"

Surely Miss Edna's talents were being misused, Shirley decided: she belonged in the military. But she didn't want to be rude. "Sure," she said. "Why?"

When Miss Edna propped her fists on her hips, her belly pushed at the buttons on her blouse. "You may not realize it, but when you say 'This . . . is . . . the'—well, on average, it'll take you close to two seconds. Now, two seconds might not seem like much, especially if you've got only one light blinking, but when three or four folks on your panel are trying to place calls at the same time, the seconds add up." She pointed at a pair of jacks in the lower left-hand corner. "These two, numbers five four four and five four six, are the lines to Camp Loring. You don't want them waiting to reach the War Department because you're saying 'This . . . is . . . the.'"

"If time's so precious," Shirley said, "shouldn't I eliminate the pause, too?"

She could tell, from looking at the woman's face, that Miss Edna didn't have much hope for her. She hadn't wanted to hire Shirley to begin with and had given in only because Fred Harney, who ran the local branch of Southern Bell, had ordered her to, and that was because Alvin promised him extra gas coupons for his Stutz Bearcat, which he liked to race on the levee every weekend. Shirley also knew all too well why Miss Edna hadn't wanted her around. If she'd committed half the sins folks like Miss Edna thought, she probably would have been content to lie down and die, figuring she'd lived her life, and two or three others, to the fullest.

"The pause," Miss Edna said, "is just a small touch of nicety, which is only right and proper. Some people might disagree with what I'm about to say, Shirley, but I believe that especially in times like these, it's important to preserve at least a *little* decorum."

That afternoon, Cassie Pickett poked her in the ribs. When Shirley looked over, Cassie pulled off her headset and gestured for Shirley to take it. Shirley slipped hers off and put Cassie's on.

She recognized one voice right away, but the other took a little longer.

"Why don't you come over tonight?" Vera Bivens said. "You haven't been over here in so long, and I get so lonesome, always waiting."

A little hemming and hawing on the other end, a word or two about work and bad weather.

"You remember how you found me last time?" Vera said.

There was a long silence. Then Kent Stark said, "Well, I reckon I might could come over."

"You *might* could?" Vera said, sounding a good bit like a kitten.

"Yeah, I think I can. I think I can."

And Vera said, "You're the little engine that could, Kent."

TWELVE

A SHORT, neat-looking fellow who always wore clean clothes, even in the field, and liked to keep a good hat, John Burns lived over on the Young place. He'd never been out of Loring County, except for one time when old Walter Young carried him over to Sunflower to pick up a tractor.

The Saturday-night dances were held at Burns's. Four or five men would seine bait before sunup, then get out there on the banks of Lake Loring with those cane poles and catch as many fish as they could before they had to hit the field. That evening, the women would fry the fish in iron skillets over an open fire, using last winter's hog lard. They'd make corn bread, too, and mix up some cabbage slaw. They did the cooking out behind the house, so that old man Young wouldn't see them if he happened to take a notion to drive down the road.

"White folks know the nigger's got to eat," John Burns always said, "but they hates to see him having a good time doing it." About the only thing they disliked more than seeing colored people having a good time, he claimed, was hearing them having it. So he never let the music start till people had eaten their fill and downed a few drinks, and that was past the white folks' bedtime.

L.C. was sitting in the dark on an overturned washtub, a tin plate in his lap and a tin cup in his hand, a warm feeling spreading from his stomach into his arms and legs. He'd eaten a mess of fish already and meant to eat more, so he stood up and walked past the fire.

They'd pulled the back door off Burns's cabin, propping it on a couple of spindle oil drums and laying out the food. He picked at a piece of fish, pulling a hunk loose to see whether or not the flesh had a yellow tinge.

"What you doing, L.C, looking for the hook?" The woman who'd spoken, a big dark-skinned lady named Doll, had her arm around John Burns, who was a good six or seven inches shorter than she was.

"He ain't looking for no fishhook," Burns said. "He trying to see is that one of them gasper gools."

"Scared of 'em, is you, honey?"

The flesh was white and flaky, most likely striped bass, and L.C. dropped it onto his plate. "Ain't a question of being scared of 'em," he said. "I just don't like the taste." What he didn't say, because Burns would have laughed at him, was that he didn't believe in catching gasper gools to begin with. When a boat passed over them in shallow water, they'd rub those little horny knots on their foreheads together, making *gooling* sounds, like they were trying to tell you something.

He often felt like animals or trees were speaking to him, sometimes even a place. When he was little, old folks'd talked about something bad happening in a patch of low ground out by Payne's Deadening, sixty or seventy years ago. Nobody ever told him exactly what it was, but he'd been over there many times, and though he'd never seen anybody, hadn't seen anything alive except a few hundred mosquitoes, he never felt alone when he stood on that ground.

Wherever he was, he couldn't help wondering who'd stood there before him. Once, when he was a little boy and they lived on the Stancill place, his momma'd found him barefoot in a cotton field, staring down at his feet as they disappeared in the rich black gumbo; he felt as if he'd grown right out of the dirt itself, as if the land, rather than a man whose face he'd never seen, had fathered him, so he asked his momma to name everybody she'd ever noticed picking cotton in that field.

"Don't get dreamy," she scolded. "Folks gone think you just lazy. They don't know you got nothing to dream with."

He had plenty to dream with. What he lacked was the means to turn the dream into a fact. He thought his hands might offer the means, but his feet still seemed like they were stuck in that gumbo. Even if he found some way to pull them loose and set out on Highway 47 north, he wouldn't make it far before an MP or one of those roving fools from the Office of Civil Defense stopped him. Once that happened, it wouldn't be any time before they'd discover he didn't have a draft card and put him in uniform. And he'd be damned if he meant to die like a dog for folks who thought he was a mule.

He ate another piece of fish and let Doll pour him another sip of bootleg whiskey. After the women cleared the dishes away,

Burns and another man lifted the door off the oil drums and laid it flat on the ground. L.C. went off to pee in the bushes. When he returned, he sat down in a ladder-back chair, placed both feet on the door and pulled his guitar out of the cotton-seed sack.

One of the men said, "When you gone learn you some of that bottleneck?"

"He don't need no bottleneck," John Burns said. "This nigger got fifteen fingers."

L.C. set the guitar on his left knee, which everybody thought looked funny, but it was the way old Fulsome Carthage had taught him to play. Fulsome had also told him not to wrap his thumb around the top of the fretboard like most folks did. "You wants to keep it flush with the neck," he'd said, offering a demonstration. He made L.C. clip the nails on his left hand down to nothing, while growing a monstrous one on his picking thumb. He mixed up an awful concoction that smelled strongly of cat piss, said it would strengthen the nail and told L.C. to drink it three times a week. When he'd asked what was in it, Fulsome said, "It best behoove you not to know."

He began to pick a rolling riff, not knowing where he was going or how he meant to get there, stomping down hard on that weather-beaten door, closing his eyes and thinking about feet you couldn't tell from the dirt they stood on, a man growing right up out of the ground.

"I *mean!*" a woman yelled.

"Sing about the bush and the bower," John Burns said. He used both terms for the place between a woman's legs, though L.C. had told him *bower* didn't cut it, that as far as he was concerned, it sounded like something off a battleship. Burns

claimed that was all right, since you entered it a man and came
out destroyed. But L.C. had more on his mind than bush and
bower.

> *go down to the deadenin'*
> *see the cottonmouth crawl*
> *see the Devil with a cane pole*
> *on his shoulder y'all*

> *spirit fish be talkin'*
> *say it time to go*
> *Devil say he gone catch you*
> *ain't gone see no She-car-go*

"How come y'allways studying Chicago?" Burns hollered,
shaking his rear right in L.C.'s face. "Up there, your young ass'll
turn to black ice."

> *man say peoples fightin'*
> *got to do your turn*
> *day that bullet find you*
> *you gone have to face that worm*

> *death tap you on the shoulder*
> *done too late to move your feet*
> *this train bound for Hades*
> *it time you take a seat*

John Burns was twirling his shirt in the air as he and Doll
were banging hips. Over near the outhouse, a pair of bodies
writhed and squirmed together, and Cooter Sam, from the

Moreli place, was doing the Lucky Duck, waddling with his woman to the woodpile and back.

Catching L.C.'s eye, John shook his head. "You gets less out of being a nigger," he said, "than anybody I knows."

In the morning, he lay on a thin pallet, with a pounding headache, listening to John and Doll, no more than a few feet away, in the bed across the room. The floor sounded like it could cave in at any minute.

Forty-nine percent of L.C. wanted to crawl over to the door and disappear as fast as he could, but this was an instance of majority rule. Doing his best not to make any noise, he shifted his position, raising his head. Moaning, Doll lay on her back, palms locked around her ankles, while Burns pumped away between her legs. If he'd been engaged in such activity, L.C. would have kept his eyes shut, but Doll's were wide open and staring straight at him.

THIRTEEN

WALKING HOME, hoping not to find his momma there, he passed a church. The parking lot was covered up with pickup trucks and cars. There was even a tractor, a fairly new Oliver, and he wondered which white man it belonged to.

Brother So-and-So's truck broke down, he imagined folks would say, *but he cares so much for the Lord that he got his whole family on that tractor and brought 'em down to church. With enemies like him, the Devil don't have a prayer.*

The Devil didn't have a prayer, not because some redneck drove his tractor to church, but because the Devil didn't pray. White folks, of course, would never see that. They believed everything had been made in their own image, and since they prayed, it stood to reason the Devil did, too.

The Devil was in each and every one of them, just as sure as he was in old Adolf Hitler, but the white folks didn't know it. The Devil had been in that glance that passed between him and Doll, in what he would have done to her, and she to him, if John Burns had wandered off. It wasn't that different, as far as he could see, from what you did when you pointed a gun at another man's heart and pulled the trigger. Wanting, you

74

willed yourself to take. One day they called it loving, another day rape.

When he stepped onto the porch, the floorboards sighed, and in that pitch he heard absence. He shifted his weight from foot to foot, listening. Must have taken herself off to church.

He stepped inside and, when his eyes adjusted to the darkness, saw her sitting near the woodstove, in her lap the raggedy old black Bible that one of her mistresses had given her. At the sight of it, he knew he ought to have had a lot more fun last night. Because what fun he'd had wasn't nearly enough to make up for the misery he was about to endure.

"You know where you gone end up?" she said. "A few miles south, down in the state penitentiary. Just like your no-good daddy."

"You never told me my daddy went to jail."

"I never told you your daddy went to Hell, neither, but I imagine that where he at now."

He walked over and laid his guitar down on his cot, then picked up a box of matches and lit the coal-oil lamp standing on the drink crate that served as his bedside table. He sat down and pulled off his shoes. "Since you ain't never told me who he was, don't tell me where he's at."

For a minute, her face lost all expression. When her cheeks went slack like that, you could see how pretty she must've been. Nice caramel-colored skin—not too dark, not so light you had to wonder if she was part white. "Don't you be telling me what to say or not say about that particular nigger. I say what I want."

"Yeah, I guess so. Reckon you do what you want, too. I'm proof of that."

She stood, laid the Bible on the table, walked over and drew back her hand.

"Hit me on the other side," he said. "I'm still sore on my left cheek from last week."

"So split the difference," she said, and slapped him hard across the bridge of his nose.

His eyes stung, and blood began to trickle from one nostril. "I ain't gone end up down south of anywhere," he said. "I'm gone end up *north*. And it won't be no few miles."

"North?" she said. "*North?*" She laughed. "Chicago, Illinois. Right? Detroit, Michigan. Pie in the Sky, Pennsylvania." Grinning, she shook her head, reached for his hand and, between her thumb and forefinger, pinched a wad of his skin. "'Less you get north of *this*," she said, "you ain't going nowhere."

FOURTEEN

"SWEE SPATS A NATTER," Dan said. He pulled his wallet out of his pocket and laid it on the floor because the seat was hard and his hip was about to kill him. "You ever heard tell of that?"

L.C. perched on the drink box, looking down the aisle at the group of sweaty Germans. Since all of the passenger seats had been removed, most of them lay on their backs or leaned against the display cases. The only exception was the tall one who was always doing his calisthenics out in the field. He sat up straight, in the very center of the aisle, hands resting on his knees.

Dan had no choice but to return them to camp in the rolling store. His mother took the truck to town every day, now that she had a job, and his uncle was over in Greenville, cooking up some deal he said would be even more profitable than the sanitary napkins. He'd promised to get back before quitting time, but he hadn't made it.

"What you say?" L.C. asked.

"Swee Spats a Natter."

"What about it?"

"This morning I was over on the Teague place, and this little colored boy that was out in the field with his momma comes over and asks me if I got any Swee Spats a Natter. At least I think that's what he called it. I told him I didn't know what the hell that was."

"Course you do." L.C. pointed at the display case containing patent medicines. "Yonder's two bottles of it."

Dan slowed so he could look over his shoulder. "Where?"

L.C. bounced down off the drink box, slid open the glass door and lifted out a blue bottle, then held it up to Dan. *Sweet Spirits of Niter*, the label read.

"Might as well be speaking different languages," L.C. said. "We don't understand y'all, and y'all don't understand us." He stuck the bottle back into the display case and closed the door. "Just like these Germans."

It had rained hard yesterday, and the road was a mess. Ordinarily, Dan wouldn't have set men to picking in such wet conditions. But before leaving that morning, Alvin had told him that rain was forecast again for the end of the week. "Better get that cotton while you can," he'd said. "They got them tower driers over at the gin now—it don't matter if the stuff's a little damp." So Dan had collected the prisoners first thing, before his mother took the pickup into town.

The closer he got to the highway, the worse the road looked. Tractors and cotton trailers had churned it into a huge batch of fudge, everybody trying to beat the next front. Several times the wheels spun on him, and he came close to getting stuck.

His uncle had bought the buses from some school district way up north, someplace that must've had a fair amount of snow, because they both had four-wheel drive. And given this mess, he decided to engage it.

Once all four wheels were pulling, the driving was much easier. But a few minutes later, when he turned onto Highway 47 and tried to disengage, something went wrong. The steering suddenly stiffened—he could hardly turn the wheel. Hearing a grinding noise, he let off the accelerator. Instead of slowing gradually, the bus slammed to a quick halt, as though he'd leaned on the brakes.

"Goddamn," he said. "The transmission's all screwed up."

In some strange way, it encapsulated everything that had gone wrong since that day last winter when he'd walked into the house and found his father's body. From that time on, it had been like he was trying to go backwards and forwards at once, like his own internal gear works were grinding themselves to bits.

He thought he might lay his head against the wheel and start crying. He was stuck six miles from town with a busload of POWs, and the only person who might help him, L.C., was just as alien to him as the Germans. For a moment, he felt the only thing to do was get mad. "If a cousin to one of them fellows sends me home in a box," he said, nodding his head to the back of the bus but looking at L.C., "you won't shed a goddamn tear, will you?"

To his surprise, L.C. slammed his fist down on the drink box, and several of the Germans flinched. "Why you ask *me* that? Just 'cause you done tore up your uncle's transmission? See, that's how y'all do. Everything come right back round to you. I been in a box my whole life, but has your ass shed any tears?"

Breathing hard, Dan rose as L.C. balled his hands into fists. Dan's first thought was that he'd have to make up some story to explain any cuts or bruises on his face, since otherwise there was no telling what folks might do to L.C. and Rosetta.

But before L.C. could swing, a curious thing happened. The German with the angry purple stain on his face stood up and, stepping around the tallest prisoner, walked forward and gestured at the empty driver's seat. "Maybe I try?"

Since that first day in the field, he'd spoken to Dan four or five times, but only when the others were some distance away. He never said a lot—*Very hot this day . . . Here is many cotton*—so Dan couldn't tell how much English he really knew, nor had he figured out why he referred to German as "their" language.

Marty had warned him not to believe anything a prisoner told him. "They'll dupe you," he said. "They fooled a buddy of mine, and he ain't coming home." And he meant to find out exactly where this one had been captured, have them check his *Solbuch* up at the base camp in Como, because there were a few things about him that didn't seem right.

Now all Dan could do was stare at him, not knowing what to say.

"Cat want to see can he get it going," L.C. said. "It was me, I'd let him. I sure as hell don't know how to make it run right, and you don't, neither."

Dan glanced at the rear of the rolling store, where every one of them was sitting up straight, watching. If they wanted, he knew, they could commandeer the bus. The question was, Where could they go, especially with the transmission locked up?

He stepped aside and let the German sit down. For a time, the prisoner studied the dashboard, then bent and looked underneath it at the pedals. Then he sat up, grabbed the stick and threw the transmission into reverse.

When the bus lurched backwards, Dan sprawled onto the floor. L.C. managed to stop himself from falling by grabbing the handrail. Bottles and canned goods tumbled off the shelves and rolled into the aisle.

Dan heard glass breaking, and several of the Germans hollering, then realized he was hollering, too.

He struggled to his feet just as the prisoner jammed the gears again. This time, the bus hurtled forward, and he smacked his head on the door. L.C. toppled backwards over the railing, his feet sticking up in the air.

The prisoner drove on for a few hundred yards, shifting from second to third, picking up speed, then slowing gradually, the bus rolling smoothly over the pavement. Finally, he pulled onto the shoulder.

Dan sat on the floor, feeling a great purple bruise forming on his forehead. L.C. sprawled on the steps, rubbing his collarbone. The aisle was littered with dented cans and broken bottles. For once, the tallest German wasn't smiling. Face pale as buttermilk, he'd wrapped his arms around one leg of the drink box, which was anchored to the floor with steel bolts.

The prisoner got out of the driver's seat. "Sorry so rough," he said.

Wincing, L.C. stood and climbed the steps, then reached down and offered Dan a hand. "Maybe we'd be better off," he said, "over there in the fight."

After signing the prisoners back into the camp, Dan dropped L.C. at his mother's house, where he didn't say a word, just trudged off across the field.

Alvin was at his store, in high spirits, sitting on the front porch, smoking a cigarette and drinking an Orange Crush.

"I had to slam the brakes on to keep from hitting a cotton

trailer," Dan said. "A bunch of stuff went flying off the shelves. Broke a few bottles and dented some cans pretty bad."

His uncle waved a hand as if brushing a fly away. "Don't worry about it." He puffed on his cigarette, and he had that peculiar gleam in his eyes. "I just made me a dandy little deal with a condom distributor. Every rubber in the Delta has to pass through my hands."

"Before use, or after?" Without waiting for Alvin's reply, he went inside, grabbed a hunk of Day's Work, then laid it down on the counter.

Rosetta peered at him over the Memphis paper, its banner headline announcing that British troops were advancing on Salerno. "Your momma told me you don't never walk out of here with no chewing tobacco. Say that nasty habit gone ruin a person's teeth."

"She's not one to talk about habits."

"Your momma do the best she can," Rosetta said, "and you may understand that someday. Then again, maybe not. You about as dumb as L.C." She folded the paper and eyed the plug of tobacco. "You want it, you gone have to pay for it, 'less your uncle come in here and make me give it to you."

"I aim to pay for it," he said, reaching for his wallet, though he'd hoped he wouldn't have to. Finding his hip pocket empty, he remembered pulling the wallet out and laying it under the seat. "Just a minute," he said, "I'll be right back."

The wallet wasn't on the floor up front, so he crawled up and down the aisle, looking under every counter and display case, but the damn thing was gone. With it went four dollars, his driver's license, a picture of his daddy and his State Guard ID.

FIFTEEN

ORDERED TO PATROL the perimeter after supper, Marty paused near the fence to look at a thicket, about a hundred yards away, at the edge of Otis Heslep's field. On the far side of the trees was the field itself, and beyond it a gravel road and Red Gillespie's place. If you flew over Loring County, everything would be broken up into neat, orderly squares, this man's world ending where that one's began, much as it had been since the early settlers moved in, poisoning and then burning the trees and clearing the land.

He was no stranger to the notion of boundaries, of lines that separated, but until now he'd always thought of them as flimsy, just some vague notion of how things ought to be. Yet there was a big difference between being on the outside of a fenced enclosure and being on the inside, between being in uniform and out of it, between one uniform and another. And between those who'd answered the call to murder and those who'd never heard it, the difference was huge.

The majority of the guards, like Kimball, had fathers who could, and would, demand favors. One of them, a boy from Tampa named Huggins, told Marty that his daddy had chosen the University of Florida over Yale because his grandfather refused to let him take his valet up to Connecticut, for fear that northern exposure would corrupt his black character. Huggins didn't know whether his family had interceded with the army on his behalf, and he didn't much care. It wouldn't have bothered him one bit, he said, to serve overseas. He'd been in the ring, beaten the shit out of others and gotten the shit beat out of him, and his little brother had once shot him on a squirrel hunt. Somebody somewhere had a reason for keeping him stateside, and he guessed it was a good one. The Hugginses owned a company that used to manufacture tennis nets but now was turning out camouflage helmet netting. And if the war lasted long enough, he might have to go home and take over, since neither his father nor his grandfather was in particularly good health.

The few guards who'd seen action rarely talked to one another, though every now and then Marty would catch himself staring at one of them and sometimes he'd feel somebody studying him. Whenever that happened, both men would look away, as if the fleeting glimpse alone had already revealed too much.

Four or five days ago, in the latrine, he'd been watching his urine splash into the trough when a guard named Brinley walked up beside him and unzipped. Kimball, the camp gossip, claimed that he'd been in the Philippines with MacArthur, but that a wound, possibly self-inflicted, got him evacuated to Australia a few days before Homma drove the Americans and Filipinos onto the Bataan Peninsula. The unit Brinley had belonged to, he said, was completely wiped out.

For the longest time, as they stood side by side at the urinal, Brinley failed to produce. Marty had been out in the sun all day, driving from field to field with Kimball, and when they got back to camp, he'd drunk about a gallon of water; had his bladder not been full, he would've shaken himself, zipped up and left, to spare Brinley the embarrassment. But that, evidently, was the furthest thing from Brinley's mind. When Marty finally finished and turned to go, he realized Brinley had not come there to piss but to jerk off, and even that endeavor wasn't working out. "I could do it," he said, "if I could just concentrate. But Christ Jesus, I just can't."

Marty had no idea what he ought to say. But he knew, as surely as he'd ever known anything, that to simply walk away would be even more indecent than Brinley's behavior.

"I had an aunt back in Saint Joe," Brinley said, giving up and tucking himself in, "my father's sister. A real nice woman, big and kind of tall, most people would probably say a little homely, because her face was on the rough side. She taught little kids Sunday school—taught me one year, too, but she was always careful not to favor me over any of the others. That's just the kind of person she was. She clerked in the Woolworth's on North First, and sometimes, when the woman who took tickets at the theater was sick, she'd fill in for her.

"I guarantee you she never had a dirty thought in her life, probably never said a cussword or took a drink. Never did anything bad to anybody—I mean, this was just a real good person we're talking about. But that don't count for much, does it? She died about two years ago. My dad wrote me a letter when I was in basic. She was only fifty when she got some kind of cancer and they amputated a leg. That didn't save her, though. It took her a long time to die, and while she was sick, my uncle Owen started running around with other women. He wasn't even there the night she died.

"And that's who I'm trying to think about," Brinley said.

"Thinking about doing it with her after she's already lost her leg and Uncle Owen don't have no use for her. I know it's wrong, and that's why I can't concentrate. The rest of the time, when I'm not trying to do it, she's all I think about."

"I meant to go to a whore," Marty said. "A colored one. They're down there on Church Street every night. At least that's what folks say."

"I been with colored women," Brinley said. "In California, before I shipped out. Hell, out there you can't always tell what somebody is. Got Mexican mixed in with colored and some- times Nip, too. I fucked a Nip in Long Beach. Never thought a thing about it."

"I wanted a colored whore because I figured she'd hate me."

"Makes sense that she would. Not saying anything against you, understand, but you're from around here, and you all don't treat colored people too good."

"That's a fact."

"Funny they'd send you back home, though—and thank God they didn't do it to me. Saint Joe's the last place in the world I'd like to be."

"I guarantee you there's worse places than Saint Joe, wher- ever the hell it is. But I reckon that's something you know, ain't it?"

Brinley's face, which had displayed such innocent baffle- ment at his inability to masturbate, now took on an altogether different cast, hard and sharp. "There ain't no good places left," he said. "Not for people like you and me."

He left Marty standing alone in the latrine, somehow feel- ing as if he were the one who'd gotten caught milking cock. They hadn't spoken again since. Whenever they passed each other, on the way to the mess hall or Supply, Brinley ignored Marty, just as Marty ignored him.

In the twilight, at the southwest corner of the compound, the one person he couldn't ignore—and had begun to think about night and day, much as Brinley thought about his dead aunt—sat with his back against the fence, arms clasped around his knees while he gazed at the sky.

Marty had gone to the trouble of listing, on a sheet of lined paper, everything about the German that struck him as suspicious. For one thing, when Marty addressed him, he would just stare back like a calf mesmerized by the sight of a painted gate, yet Dan claimed he'd spoken English to him, and Dan didn't lie. And he never put on the German uniform in the evenings, content instead to loom around the camp in his dirty, sweaty prison clothes. You never saw another prisoner have anything to do with him. Most important, though, there was Marty's own certainty that he and this man with the ruined face were somehow linked.

Sometimes he was sure he was the soldier who'd pointed a Gewehr at him while he knelt in the ditch on the Niscemi road, begging for his life. The rifle had what looked like a silencer on it, which was absurd, since the din all around was deafening, the pop and crackle of small-arms fire melding with the low-frequency whooshing sound of mortar rounds, followed by the dull thunk of concussion. The German's face, it seemed to him now, had been discolored, a purple band spreading from his neck and onto his cheek, and his eyes, in recollection, devoid of malice. The middle joint on the trigger finger whitened, and

Marty shut his eyes. When a voice hollered "Hands!" he thought of his own helpless hands, already in the air, and the other man's—the hands that were about to destroy him. A lifetime passed before he understood that what he'd actually heard was *"Hans!"* When he opened his eyes, he was alone and, in a manner of speaking, still alive.

He paused before the German, who looked at him for a moment, then cleared his throat, got up and brushed dirt off the seat of his pants. Then, instead of nodding and walking away briskly as he usually did when their paths intersected, he just stood there.

Marty's fingers grazed the stock of the rifle hanging from his shoulder. "I got a feeling you're a liar," he said. "Sometimes I think you killed a buddy of mine. Sometimes I think you almost killed me. Sometimes I think you didn't do either one. But there's still something about you that don't seem right."

"Not German," the man said softly.

Whatever internal mechanism kept time in Marty's body all but failed. "Not German? Then what the fuck are you?"

"Polish. I am Polish. From border place." The prisoner raised both hands in front of his chest and brought them together as if squeezing an accordian. "They *make* me to fight. But I kill no one. *No one.*"

When he put out his hand, Marty stepped backwards and jerked the rifle off his shoulder.

"No," the man said, shaking his head, eyeing the hole in the end of the quivering barrel. "No. I mean not to harm. Please."

"Please? You asking me to show a little faith in you? Jesus, have you picked the wrong fellow." As best he could, Marty leveled the rifle at him, though he couldn't keep his hands from

shaking. "Go on! Turn your ass around. We're going to see the captain."

He poked the prisoner with the tip of the barrel, then shoved him as hard as he could with the butt, and with a shout, the German fell forward onto his hands and knees.

From different directions, Kimball and Huggins both came running, Kimball shirtless and with shaving cream on his face. Instead of a rifle, Huggins carried a tennis racket that was missing half its strings.

Marty stood over the prisoner, pointing the barrel at the back of his head.

Because of the shaving cream, Kimball resembled a stunned young Santa. "Stark?" he said. "What the fuck is going on?"

The trigger teased him as no woman ever would. "This son of a bitch don't know who he is."

"Well, these days," Kimball said, "who the hell does?"

Huggins swatted an imaginary ball. "I do," he said.

SIXTEEN

"AT EASE," Munson said.

Kimball relaxed, but Stark didn't, because he couldn't, and Huggins didn't need to. Huggins never really came to attention to begin with, most likely because he knew his grandfather had gone to college with Henry Stimson. Word had come down to Munson that all this private would need, if he wanted to reach the secretary of war, was a nickel and a pay phone, and he'd get the nickel back.

The rest of his face as inflamed now as the scarred part, the prisoner stood at attention between Kimball and Stark. Stark's rifle was at sling arms, but he kept caressing the stock with his fingers—a fact Munson noted with some nervousness. "What's the problem?" he said.

"This prisoner, sir," Stark said. "I spoke to him the day I reported for duty. Spoke English to him, I mean. And he acted—"

"Would you speak German to me, Private?"

"Sir?"

"I asked if you'd speak German to me?"

"No sir."

"Of course not. Because I'm not German."

"No sir."

"So why would you speak English to him?"

"Well, sir, I can't speak German."

"You're not here to carry on conversations with the prisoners, Stark. If you're lonely, I'm sure that Huggins and Kimball would be happy to chat with you about the fortunes of your favorite football team or the vicissitudes of romance, whatever you'd like. But these Germans are here to be prisoners, and you're here to help them fulfill their obligations as captured enemy soldiers. Is that understood?"

"Yes sir."

Stark's cheeks, Munson realized, were about the same shade now as the German's. In the small-unit seminar at West Point, commanders were always urged to pay attention to what they liked to call "the stress points"—the fingertips, the mouth, the jaws—because it was your duty to help keep a man from exploding, unless you wanted him to explode. In this case, Munson didn't. He hoped that if Stark ever exploded, he'd be so far away that he'd never even have to hear about it. "So," he said, easing off a little, "you spoke English to him."

"Yes sir."

"And what happened?"

"He acted like he couldn't understand me. But the fact is, he speaks at least some English. He talks some with the fellow he's working for—and that's Dan Timms, who I've known all my life—and just now he spoke it to me. He told me that he's not German. Says he's Polish and the Germans made him fight. I think he's lying, sir, but I don't know why. I just got a funny feeling about him. I think—sir, I know it's not my business to make decisions, but I think maybe we ought to look at his *Solbuch*.

There's something creepy about him, and the way he's been acting proves it."

Munson himself had a friend or two in the War Department. They claimed to be working feverishly to wrangle him a combat assignment, to get him transferred out of this backwater that would always be considered a stain on his record, just as he claimed to be itching for action. But in truth, he wanted to stay right here, or another place like it, until the war was over.

His best friend at West Point, a guy from Medford, Oregon, who could bring a tear to the eye of the crustiest topkick when he sang "Danny Boy," had died during the Torch landings in November. Munson knew a lot of men who'd died, and more still who were going to. In some instances, he knew their wives or girlfriends, their parents or children, and where they'd grown up, what kind of music they liked, what their favorite foods were. Much as he loved them, he didn't want to join their ranks. He wanted to live a long time, to see his daughter grow up and get married, to watch while his wife's hair turned gray, and his along with it. He longed for no greater glory now than the rigors of old age.

Nevertheless, he'd always done his job and would continue to, no matter the consequences. And from those same friends in the War Department, he knew that plans for reeducating POWs were already being hatched. The first step would be to identify the anti-Nazis, who could then be separated from the rest, given training and ultimately be used to de-Nazify the others. His duty was to investigate. If he uncovered information that drew favorable attention and got him promoted into a combat assignment—well, that would be the hand fate dealt him. And he'd play it.

He stepped closer to the prisoner. "Do you speak English?"

"Little."

"Little, *sir*," Kimball snapped.

"Shut up, Kimball," Munson said. "I can guarantee you that no man who served in the Afrika Korps requires instruction in military etiquette from you." He looked into the prisoner's face. "Are you Polish?"

"Polish, yes."

He walked over to his desk and picked up a pad and a pen. "What unit did you serve in?"

"Schutzen Regiment Hundred Four."

"Where were you captured?"

"Name of place . . . I don't know. English capture."

"What's *your* name?"

The prisoner told him.

"Spell it."

The prisoner hesitated. "Please?" He extended his hand.

Munson gave him the pad and pen. The prisoner stepped over to the desk, laid the pad on it, wrote his name.

Munson looked at what he'd written. *Gerard Szulc.* "I've seen your name on the roster," he said, "but there it's spelled S-C-H-U-L-T-Z."

"I write Polish. German spell different. My family Polish."

"From what I know, if your family's Polish, you wouldn't have been in the Afrika Korps."

"Like I told you, sir," Stark said, "there's something spooky about him."

Munson decided to ignore him, though if Kimball had interrupted, he would have rescinded his privileges for a couple weeks. "You're anti-Nazi, I take it?" he asked the prisoner.

"Not Nazi. Yes. No one in family."

"What about the other prisoners?"

This time, he didn't answer.

"Just the ones in your own work detail, say. Are any of *them* Nazis?"

The man moved his feet but still didn't speak.

"Are you afraid to answer that question?"

"Afraid, yes."

"Why?"

Again he remained quiet.

"Okay, Schultz." Munson thumped the pad against the desktop. There was no point in prolonging the encounter. Besides, he wanted to be alone, so he could write his wife a letter, as he'd done every night they'd been apart; some days, he'd written two, one in the morning, another that evening. "We'll check out what you've told us. It may be that some other people will want to talk to you. In the meantime, for better or worse, you're a field hand. You'll pick that cotton till your thumbs fall off."

He told Kimball and Huggins to escort the prisoner out. "But don't go with him any farther than the rec area. Just leave him there and get back to your own business. Stark, you stay."

He waited until the others had left, then he glanced at the pad once more before putting it in his desk drawer. "Stark," he said, "on the subject of what is or is not creepy?"

"Yes sir?"

"I believe you are."

"Yes sir. Whatever you say, sir."

"Do you find yourself creepy?"

"At certain times, sir."

"When?"

"Most times, I guess. These days."

"Were you always that way?"

"I don't believe so, sir. In fact, I know I wasn't."

"Stop touching that rifle stock."

"Yes sir."

"This instant."

"Yes sir."

"I don't want to see you fooling with it like that again. If you have need to lay your hands on it, then *lay your hands on it,* by God. It is *not* a woman's breast, Stark. Are we *goddamn* clear on that?" Despite the fact that he'd always been regarded as a calm person, and was doing his best to remain calm now, he was screaming. And as he advanced on Stark, stopping when their faces were only inches apart, it crossed his mind to wonder how he'd behave in dense undergrowth, in unknown country, with dark shapes closing in from all sides.

SEVENTEEN

WEDNESDAY EVENING, Dan put on his State Guard uniform and drove the truck to town. Alvin had loaned him a few dollars, and he meant to do something he hadn't done in a good while—treat himself to a burger and a shake. He loved a good burger more than just about anything, and Kelly's were the best, but he'd been staying away from the snack bar. To begin with, he didn't have money to waste on restaurant food. More importantly, he didn't want to encounter Marie Lindsey, as he stood a fair chance of doing at Kelly's.

Tonight, though, he wasn't feeling so cautious. Having his wallet stolen had reminded him that there wasn't much point in denying these little pleasures. You could hold off and hold off, and the next thing you knew, you might not have anything to buy your pleasure with. You might not even have yourself to please.

Marie wasn't in the snack bar, but one of her friends, Sally Mankins, was sitting in a back booth with Tom and June Gaither, whose father had just taken over from their grandfather at the bank. The three of them were still in high school, and when Dan saw the schoolbooks stacked up beside their empty soda glasses, he felt a flush of anger. With Gaither's luck, the war would end before he ever had to go fight, and in another year or so, they'd all be strolling around the Ole Miss campus, doing whatever college kids did.

That was the thing about the war: if it ended, he'd be stuck right here for the rest of his life; if it didn't, he'd be trying to kill people who in most cases wouldn't be so different from him, and he hadn't really understood this until he got out in the field with the Germans. His father had attempted to tell him as much, but the way he'd put it didn't make any sense at the time. "If everybody went naked," he said, "war wouldn't work."

He and Dan were out back, stacking firewood under the eaves, and the house was empty. Shirley had gone to Jackson to see her ailing sister, and Alvin had business down there anyway, probably with a bootlegger.

"It's the uniform does it," his father said. "Once they put it on you, you start thinking, *I'm green and they're gray*—or *they're green and I'm gray*. Or *blue*. Or *brown*.

"Course, the uniform itself ain't enough. Too many folks got exactly the same one, and how can that be worth having? So they'll try to instill unit cohesion, but ain't enough if you only cohere with folks from Loring County, or from Mississippi. You got to cohere with folks from Blytheville, Arkansas, and Bossier City, Louisiana, maybe even some from Illinois. So a bunch of you'll get the same kind of patch on your shoulder— and it'll have something to do with making bones."

Dan had no idea what the hell he was talking about. Some people thought his daddy was drunk a good bit of the time, but he hardly ever drank. "Sir?" he said.

"Making bones, Danno, making bones. See, if that patch was a color, it'd have to be red. And anybody wearing it has got to be ready to give up all the red they got in 'em. For their momma, their daddy, for their sister or aunt Sue. Make yourself a bone—but not till you've made some other folks bones first.

"Now, my job in the war was looking after a bunch of four-legged Fords, otherwise known as mules. And even that was about making bones. They sent me over there in the belly of a transport in the spring of '17, me and a whole drove of the poor beasts. You should've seen how they crammed 'em into that ship. Put 'em on a pallet and lowered it down there into the hold and shut 'em up in stalls, and don't let nobody ever tell you a mule can't get seasick. Every day, for twenty-four straight days, them mules puked and shit, and I puked and shit right along-side 'em. Difference was, I had to clean up their mess.

"I made bones out of them mules," his daddy said, a few flecks of white foam on his lips. "I made bones out of boys like myself, and they made a bone out of me."

Two days later, on the afternoon his mother was due back from Jackson, Dan got off the school bus, walked into the house and found his father in a pool of red, still clutching his pistol.

Lizzie was behind the counter, wearing the same outfit she always had on. It looked like a nurse's uniform. Dan had never once seen her out of it, not even on those few occasions when they'd met in the street. She was the face of Kelly's snack bar, a small dark-haired woman who could have been any age between thirty-five and fifty.

"Hadn't seen you in a while, soldier," she said, setting a glass of water before him.

"I'm not a soldier. Not yet anyhow."

"You will be. Before long, they'll have stray dogs in uniform. Fact is, they already got one or two." She glanced at the far end of the snack bar, where the little sergeant from Camp Loring was snickering over a stack of comic books. She shook her head, then leaned over the counter as if intending to say something mean, and her breasts almost spilled out of her blouse.

He must have taken too long to look up. "They better put you in the artillery," Lizzie said. "You're pretty good at zeroing in on targets."

He couldn't decide whether to act like he didn't know what she meant or to hang his head and apologize. "Sorry," he finally mumbled.

When she laid her hand on top of his, he almost jumped off the stool. "Don't be stupid," she said. "What do you want?"

"A burger," he blurted. "And a shake."

"Hot and cold. You got it, Captain." She turned and walked over to the grill, where the elderly Negro fry cook stood turning burgers. "One more," she said.

The burger was big and juicy, the milk shake so thick, he had to eat it with a spoon. He was just finishing when he heard the door open. In the mirror behind the counter, atop the inverted stacks of cups, his eyes met Marie's. Her hair looked different, like she might have dyed it. He didn't remember it being such a white shade of blond.

"When she gets to be about thirty," his mother had told him last fall, "Marie won't be worth having. Every woman reaches that point sooner or later, but for her, it'll be sooner." That was all she had to say on the subject, and he was glad, because by then Marie had been wearing his letter sweater for more than a month. She wore it to school every day until the

Monday after his father's suicide, when she handed it back to him, washed and neatly folded, in the hallway between classes and said she couldn't see him anymore. When he asked her why, she said she was sorry, then turned and walked into the girls' bathroom.

At that point, he made what the principal told him was the worst mistake of his life: he pushed the door open and barged in after her, shouting and kicking the doors to the stalls, knocking one right off the hinges. Girls began screaming, cowering in the corners, and it took the chemistry teacher and the baseball coach to haul him out of there. Later, in his office, the principal said he wasn't going to expel him, because he was so close to graduating, but that if Dan didn't get hold of himself, he'd end up like some of the other men in his family. That was a hard thing to say, he added, and he knew it was a hard thing for Dan to hear right now. Then he got up from his desk—a big man who doubled as the football coach, and who'd paddled boys so hard that they had to ice their butts down—and put his arms around him, pulling him to his chest. "Aw, Danny," he said. "Goddamn it, son. Goddamn it."

Marie wouldn't say *Goddamn it* now, but Dan bet she was thinking it, wondering, in her surprise, why she'd picked tonight to come to the snack bar. Spooning up the last of his milk shake, he let her have a few seconds to decide what to do. Out of the corner of his eye he saw Gaither leaning across the table, whispering something to his sister and Sally Mankins, probably hoping to find a way to help Marie save face.

But evidently, she decided to save face herself. Instead of turning and walking out, she came over to the counter and sat down beside him. Lizzie looked at her sharply, then grabbed a stack of dirty dishes and piled them in the sink.

"Hey, Dan."

"How you doing, Marie?"

"Not too bad."

"Well, that's good."

"You got drill tonight?"

"Yeah."

"I thought so. Y'all do it every Wednesday night, don't you?"

"Three out of every four."

"How long before you go in the army?"

"I aim to join up at the end of the year. That's when I turn eighteen."

"On December seventeenth," she said. "Did you think I'd forgotten?"

"Well, I don't know."

"I didn't forget." She pulled a paper napkin from the holder on the counter and began tearing off bits. "I'm not as bad as your momma says I am."

Before he could reply, Lizzie said, "This ain't the time to be tearing napkins to pieces. Those are the last ones we've got. If you're nervous, why not bite your nails?"

For a moment, all conversation stopped. Lizzie went right on washing dishes, her hands submerged in soapy water. Marie looked as if she'd been hit in the belly with a baseball bat.

Dan said, "Why don't we go take a walk?"

Marie said nothing, just nodded, and he dropped some coins on the counter. "Thanks, Lizzie," he said.

She never looked up. "Sure thing, Captain. March hard."

Outside, the streetlights had come on. A brisk wind was blowing in from the west, and looking above the buildings on the far side of the street, he saw a purple mass of clouds. "I wouldn't mind if it rained tonight," he said. "We just keep doing the same drills over and over. It don't amount to much."

She walked along beside him, step for step. They weren't really touching yet, but once or twice her elbow grazed his. He'd thought they never would share a sidewalk again.

"That's what you do in the army, isn't it?" she said. "Just the same things day after day?"

"Yeah. Till somebody starts shooting, anyway."

"Nobody'll ever shoot at you. The war'll be over by next summer."

"Who told you that?"

"That's what everybody's saying."

"Yeah, well, let's hope everybody's right," he said. "What'd you mean—what you said about my momma?" He knew what Shirley thought, of course, but he couldn't believe she would've said anything to Marie.

"She stopped my mother in Woolworth's. Not long after we broke up. She really gave her what-for, about me being two-faced and all, and Mother started crying. She told your mother it wasn't me and it wasn't her, that it was Daddy that made me break it off. And then your mother—well, she used foul language about Daddy and asked where he was right then, like she meant to go after him, too. When Mother said he was at work, your momma grabbed her arm and stuck her face in Mother's and asked if she was so G-D sure about that."

The shoes Mrs. Lindsey was wearing during the encounter probably cost more than all the clothing his mother owned, but you couldn't call Shirley Timms a coward. Tomorrow, he might feel a little proud of her, though it wouldn't do to show it now. "Seems like everybody's going crazy," he said. "You probably remember me mentioning L.C.? Now, I've known him since I was seven or eight. Me and him's tromped cotton together, pitched baseballs back and forth for two, three hours at a time. But the other day my wallet went missing, and I'm pretty sure he stole it."

"Sooner or later, that's what they'll do. You can't even blame them. None of 'em have any money or ever will. Mother's been through more housekeepers than I can count, and I don't even know what the current one's called."

She allowed him to take her hand. And right when things were going the way he wanted them to, some flaw in his makeup—the same flaw, he decided later, that had provoked his remark about L.C. not having a grandfather, or his telling Marty about the prisoner speaking English—made him say, "So, *was* your daddy at work?"

Right in front of Delta Jewelers, while the wind whipped her hair, Marie stopped walking and backed away from him, her hands clenched at her sides into tight little fists, until a parking meter halted her retreat. "Oh God," she said. "Everything Mother said about you was true."

"And what was that?" he asked, knowing he wasn't going to like the answer.

"Jesus. It really does run in your family."

She turned and ran back down the street, then slowed as she neared Kelly's. Stepping off the curb, she pulled her sweater tightly around herself, strode purposefully across the street and disappeared into the alley between Woolworth's and the Western Auto.

Yeah, Dan thought, sticking his hands into his pockets, *and plenty of things run through some other families, too.*

EIGHTEEN

HEADED TOWARD the football field, he nearly bumped into Marty, who darted out of the pool hall with a big bag of popcorn tucked under his arm. You could tell he'd been drinking. His tie had come unknotted, his zipper was partway open and there was a dark stain where he'd spilled beer on his class A's.

"You going to drill?" he asked.

"Yeah."

"Who's y'all's commanding officer?"

"Captain Hobgood."

"*Ralph* Hobgood? From the Highway Patrol?"

"Yeah."

"He drill y'all in how to write a traffic ticket?"

He was loud and insistent and thick-tongued, and Dan had never liked talking to anybody in that shape. "We do close order," he said. "And last month we went to the firing range down at Camp Shelby."

"We did all that shit in boot camp," Marty said, falling in beside him. "It's completely useless. The one thing you really need to know, they don't teach that."

"And what might that be?"

As if to reclaim some vestige of dignity, Marty handed Dan the bag of popcorn, then zipped himself up and started knotting his tie. "I couldn't say," he said. "I just know I never learned it."

Armed with a 1917 Enfield, Dan and seventeen other State Guard members stood at midfield while Corporal Bunch, under the watchful eye of Captain Hobgood, demonstrated the proper use of a Thompson submachine gun. A handful of high school girls, and another of old men, sat in the bleachers on the home side, glancing up into the stadium lights every few minutes, wondering when to head out in order to beat the rain. Marty sat alone on the visitors' side, a row from the top, and kept right on eating his popcorn.

Corporal Bunch was in his late twenties, a tall, broad-shouldered man who worked in the shop at Loring Chevrolet. He'd moved up from around Yazoo City a few years ago, and nobody knew much about him except that he had both "military experience," which accounted for his Guard rank, and a "chronic condition," which accounted for his exemption from active duty. Nobody liked him. If Captain Hobgood met you on the street, he'd call you by your first name. But Bunch would say, "Step out, there, Private," then grin like you were supposed to find this funny.

"The Thompson submachine gun fires forty-five-caliber ammo," he now informed them. "It's the most advanced weapon of its type. This thing will kick the living shit out of the Schmeisser."

"Watch your language, Corporal," Hobgood called. "There's young ladies over yonder."

"Right, *sir,*" Bunch barked. He held the Thompson at port arms and slapped the stock. "Say that some months from now y'all find yourselves in a street-fighting situation in downtown Berlin. We use mortar fire on the buildings, call in some tanks and artillery to blast holes in 'em, then you pitch a grenade in there and, right after the explosion, jump through the hole and spray the sorry—you spray the enemy with fire from this exquisite weapon. Well, the problem, gentlemen, is that this thing packs a punch. Even if y'all got forearms made of tempered steel like yours truly, the barrel's bound to climb. So the designers of this lovely lady built her with a detachable stock. Now, y'all no doubt noticed the sling's attached to the stock *and* the barrel. So what you gone do is detach the stock—" he popped it loose—"and then let gravity work her magic."

The stock hit the ground.

"And then you gone plant your foot *firmly* on that baby—" he stepped onto the stock with one boot, then dropped into a shooter's crouch—"and you gone squeeze—"

"Goddamn it, Bunch!" Hobgood snapped. "Is that thing loaded?"

"Yes *sir.*"

"With live ammo?"

"No *sir.*"

"Give me that son of a bitch." Hobgood snatched the Thompson out of his hands, then jerked on the sling until the corporal lifted his foot. Jamming the stock into place, Hobgood said, "Y'all can just forget all that shit. You jump into a room full of Germans, you got worse problems than a bucking barrel. The last thing in God's world you want to do is get yourself where you can't move because your foot's stuck on the stock of your goddamn weapon. Might as well step on your own dick."

The captain was breathing hard. He'd fought in the First War, got captured and stuck in that underground cell with Jimmy Del Timms and two other men from Loring County, neither of whom made it home. For many years, every so often he'd come out to the house, where he and Dan's father would sit together on the porch steps, not saying much, occasionally mentioning a name and shaking their heads. Dan once heard them talking about a wagon that had pulled up outside the prison every morning—they could see the wheels through a small window up close to the rafters. Three Germans would enter the basement; the one with the stethoscope around his neck figured out who'd died during the night, then motioned for the others to wrap a chain around the bodies, which were then hauled up to the street through a coal chute. A great many of the prisoners, Hobgood included, had pneumonia. They wasted away on bread and water, an infrequent bowl of meat-less soup. When they were finally liberated, only twelve men out of nearly a hundred had survived.

Hobgood finally got his breathing under control. He glanced up at the girls in the bleachers, but they were chattering among themselves and paying no mind to the men down on the field.

"We gone do some drill now," Hobgood announced. "It's useful, since moving's the most important thing you'll ever do."

Shortly afterwards, the storm rolled in and the bleachers emp-tied out. Though Dan expected Hobgood to order them back to the armory, for some reason he kept drilling them, and Marty continued to sit there, even as the rain pounded down.

"To the rear, march!"

Dan stepped out with his left foot, then executed a perfect pivot and headed back with the others toward the west goalposts. He didn't exactly enjoy this part of it, but he didn't hate it, either. When you were marching, nothing mattered except where you put your foot, and he always put his in the right place.

"Left flank, march!"

The rain fell in sheets. A thunderclap shook the ground, making everybody jump and look up into the night sky streaked with gold and silver.

"Column right, march!"

The principal wasn't going to like having the field all torn up, but it belonged to the American Legion, not the high school, so State Guard drill took precedence over football.

"Step it up there, Kennison," Corporal Bunch hollered. "A little rain don't stop the—"

Suddenly, a bolt of lightning struck the press box and the stadium lights went out, the air thick with the green-peanut odor of nitrogen and sulfur. As they stood there paralyzed, lightning hopscotched eastward from the far end of the field, each strike followed by another, as if a giant were strolling the Delta.

"Drop them rifles and scatter!" Hobgood yelled.

Dan flung his weapon aside, bent over and sprinted for the vistors' sideline. Another bolt shattered the darkness, and he threw himself forward, landing in a puddle and sliding onto the cinder track.

When he looked up, Marty was perched above him in the gray electric light, still sitting in the same row and pawing through the bag of popcorn for a kernel dry enough to eat.

NINETEEN

FRIDAY MORNING, while waiting for Dan to bring the pickup back so she could go to work, Shirley decided to curl her hair. For a good while now, she'd been letting herself go, even though she'd promised herself she wouldn't. She came from Irish Protestant stock, and nobody in her family'd ever had it easy. Her father was born with only one good arm; on the end of his right one, he wore an ugly metal hook. But when you knocked him down, which a few men had done, he didn't just get up. He got up and knocked you down, too, and then he did his level best to claw your eyes out with that hook. If there had been anybody whose eyes needed clawing out, Shirley might've done it, but the only eyes she saw any fault in were her own. Last night, while Dan slept in the bedroom next door, she'd brought herself to orgasm. Though she'd bitten down hard on the pillowcase, she couldn't believe he hadn't heard her cry out. The hell of it was, she hadn't even enjoyed it much, the greatest pleasure being the utter helplessness she'd felt.

Once or twice at night, she'd heard him doing the very same thing—the telltale creaking of the bedsprings as he did his best to keep quiet. A few months from now, wherever they sent him for training, he'd do it on leave with a living, breathing partner. The act would finally take place in tawdry surroundings, and when he looked back—if he lived long enough to—he'd probably be surprised that he thought it was anything special.

The only man she'd ever known who felt the same way she did about making love was Alvin. Any day on which he did it was by definition a good day, no matter how many other things went wrong. He never rushed. Sometimes he wouldn't even put himself in—he wanted to sit and touch and look for hours. He loved the parts of her body men normally didn't notice: her armpits, her knees, her heels and ankles. He loved them so much, in fact, that he would no longer touch them.

Some people had electric curling irons, but she wasn't about to squander any money on that when the old kind worked just fine. She lit the coal-oil lamp on her bedside table and stuck the iron in the glass chimney. While it was getting good and hot, she walked over to the dresser and opened the middle drawer, reaching for a clean pair of panties, and she saw motion down in all that soft fabric.

The snake had dull brownish skin, its body a little thicker than a broom handle. Back when they moved into the house, Jimmy Del had told her that cottonmouths hated dry spaces or being very far off the ground, so odds were that any snake she ever saw inside was just a chicken snake. "Stay calm and call me," he'd said, but that was no option now. If she let the snake escape, she'd worry every time she opened a drawer or a cabinet and might as well just run out the front door now and keep going.

She looked around the room but saw nothing that could serve as a weapon, so she hurried into the hallway, jerked open the closet door and grabbed Jimmy Del's shotgun from where it stood propped in the corner. She hadn't fired it in years, but she shucked the action and heard a shell slide into the chamber, then ran back into the bedroom and got as close to the drawer as she dared. The snake raised its head, the alert eyes indicating an intelligence that she hoped wasn't there. When it opened its jaws, she squeezed the trigger.

The blast knocked her backwards and blew the snake to bits. She stood there rubbing her shoulder and poking the barrel through what used to be her underwear drawer. Blood and snake guts were soaking into her panties and stockings. The whole dripping mess had fallen through the splintered wood into the next drawer, where she'd folded the white blouse Alvin had bought her last Christmas.

Shaking, fighting the urge to sit down and cry, she pulled everything out of the undamaged top drawer; then she got Jimmy Del's handcart off the back porch and rammed it under the dresser and wrenched and pulled until its weight shifted and she could roll it down the hall and off the edge of the back porch.

Back inside, she took a bath and then, because she'd made herself a promise to curl her hair, marched back into the bedroom and picked up the curling iron, not thinking how hot the rods must've gotten by now. Spinning around, she looked in the mirror at the very moment her hair caught fire.

TWENTY

THE OFFICE of the local draft board—or "*see*lective service," as the chairman, Jasper Sproles, called it—was located in a glass-fronted building right across Second Street from the courthouse. Under a poster proclaiming the urgency of the cause, a couple white boys fresh out of high school sat nervously in stiff-backed chairs, accompanied by their mother, whom Alvin knew well enough to nod at. Three or four Negroes stood off to one side, holding their caps, waiting to be called.

Jasper was just coming out of his private office. He grinned at Alvin and raised one finger, then leaned over and whispered something to his clerk, who happened to be the mayor's wife. When he finished, he looked up and said, "Alvin, whyn't you come on back here? You and me's just gone take a minute or two, and then I'll get to these good folks." He smiled politely at the white boys and their mother, ignoring the black men altogether.

His desk was littered with files and applications for deferments, as well as a number of personal letters with return addresses that Jasper said Alvin would most likely recognize.

Some folks were reluctant to put their name on an envelope going to the selective service office, he said, but anonymity was a big joke anyway. Buddy Baker, the director of the Office of Civil Defense for Loring County, could walk into the post office and order any piece of mail opened if he deemed it necessary. When Alvin asked if that was federal policy, Jasper laughed and said it unofficially was, state by state.

Jasper found many things funny, not least of all the fact that a man who'd had two businesses foreclosed back in the thirties was now in a position to decide if the banker's grandson would go to college or hide in a foxhole. Kind of interesting the way things sometimes work out, he said. For instance, McNabb's Paste and Glue Company, which he'd married into, was only moderately successful until it started producing the glue that went on the flaps of every envelope licked at the War Department.

This morning's post had brought Jasper even more entertainment. "You know much about Mennonites?" he asked.

"I know what they are," Alvin said. "Don't know as I've ever met one, though."

"Oh, you've met 'em, all right, you just didn't know it. Fact is, we're surrounded by Mennonites, Jehovah's Witnesses, even got a Quaker. If my mail's any indication, it's amazing there's any Baptists and Methodists left, not to mention the purely unrepentant."

"They claimin' conscientious objection, I reckon."

"Oh yeah, right up until you tell 'em they'll most likely get assigned as medics, at which point they want to have a rifle and a chance to shoot back."

"Last time around," Alvin said, "you and me would've pulled the same kind of stunt, I imagine, if we'd had to."

"Would we?"

"I imagine."

"You don't believe in nothing, do you?" Jasper said.

"I believe in about as many things as you do."

"Well, that's why if old man Gaither walks in here and puts a bullet in me for sending his grandson on a surfing vacation to Honshu, I'd choose you as my replacement."

"You're nuts."

"How come?"

"You know how come."

"You mean because you're not respectable like I am?"

"To some folks."

"Like who?"

"Them that believe the line between what's strictly legal and what's not isn't just a thin streak of bullshit."

Jasper threw his head back and laughed so loudly, they could probably hear him across the street in the courthouse. "You're something, Alvin," he said. "Lordy."

"You didn't ask me to come by just so you could point that out."

"Naw, I sure didn't. You know old Frank Holder, don't you?"

"Know him when I see him."

"That very often?"

"Comes in the store from time to time, buys hisself a cold drink or a plug of tobacco. Don't usually say much. At least not since his boy got killed."

"A person might conclude that a man like Frank couldn't cause him no problems," Jasper said. "And in normal times, that'd probably be so. Thing is, these times ain't normal, and Frank's wife, Arva, is kin to Senator Bilbo." He smiled broadly.

"Now you probably wasn't paying a lot of attention along about November of last year when the senator addressed his colleagues on the subject of colored participation in the war effort, but he allowed as how he found it unseemly that a state like ours, with a colored population of close to fifty percent, should send only white men to the front. Said he wanted to see some coloreds in uniform, too, even if all they did was drive trucks and clean latrines. And ever since, the *see*lective service has been real careful to send up a fair number of our darker brethren."

He then explained, at tedious length, that Senator Eastland could always be reasoned with, since he owned a cotton plantation and knew what work needed to get done. "But old Theodore don't own much of anything, so if he found out about some colored boy that hadn't even registered—especially one that strikes some folks as cheeky—he *might* get hisself all worked up, you know."

"Are you telling me, Jasper, to bring L.C. in and sign him up so you can pack him off to the army?"

"Aw, Alvin, you know I ain't one to cave in to pressure."

"That's right. You're more likely to apply it, particularly when there's something you want."

"What could I want that I don't got?"

"Seems to me I recall you like that bootleg whiskey."

"Yeah, and that case you brung over when we talked about your boy last spring was good stuff. But fact of the matter is, I could get another case just like it by sundown. See, I own a big chunk of a thriving business. I can't be bought, 'cause the war's done let me purchase myself. I hope it does the same for you. And that colored boy, too. Till it does, though, he needn't attract no undue attention. And if you don't mind me saying so, you ought not to, neither. An august individual might question your patriotism."

He rose, so there was nothing Alvin could do but rise with him. And even though he knew he ought to keep his mouth shut, he said, "I need to ask you something, Jasper."

"Fire away, Alvin—fire *away*."

"If you were colored, would you die for this country?"

The man's face broke into a wide grin. "Not unless somebody shot me."

TWENTY-ONE

FOR A GOOD MANY years now, on Friday evenings Alvin had let Rosetta go home, trusting L.C. to operate the register. That first night, he told him not to let any of his friends beg candy or drinks from him, and after that he never mentioned it again.

"Mr. Alvin know a thief when he see one," L.C.'s momma said, "because that's what he is. And he know you ain't."

L.C. was only thirteen at the time, so he didn't argue with her, but how could Alvin tell he wasn't a thief when he didn't know that himself? He figured he'd steal whatever he could, whenever, so it had puzzled him, as the years went by, to discover that the urge to steal, even from white folks, just wasn't in him.

John Burns regarded this as a serious deficiency. Once, L.C. had wandered over to his place to drink a little whiskey, and when he walked in, the first thing he saw, hanging right there on the wall, was a black suit tailored for somebody about half a yard taller than his friend. "That old man Young's," he said, "ain't it?"

"Was his," Burns said.

"Aim to have it took up?"

"You think I wear that ugly thing, you dreaming."

"Why you hook it, then? You aim to sell it?"

"Hell no, I gone bury it. See, when old man Young went over yonder to Arkansas for a week, he done locked the back door and left the front open. Now what that tell you?"

"That he done forgot to lock his front door."

"You a waste at school, nigger, you can't do no better than that. What it say is, old Young thinks no white folks steal and no nigger ever go to the front door. So when he come back, he can lay awake in that bed to wonder how *that* shit done happen."

L.C. doubted Young would have to wonder very long before deciding what happened. But since tractor drivers and hoe hands were now scarce, he wouldn't run Burns off like he would've a few years back. Instead, he'd determine what that suit had cost him, multiply it by two or three and take that sum out of John Burns a nickel at a time, week after week, year after year. To get even, the only thing Burns could do was watch for another unlocked door.

Alvin had left plenty of doors unlocked when L.C. was around, including the one to his office safe. He'd send him in there to sweep up when it was hanging open, leaving the office himself so as not to get in the way. L.C. never told Burns about it, because he'd think he was crazy for not seizing the opportunity.

The thing was, L.C.'s feelings about Alvin Timms were complicated. There were times he hated him—like the day last spring when Alvin came back from town in a high mood and told him not to worry, that he'd cooked up some deal with the draft board to keep him from having to register. He'd wanted to escape the draft, but not because Alvin needed him to pick cotton, sweep the floor and sell Popsicles; that robbed him, at least for a while, of the biggest hope he'd ever harbored, along with all the others, and you couldn't help but hate a man for taking that from you.

But at other times, Alvin gave back some of what he'd taken. Late on Friday nights, after they'd turned the porch light off and latched the front door and nobody else was around, he'd pull out a bottle of whiskey and pour two glasses and, after L.C. had a swallow or two, ask if he'd mind making a little music.

The first time, it threw L.C. into the worst kind of confusion, which Alvin must've realized. "I was over on the Young place the other night," he explained, "heard the singing over by them shotgun houses and recognized your voice. Sat on the road in my pickup to listen awhile. I ain't never heard anything quite like that before, and I sure did like it."

L.C. sang that night, slapping his knee for rhythm, and the next Friday night, too. Before long, he was carrying the guitar to the store on Fridays, leaving it in the closet in Alvin's office. Just as John Burns craved the bush and the bower, Alvin Timms loved to hear about the Devil and his various guises, how the old one would make himself pretty if you thought he was ugly, then uglify himself right back.

"You ever seen Satan?" he finally asked one night.

"Not that I know of," L.C. said.

"You believe he's out there?"

"Could be."

"I believe he's in here," Alvin said, rapping himself on the chest. "I think I've had him in me since the day I was born."

L.C. picked a riff. Dark and slow. "What make you say so?"

"There's stuff inside me that nobody else could've put there."

L.C. thought he knew what Alvin meant. He'd heard his momma say stuff—just talking to herself—about Alvin and his brother and Dan's momma.

"You know what I'm talking about?" Alvin said.

"No sir."

"I think you do. And just between the two of us, I believe you got the Devil in you, too." Alvin poured himself another shot of whiskey, then drank it down and set the glass on his desk. "But I'm here to tell you, L.C., I hope it ain't so. Because that old boy can cause some real trouble."

Tonight was Friday. But instead of heading for his office like he usually did after the last bunch of field hands had been in and bought some Vienna sausages and as much hoop cheese as they could afford, Alvin hoisted himself onto the countertop. "L.C.," he said, "you and me's got to talk."

L.C. paused with the broom in his hand, feeling, already, like the worst kind of fool, a white man's dream of the ideal darky. His guitar was standing in Alvin's closet, right where he'd put it this morning.

"You know Mr. Frank Holder?"

Not *Frank Holder,* which is what he would've called him back there in the office with the two whiskey glasses on the desk. *Mister* Frank Holder.

"Yes sir."

"Hasn't nothing happened between you and him, has there?"

What in the name of God, he wondered, could happen *between* him and a white man? "No sir."

"You stop over there on his place on your route, don't you?"

"Yes sir. Stop there sometimes, anyway. Hadn't lately."

"And you can't think of no reason why he'd get it in his head you was smartin' off?"

Slowly, L.C. leaned his broom against the counter. Alvin's gaze lit on the handle for a second or two, then flicked back to L.C.'s face.

"I can think of one thing I might've did."

"All right. So what was it?"

L.C. scratched his head. "Well, maybe two—naw, now I don't want to be lying . . . it seem closer to three weeks ago. . . . Yes sir, it sure was three weeks ago that I stopped on my route there one day, long about three-thirty in the afternoon, and looked Mr. Frank Holder right square in the eye."

For a long time, Alvin said nothing. Then he shook his head, chuckled and jumped down off the counter. "Okay," he said. "Come on, let's drink us some whiskey. Where you gone end up, you'll need a little alcohol in your bloodstream."

The next morning, when he walked out onto the porch, the sunlight almost knocked him over. Dimly, he recalled that before Alvin had driven off and left him there in his office, they'd sung "Swing Low, Sweet Chariot."

He wanted to slip off somewhere and rest till his momma left the house for work; then he could get in the bed and give his head a chance to quit hurting. Hoping to God he wouldn't run into her, he set off the longer, roundabout way and was crossing the gravel road when he saw a pickup coming toward him. As it got a little closer, he recognized it. He raised his hand, intending to wave it down, but Dan just nodded and drove on by.

TWENTY-TWO

WAKING, Marty had discovered, was a lot like being born: unsettling but unavoidable. Light seeped in through the folds in the tent flaps, until it became a fact he had to acknowledge. Sooner rather than later, this being the army, you had to climb out of the cot, pull your clothes on and step outside. What you didn't have to do—and he began each day that fall knowing he wouldn't—was pick up a newspaper and read the new figures, the ones that told you how many more were dead. They didn't list how many others might as well be.

In the shower, he did his best to banish the chill he always woke with, letting the hot spray knead his neck and chest while Huggins and Kimball and one or two others hollered back and forth, the topic the same as always.

"You know whose bank I wouldn't mind making a deposit in? That little dark-haired thing down at the snack bar."

"*Lizzie?*"

"I never note their names. To me, they're all just *Honey*."

"That woman's probably forty, man, maybe more. Jesus

Christ." Kimball's horror sounded genuine. "What's the matter with you? You got the urge for a gray cootie?"

"California must have the worst educational system in the country if you got cooties confused with pubic hair."

"Whatever it is, I don't want to see anything gray when I look down there."

"You're not supposed to eyeball it, you're supposed to rout it out."

Kimball gestured at Huggins's crotch. "With what you got, about the only thing you could rout out is somebody's ear canal."

When Huggins made thrusting motions with his hips, Kimball hurled a soap bar at him, and a few minutes later, as Marty stood in a corner, toweling off, they were still in the showers, laughing and belittling each other.

His main concern now was the one of identity.

With so few guards in camp, nobody got liberty very often. But the last time they'd turned him loose, he'd gone home and, while his mother sat downstairs, scrounged through the attic until he found his father's 1920 Loring Separate School District yearbook. He'd turned to the student portraits and, not even looking at any of the faces, torn out those pages.

Back at camp, he'd sat on his cot, examining the photographs and, without referring to the names listed in the margins, trying to see how many he could correctly identify. About half the time he succeeded, because it was the mother or father of one of his high school friends and the family resemblance was obvious. But the man he thought was Harvey Finch, whose son Teddy he'd played basketball with, turned out to be somebody named Zenus McGhee, whom he'd never even heard of.

Still, he was batting about .500, if you wanted to see it in those terms, though that didn't seem too good, given that he'd known most of these people, in various incarnations, all his life. He thought he should give this test to somebody else—Dan, maybe—but was sure Dan would have said he was crazy.

So it disconcerted him when he walked into the tent after showering and found Sergeant Case flipping through the yearbook.

"Give me that," he said, snatching it out of his hands.

"Hey, hey—what's this?" Case said. "You ever heard about the chain of command? You know, treating your superiors with respect? I got a good mind to make you do some push-ups."

Marty jammed the yearbook into his footlocker and snapped it shut. "If I push anything up, it'll be you."

Backing away, Case leveled a finger at him. "And you'll end up in the stockade. Or the fucking nuthouse."

"Either one'd be an improvement on this, unless you're in there with me."

Case backed all the way out of the tent, then stuck his head in through the fly.

Marty couldn't help but crack up. His NCO looked like one of those clowns at the county fair: hit him on the head and win a nickel or take a ride for free.

"Captain wants to see you," Case said. "Right now. So get your loony ass moving."

To see Munson without a file at hand was almost like seeing him naked, and this morning he was also out of uniform, with a robe over his pajamas, and suffering from the flu. On his upper lip was a bright red cold sore.

He pulled a handkerchief from the pocket of his robe and blew his nose. "You ever find yourself in a position, Stark, where you really wanted to do the right thing, and you had what looked like two clear choices—not three or four, not five or six, just two—but you still couldn't tell which was which?"

"Yes sir. I guess everybody's been in that position at one time or another."

"And that's the position I'm in right now. You say you recall being there yourself?"

"Yes sir."

"Care to tell me about it?"

"No sir. Not really."

"Would it surprise you to know that *my* being in that position has something to do with you?"

"No sir."

"It wouldn't."

"No sir."

"There's not much that surprises you, is there, Stark?"

"Not really, sir. Not anymore."

"Would it surprise you," Munson said, "to know that some documents relating to the prisoner you're so interested in are missing?"

Word was, Patton took his own pulse whenever he came under shelling and somehow had learned to hold it steady. That was one skill, among many, that Marty Stark would never master. "No sir."

"I didn't think it would. And frankly, that worries me."

"I'm sorry, sir."

"The prisoner himself has nothing to do with the screwup.

In combat situations, rules are often forgotten. A *lot* of things are forgotten on the battlefield."

"Yes sir. They sure are, sir."

"That's right. Soldiers forget their training. Our men have been told, for instance, not to hunt souvenirs, yet they do. They swipe medals, steal decorations, sometimes even steal identification and documents. And because of this, it turns out that registering some of these prisoners can be a real nightmare."

Marty said, "Sir . . . if I could ask a question?"

Munson waited.

"Where was hc captured?"

"We don't know. His *Solbuch*'s gone. And unfortunately, that's not all."

He explained that the prisoner's serial number began with 81, indicating capture in North Africa. The problem was, no record of the serial number could be located at base camp; an entire box of files was missing, and his must have been in it. Right now, the army didn't even know which convoy had brought him over. The processing center had either lost or misplaced every shred of information on him. Practically speaking, he didn't exist.

Munson paused to see if Marty would offer an observation. When he failed to, the captain asked, "What does this news suggest to you, Stark?"

"Nothing, sir."

"Nothing?"

"No sir."

"In other words, you're buying my explanation—that some poor, dumb, overworked clerk screwed up somewhere in New Jersey, but that in the end these records will be found, proving this prisoner's exactly who he claims he is?"

"Yes sir."

"That's good, Stark," Munson said. "That's exactly the answer the army wants to hear."

"The *army*, sir?"

"That's right, it's what the army wants." Munson blew his nose on the handkerchief again, then gazed at it with disgust. "And believe it or not, Stark, the army also wants to ask you a favor."

TWENTY-THREE

September 29, 1943
Camp Loring, Miss.

Dear Stella,

First of all, since I know you like to envision the circumstances under which I'm writing, I should let you
know that it's midafternoon. I'm sitting on my cot,
wearing, if you can believe this, a pair of pajamas and a
robe cadged from the infirmary. I've been running a
slight fever—well, not that slight, above 102—so I'm
spending the day in my quarters.

I can't help wondering what it would be like to be
sick when you were actually on the front lines. That's a
strange thing to think about, isn't it? (And that's all I'm
doing, thinking on the page.) I remember that when I
was growing up, Mrs. Jorgenson, who lived down the
street from us in Wynoka, was diagnosed with cancer.
(The only reason we knew this was that her doctor,

another neighbor, told my father.) Of course, anybody could see that something was wrong with her; she began to lose weight, and her skin gradually took on a strange cast, almost greenish.

She and Mr. Jorgenson were childless. They ran the only drugstore in town, and each of them had been known to slip some of us kids candy. They liked children, in other words, and everyone agreed it was sad they never had any. My impression, and everyone else's, was that they were totally devoted to each other. You would see the two of them walking together in the park on Sunday afternoon, strolling along the creek, throwing bread on the water for the ducks. Or they'd ride around the countryside in their Model A, carrying a picnic basket with them and stopping wherever they felt like it, then spreading a blanket on the ground and having a leisurely lunch.

They were in their mid-forties when she got sick. When it became apparent that she wasn't going to recover, everybody wondered if Mr. Jorgenson would live long after she passed away. I think we all believed it would be one of those situations where the health of one person in the marriage determines that of the other.

In fact, he didn't live very long after she died—less than four years, if I recall this accurately, so he was probably no more than forty-nine or fifty when he died. It would make a more symmetrical story if he'd died of cancer himself, just as she had, but in fact he was up in a big oak tree in their front yard on a Saturday morning,

pruning some branches, when the limb he was standing on suddenly collapsed. Somehow or other, he managed to come down right on top of his head. It didn't kill
him, but he was unconscious when a neighbor walked
by and saw him, and by the time they got him to the
hospital, there was some type of swelling in his brain.
His head actually grew misshapen. He was in a coma for
the better part of two months, and then passed away
quietly one afternoon.

But the point of this story is that during the time
when Mrs. Jorgenson's condition was growing worse
and worse, you'd see the two of them at local sporting
events. At a basketball game, say, when we scored a
basket, Mrs. Jorgenson would scream at the top of her
voice, and Mr. Jorgenson would, too, just as if neither
of them knew that she would soon be gone.

You will probably think the connection I'm trying
to make here is tenuous, and I'm probably not making
it too well. But I sometimes wonder if, in life-and-death
situations, the only thing that matters is staying alive. If
it is, would a person stop loving the taste of smoked
salmon—even if, like me, he'd always enjoyed it more
than any other food in the world? In other words if, in
his rations, you gave him smoked salmon (not likely, of
course, in this army), would he notice what it was and
take pleasure in it? Or would he just shovel it down and
get on about the business of keeping his head low? I've
never thought about things like this before. It is un-
characteristic of me, probably a waste of time bought
and paid for by the army, and I would never express

such thoughts to anybody but you. Put it down to the fever, if you will.

Speaking of fever, the guard I've been worried about shows signs of cooling off. I know that from time to time he drinks when he's on duty, and you can rest assured I'm keeping an eye on that. But whereas a week or two ago after the incident I mentioned, I believed he posed a risk to the prisoners and perhaps even to the other guards, he has caused no further trouble. It's not my business to say if it was a good idea or a bad one to assign him to a camp in his hometown, but at any rate he's in a position to be particularly useful if, as I have some reason to hope, he so chooses.

Now, regarding your father's proposal: please tell him I'm flattered. I suppose that he's making a certain kind of sense—that "selling" the army is not that different, in the end, from selling real estate. But I'm not a recruiter. The people I "sell" the army to—since they are already in the ranks—have no choice but to buy what I'm selling. I'm afraid that if our livelihood were ever to depend on my ability to move a given piece of property, we'd surely starve.

But you don't need to say no just yet, because, for one thing, this war's far from over. I'm glad civilians are optimistic, since it would make prosecuting the war much harder if they weren't. But if they knew more about the enemies we're fighting, they'd realize that some of these people, at least, are a long way from giving up. Maybe some of them never will.

I don't want to end, though, on a somber note. So

I'll conclude by saying that I wish I was holding you in my arms, that I wish I could pick Elizabeth up and twirl her in the air, and that if I were with the two of you just now, it wouldn't matter to me one bit if I looked out the window and realized I was in Philadelphia!

How's that for devotion?

Love to you, as always,
Robert

TWENTY-FOUR

DAN WALKED into the living room, to find his mother sitting on the couch in her bathrobe, a plastic net on her head and a listless look in her eyes. She'd been like that all weekend, and then this morning she hadn't gone to work, even though she'd told Miss Edna Boudreau she'd be in on Monday. He hoped the phone company wouldn't fire her. Knowing she had a job, even one that didn't pay well, had eased his conscience. She still hadn't given up hope that he might not enlist, that the war would end before the army called him up.

"Anything you need?" he said, fingering the keys in his pocket.

"Yeah. I need my hair back, so that I can stand to look at myself, since nobody else ever does."

When he'd played football in high school, he discovered he couldn't get mad unless somebody hit him in the nose. When that happened, he'd kick, bite, gouge and grab the other fellow by the nuts if, in his blind rage, he could find them.

In a manner of speaking, she'd just poked his nose. His father had been willing to look at her right up until the day he took his life. "You want somebody to look at you?" he said. "Get up off the couch and go to town. Somebody'll look at you then. Quit sniveling around, waiting for you know who."

She crossed her arms over her chest, regarding him with the kind of intense interest she'd probably shown him in the cradle. "I *do* know who," she said. "Do you?"

He withered. "Hell," he said, "I don't know."

"What don't you know?"

"Look, I didn't mean anything."

"Oh yes you did. You meant one hell of a lot."

"I'm going to Greenville," he said, "with Marty Stark. Shoot some pool, maybe. You want anything?"

"I want you to tell me who I've been sniveling around after."

He didn't answer, and couldn't look at her now.

"Do you know *why* I'm sniveling around?"

"Just forget it."

She rose and stepped around the coffee table. He smelled whiskey mixed with Vaseline. "Go to Greenville, Danny," she whispered. "Right this minute."

He'd offered to swing by the camp, but Marty said he'd be downtown anyway, so they met in the Piggly Wiggly parking lot.

"Last time I talked to your daddy was right here," Marty said as soon as he climbed into the truck. "On a Saturday morning. Right before I left for the induction center. I don't reckon he ever mentioned it?"

"No. But that last year or so, he was pretty closemouthed. Except right at the end."

Dan pulled into the street, drove through town and turned onto the highway. Except for his rolling-store route—which, after all, never took him out of the county—he hadn't been anywhere, not even to Greenville, for close to a year. His father used to talk about all of them visiting New Orleans one day, maybe even spending a night at the Ponchartrain, but that had never happened.

The sun was almost down. In one or two fields they saw a few pickers, old black men mostly, some women and children, a handful of teenagers. The Negro schools didn't open for fall until everything but the scrap picking was done, and that wouldn't be for several more weeks.

"I used to love this time of year," Marty said.

"Beats the other times, I guess."

"You sound like you already been at the front."

That, Dan thought, depended on how you defined the term. He hadn't been where they were fighting, and he figured when he got there, he'd have a new set of problems. Then maybe the old ones would matter a lot less.

Over close to the levee, two or three miles north of Greenville, there was a restaurant and bar that Marty said he'd been to a couple years ago. "Ain't got pool tables," he said, "but the truth is, I don't know how to shoot pool. I tried it once when they let me loose during basic. Hit some fellow in the ass with the butt of my cue stick. He spilled his drink on the woman he was bird-dogging and decided to nail me instead."

Inside, behind a burnished wood bar, a big fellow with a red mustache plinked down cold bottles of Jax without asking for proof of drinking age. Marty ordered two bowls of salted peanuts, which they carried with their beers over to a booth.

Five or six pilots from the air base sauntered around the

place, all of them wearing the dark khaki tops and beige bottoms of the Army Air Corps, feeding coins into the jukebox and bragging about stunts they'd performed. Every time an unaccompanied woman walked through the door—and three or four did—the airmen drew straws to see who'd get the first shot. Mostly, winning cost them money. They bought the women beers and, in return, got conversation only.

Conversation, though, was what Marty wanted. Specifically, to talk about his commanding officer. After they'd each downed a couple beers, he said, "He's from someplace up in Minnesota. One of those little towns where everybody's a son. Munson and Brunson, Swanson or Johnson. Word around camp is, his father taught high school. I don't know what subject. Biology or some shit. They say Munson did pretty well at West Point, was even a champion marksman with the forty-five. But somewhere along the line, somebody made a determination."

"What kind of determination?"

"That he couldn't cut it. Or that he wouldn't anyway. But I got a feeling they're wrong. I think he'd cut it, right up to the minute it cut him. And I guess that's what you need to win a war—somebody that's eager to bleed."

"What about somebody that just wants to do what's right?"

Marty grinned, lifted his beer, took a swallow and shook his head. "I knew that's what you'd say. I told Munson so just the other day."

"You talked to the captain about me?"

"Sure did, buck. For a solid hour, maybe more. He's got the *Life and Times of Timms* down cold. He *knows* about that goal-line tackle you made against Belzoni after that swivel-hipped dago—what was that little bastard's name? Number twenty-nine."

"Joey Malatesta."

"After that little bastard faked me out of my britches. He knows you're good in English, bad in math, worthless with women and completely without guile."

"What the hell is guile?"

"You don't need to know—you ain't got none."

One of the flyboys cleared his throat and sidled over to the door. A young woman in a plaid dress had walked in, clutching her purse strings so tightly, her knuckles had blanched.

"Allow me, ma'am," the airman said, "to introduce you to a gentleman who this very afternoon flew a magnificent AT-six underneath the Greenville bridge."

"Why would anybody do that?" the woman said. "I don't want to meet anybody who'd do that."

Marty burst out laughing.

The pilot looked at him, red-faced. "You hear something funny, bub?"

"Naw, I just choked on a peanut." He kept his mouth shut until the man had cajoled the woman into sitting down with him and his buddies. "What you got that I don't have," he then told Dan, "is a quality Munson prizes: you just want to do what's right, and you think you know what that is."

"Sounds like you think I'm the dumbest piece of shit in the outhouse."

"Don't take offense, buck. Me and you's pissed in the same bushes many a night."

"How come the captain's so interested in me?"

"Well, he's mostly interested in that prisoner with the boiled face, and hoping you might learn a little something. Guy claims he's not a German, you know. Says he's from Poland. He ever mention that to you?"

"No, he's been pretty quiet lately." In fact, the POW hadn't said much of anything for two or three weeks—since the day he'd popped the gears on the bus. The next day, Dan had approached him near the end of a row, intending to thank him, but the guy'd kept his eyes fixed on the cotton stalks. Dan had looked up, to find the tall prisoner who always did exercises staring right at them. "How the hell could he be Polish and serve in the German army?" he asked.

"Bastard's probably lying."

"Don't y'all have any records on him?"

"Army says everything relating to him's missing. They can't even find a record of his serial number. All the insignia's been stripped off his uniform, too, but apparently nobody found that odd till now. He don't have a thing in his duffel bag except the German uniform he never puts on, a shaving kit, a couple knitting needles and some thread and a small stuffed bear with an ear tore off. He ain't written a letter, or got one."

"How come the army don't send somebody down here to investigate?"

"That'd make sense, wouldn't it?"

"Would to me."

Grinning, Marty grabbed a handful of peanuts. "Well, that's why the army don't do it." He stuffed the nuts in his mouth and started crunching.

An argument had broken out among the airmen, clearly being staged for the benefit of the women at their table. The pilot who'd exchanged words with Marty bristled at the suggestion that he lacked the skill to land a training craft on top of the levee. "I could do it in the dark," he said.

"Go on, you crazy Okie. You couldn't land on it in broad daylight if you had Charlie Lindbergh holding your hand."

"Why would anybody want to land on the levee?" the young woman in the plaid dress asked. "There's cows out there."

Shaking his head, Marty drained his third beer, then motioned at Dan's bottle, which was almost empty. "Want another one?"

"I don't know. I got to get them Germans in the field tomorrow morning. What time is it?"

"It's still early. " Marty rose, went to the bar and returned with four bottles, rather than two.

Dan sat there eyeing them. "You're drinking a lot, ain't you?"

"Maybe, but not nearly enough." He turned a bottle up and chugged about half of it before stopping, then wiped his mouth on the back of his sleeve and explained the plan. If Dan was willing to talk, he said, he and Munson could meet briefly somewhere in town, maybe at the armory. The captain didn't want him coming inside the camp, because the prisoners might start to wonder if he was something besides a labor contractor.

Dan couldn't help but feel flattered, but he didn't intend to validate Marty's notion that he was eager to please. "Sure, I can talk to him," he said, "but what exactly does he want me to do?"

"He wants you to sound out our Polish friend. If he drops his guard any, you can try to find out when and where he was captured, that kind of thing. I got a feeling they're hoping to turn him. See, there's plenty of gung ho Nazis in that camp, and as far as those boys are concerned, Paulus didn't surrender at Stalingrad and's already halfway to Moscow. So the brass is starting to wonder what to do with bastards like that when the war *is* over. Send 'em back the way they are," Marty said, "and they'll start the same shit again."

"You really think they're so much worse than we are?"

"When it comes to *Germans*—"

Just then, the pilot from Oklahoma jumped up from the table. "You're on! Fifty bucks says I put that baby down on the levee like you was parking your momma's car."

Marty smiled. "When it comes to Germans, I don't think a goddamn thing."

As a condition of the bet, the airmen agreed to commandeer vehicles and train their headlights on the berm, and one of them had approached Dan and Marty's booth. "You guys wouldn't be the owners of that pickup parked next to the propane tank, would you?"

Dan said, "Yeah, it's mine."

"Come on out and watch the spectacle. Beer's on us."

"I need to get home pretty soon."

"Consider it training," Marty said, standing up. "You'll spend plenty of time these next few years seeing matériel misused and abused."

They parked a handful of pickups and cars in a row on the east bank of the levee, their headlights shining upwards at a forty-five-degree angle. The night sky was perfectly black.

"How long you reckon it'll take him to get here?" Dan asked.

"He'll land on this levee about the same time Tōjō says he's sorry," one of the pilots said, laughing and leaning against the fender of the pickup next to Dan's. He looped his arm around a much older woman, a tough-looking brunette with deep lines around her mouth, but when she shrugged him off, he appeared not to notice. "Parker's the worst pilot at the base. They're training a group of women ferry pilots over there, and every damn one of 'em can already fly better than he does."

"What's a ferry pilot?" the brunette said.

"They fly new planes from the factories to their designated bases so we don't waste real pilots that could be out flying combat."

"Are you an example of a real pilot?" she asked.

"Sure am, hon."

"Then how come you're not flying combat?"

Another pilot, standing near the foot of the levee, scanning the sky, hollered, "There's Parker."

The night was cool and still, a perfect night to be out having a good time. Listening to the bullfrogs croaking down in the bar pits, Dan was reminded of the nights when, after ballgames, they'd gone out to Lake Loring and sat on the banks, listening to similar sounds.

"The son of a bitch sees us," a man yelled.

The women, particularly the young one who wore the plaid dress, had made all the men want them, whether they'd invested much heart in their efforts or not. Even the hard brunette with all the lines on her face. If she were two or three years older, she could've been Dan's mother, but he wished he had the nerve to throw his arm around her shoulder. She could step out from under his arm, too, and he wouldn't care. If only he could hold her for a moment.

"He's lining up."

An evening like this could overwhelm a young man far

from home, and even one who lived nearby. Now he wished he was up there in that cockpit, centering the nose cone on an imaginary spot and angling downward.

"The stupid son of a bitch means to try it."

A red light flashed on the left wing, a green one on the right. The drone of the propeller changed pitch.

"This'll be the crowning achievement of the poor bastard's life."

They were out there, just as the girl in the plaid dress had said they would be, five or six Jerseys. Good grazing land lay beyond the levee, and the noise and the lights must have spooked them.

"There's cows on the levee!"

Debate would be waged later. If Parker had just plowed into them, everything might've worked out fine. The landing gear would've collapsed as the propeller carved a little steak, and Parker himself would've probably emerged bruised and battered. Whoever owned the cattle would've had to be paid off, because he'd had a grazing permit and the cows weren't anywhere they didn't belong. Parker would've been grounded for thirty days, his pay docked to help cover the damage to the trainer, but his status among his peers would've been immeasurably improved.

But Parker would not have been Parker, the assembled pilots agreed, if he'd had the faintest notion of how to behave. So it was exactly in his character to slam a foot down hard on the left rudder pedal, spinning the AT-6 off the levee and right into the brunette's Chevrolet.

TWENTY-FIVE

DRIVING BACK at two in the morning, with the odor of burning metal in his nostrils and the airman's cries still ringing in his ears, Dan said, "What'd you do over there in Sicily? To make 'em send you home?"

Marty hugged the armrest. "I don't know. I know what they told me I did. But it don't seem like me."

"You don't remember it?"

"Yeah, I remember it. In bits and pieces. But it still don't seem like me. And this may sound crazy to you, but it wasn't me. I remember stuff I did when I was ten, and it was me. Shit I ain't proud of. Like one time my cousin from Jackson came to visit, and he had a straw hat on and everybody thought he was so cute that they just carried on and on until I couldn't stand it. I grabbed that hat and stomped it flat on the porch, and when he started bawling, I shoved him off and jumped on him with both feet. I would have killed him, I reckon, but my granddaddy like to beat the hell out of me. I remember other stuff I did two or three years ago, and that was me, too. But what I remember back on that damn island, that's different. I can see the fellow that did it, and he's got my face, moves like me and whatnot, but I ain't him."

"Did you run?"

"Run? Everybody's running all the time."

"You know what I mean."

"Yeah," Marty said, "I ran like you mean. I sobbed and shit and pissed on myself, too, and when a buddy of mine lay on the ground just a few feet away, shot all to pieces but still able to holler, I buried my head in the dirt. I done all of that, and I remember it just fine. It was me. That ain't why they sent me home, though. If they sent folks home for that, wouldn't be nobody left."

The highway was empty, a long, straight stretch through the heart of the Delta, a road they'd traveled together more times than either of them could count. Whatever he was going to learn, he might as well learn now. "So why did they send you home?"

The voice that answered was one he'd never heard before. "They say I shot some Germans that was already dead."

TWENTY-SIX

DAN'S GROUP of prisoners waited just inside the gate, the only ones left. When the little sergeant with the northern accent saw the pickup pull onto the shoulder, he swatted the air with his clipboard, then glanced at his watch, as though he wanted Dan to understand that by keeping the army waiting, he was undermining the war effort. Last night, Marty had told him the sergeant didn't do anything all day long but sit at a table in the duty hut, drawing up lists. He made lists of prisoners who'd reported to the infirmary, of those who'd received or written a letter and probably, Marty said, of anybody who'd experienced a bowel movement in the last twenty-four hours.

"Son, when you join up," the sergeant said as Dan climbed out of the truck, "you'll learn one thing. Late ain't great. The army don't wait, not for nobody."

"Looks like you waited for me."

The sergeant shook his head. He glanced at the Germans, who were watching him through the wire mesh. "Can you gentlemen of the Teutonic persuasion imagine what *Oberkommandur* So-and-So'd do if confronted by such disrespect? I got a good mind to rescind this young man's right to my stable of Prussian ponies."

Dan was in no mood for one-upmanship. He had a headache and had felt nauseated ever since he woke. He couldn't eat his breakfast. Drink had something to do with his queasiness, but drink was not the whole story. The remnants of night lingered, and they were full of noise: metal tearing, flame whooshing into the air, a boy crying for somebody to please call his grandpa in Ponca City, Oklahoma. And one more noise, which he had not heard and could therefore only imagine: the sound a high-caliber slug would make when you pumped it into a body at close range.

"If you don't want me to take the prisoners, just say so, and I'll turn around and go home."

"Don't nobody appreciate sharp wit down here?" the sergeant said. "I guess when a comedy comes to town, the picture show stays empty." He looked at his clipboard and began shouting out names.

The prisoners strapped on their sacks and started picking. Normally, Dan left as soon as they were in the field; he always dropped the truck off for his mother, then stocked the rolling store and headed out on his route. But today, he decided, the route could wait. He'd do it if he felt like it, and if he didn't, he wouldn't. Alvin could survive the loss of a day's income. He could survive the loss of anything. Or anybody.

He stood on the turnrow, watching the prisoners, who moved so slowly, they might have been figures on canvas, the work of an artist's brush. A notion he'd heard expressed more than once over the last couple weeks was that the prisoners were happy. They didn't want to be back with their units, hugging the ground while bullets whizzed by inches above their heads. They were worried about their families—anybody would be—but until the war ended, they wouldn't trade where they were for where they'd been, no sir, not for one minute. Dan would have agreed with that as late as yesterday, but now he found it hard to believe. He figured wherever they'd been, whatever they'd seen and done, was with them right now out in the cotton field, half a world away from all the fighting.

At the gate this morning, he'd looked straight into the eyes of the tall fellow with the miniature ears. For all his Nazi swagger, the prisoner hadn't been able to stand the gaze of a seventeen-year-old. He'd dropped his head and shuffled his feet. As soon as they reached the field, the first thing he did was jump out onto the turnrow and snap off a few toe touches, grunting like a hog—working off his anger, Dan bet, at having his weakness exposed.

"The world ain't upside down," Marty had said last night as they drove back to Loring, "because the damn's thing's round. It don't have top nor bottom. But there ain't shit for sense in nothing. The whole purpose in shooting a German's to kill him, but if you shoot him after somebody else done the job, everybody gets nervous.

"Course, if you shoot him without knowing somebody did it once already, that ain't a problem at all. So what I pointed out to this little major that served as the division psychiatrist was that what's left of the German don't know the difference between a bullet that was fired with one intent and a bullet that was fired with another. 'Well,' the major tells me, 'it's not the German we're concerned with.'

"Now if that makes any sense to you, buck, I reckon you're

normal. Because where I was, I didn't think we was concerned with anything in the world *but* Germans. Germans was all I heard about for so long, I got to where I used them to fall asleep, counting Krauts instead of sheep. And every time one went over the fence, I potted him right in the nozzle. But I never once asked myself if it was a live German going over the fence or a dead one. Truth is, I've seen dead bodies do stranger things than jump a fence."

Dan walked over to the truck and got in. Hearing the door slam, most of the prisoners glanced in that direction, then went right back to work. For several seconds, he sat there on the turnrow, pumping the accelerator until he was sure he'd flooded the engine. Then he switched on the ignition. The engine coughed once or twice. He pumped the accelerator a few more times and hit the ignition again, with the same result.

He opened the door, hopped out and slammed it good and hard, as if pissed off, then hurried around to the front of the truck to pop the latch and raise the hood. Leaning over, he loosened the nut on the sediment bowl. The smell of gasoline almost made him choke. He stood there for a few moments, pretending to examine the engine. Finally, he shook his head and started into the field.

Most of the prisoners had picked about halfway down their rows, but the tall one was way out in front. The guy with the disfigured face, as always, brought up the rear. Dan would've bet that if you threw this particular collection of Germans into an attack, they'd arrange themselves in roughly the same order.

"Hey," he said, stopping a step or two away from the last prisoner. "Schultz, is it?"

All of them quit picking and straightened up to watch.

The prisoner wiped sweat from his eyes. *"Jah?"*

With his thumb Dan gestured at the pickup. "It won't start. *No go*. Can you take a look at it? My truck?"

"*Jah*. Maybe I look." He shrugged, then slipped the canvas strap off his shoulder.

"Don't know what's wrong with it," Dan said as they walked back to the turnrow. "Acts like it's low on fuel, but the gauge reads half-full."

When they reached the truck, Schultz leaned over the engine, sniffed once, then looked at the sediment bowl and saw the gas seeping out around the fitting. "There." He pointed.

"Damn. Bad filter?"

"No, just loose. I fix." He reached in and tightened the nut. "Now try."

Dan walked around to the driver's side and got in. When he hit the ignition, it sputtered, then caught. A cloud of smoke billowed up from the tailpipe. He sat there for a moment or two, waiting to see if the engine would die, but it didn't.

He got out and walked around to the front of the pickup again and slammed the hood down. "Thanks," he said.

Schultz reached up and touched his forehead in a one-finger salute, then turned back toward the field.

"Hey," Dan said, "you're pretty good with automotive stuff."

The others were nearing the ends of their rows, all except for the tall guy, who'd already turned around and started back.

"Automotive," Schultz said. "Yes. In my own home I fix."

"What town did you live in over there in Europe?"

Rather than answer his question, Schultz said, "With camp guard you are friends, yes?"

Dan moved up beside him. A hundred yards away, the tall prisoner had stopped picking. He stood erect, fists propped on his hips, a dark cutout against the sun. He seemed to be staring right at them.

"Yeah, me and Stark's friends," Dan said. "I've known him for a long time. What about you and that tall fellow out yonder?"

"Voss."

"Yeah."

"I don't know long time. But I know enough."

"You and him friends?"

"No," Schultz said. "Not friends."

Crossing his arms, Voss shook his head as if in disgust.

"Is he a Nazi?" Dan asked.

Schultz toed a big clod. "I don't know word," he said, "to say what is Voss. Or your guard friend."

"You don't know the English word?"

"No word in no language. Your. Mine. Their."

"I heard tell you're Polish," Dan said. "Is that so?"

"Polish?" Schultz said. "I don't know. Maybe no word for me, neither." He looked down at the ground, where the clod slowly dissolved beneath the toe of his work shoe. For a moment, he seemed captivated by the sight of the clod being broken up, transformed from something substantial into hundreds, if not thousands, of particles.

TWENTY-SEVEN

ETERMINED TO appear at work, Shirley had risen right after Dan left the house to pick up his work detail.

She'd heard him come home in the middle of the night, stumbling into something, maybe the coffee table. In the kitchen, he turned on the tap, and the drain began to gurgle. After a minute or two he shut off the flow.

Floorboards sighed as he moved toward the bathroom. The hinges on the toilet seat creaked. His stream splashed into the bowl, full of beer and vigor. Then the seat crashed back down and she heard her son grunt.

"They talk to you a lot about *evacuation*," Jimmy Del had said the night before she went to Jackson with Alvin. He'd sat there in the darkness, propped up against the headboard, smoking a cigarette while she lay with the covers pulled up to her neck. "They tell you to discharge your bowels at every opportunity. That was the first sign to me that things wasn't what I thought. It give me a creeping feeling. I was a private, but I didn't have no privacy. My bowels wasn't mine—they belonged to the United States. I wasn't no more than a sausage, and I should of known it before somebody went and told me. That's what they'll make

151

of that boy in yonder, too," he said, gesturing with the tip of his cigarette, "unless somebody does something to stop it. Me, I got a little idee."

He never said what his little "idee" was, or, if he did, she failed to hear him. She pulled the covers up over her head, pressing the heavy quilt around her ears, doing her best to muffle the sound of his voice, which droned on until she finally fell into herself.

Dan appeared late, at a quarter till nine. Waiting on the front porch, she made no effort to conceal her annoyance. With her charred hair on display—she'd decided to forgo the plastic net—she knew she must have cut a ridiculous figure.

"One thing your grandfather always told me," she said, "was that if I went out and got skunk-drunk, I'd better be able to live with the odor. You've made me late for work. Where were you? Asleep in the bushes?"

His skin looked as if it had been pasted onto his face. "I've been doing something for the military."

"The military?" she said. "That's a new one. Is the army paying boys to barf their breakfast?"

Her question infused his cheeks with much-needed color. On some level, it felt good to rouse a male to anger, since anger was a form of engagement.

"I didn't barf my breakfast. I never ate any. And by the way, I'm not a boy."

"Well then, that's one thing we got in common, because I'm not a boy, either." She held her hand out for the keys.

"The army asked me to help 'em collect some information,"

he said. "One of those POWs I'm working's got 'em suspicious he may not be what he says he is."

"What does he say he is? Or is that a military secret?"

"He claims he's Polish."

"Is this a joke?" she said.

He actually stomped his foot, and he looked so much like the child he'd once been that she wanted to throw her arms around him, to protect him from himself. But the time for that had passed.

"No, it's not a joke," he said. "Or if it is, then I guess it's on me."

"Oh, Danny." She shook her head. "Just let me have the keys."

When he handed them to her, she walked over to the truck and climbed in. Driving off, she looked in the rearview mirror and saw him tentatively place a foot on the lowest of the front steps, as if doubtful that it could support his weight.

In the fall of '43, she saw sex as a sentence, believing that women bore their femininity, the urge to be touched and held and talked to, like men bore arms. She watched women weep over nothing at the grocery store, saw them walking down the sidewalk late at night, glancing furtively in other people's windows. Once, when she was just a little too slow to unplug her headset after connecting two parties, she heard Margaret Strawbridge, whose husband was on a carrier in the Pacific, talking to her sister long-distance. "Me and the kids ate us some cottage cheese and fruit last night," she said. "Peach halves. And I looked down at one of 'em on my plate, and I thought, *That's me*, and stupid as it was, I had a minute there where I got scared that if I didn't scoop another one up real quick and lay it right beside the first one, I wouldn't see Bud no more. And so I did it. There's nothing for us to do but wait and hope for a chance to put things back together."

Shirley often recalled that comment, and after a while she began to think of the war years in different terms. Most women, she now saw, had reacted like Margaret: having no choice in the matter, they'd waited for a chance to put things back together. They remained, more or less, in a hopeful frame of mind, and they learned to live beyond their own bodies.

If any sentence had been handed out, it was men who served it. The war had wrought destruction, of one kind or another, on almost every man she knew. Those who might have led ordinary lives, minding the counter at the hardware store or raising cotton on Choctaw Creek, came to see themselves as cowards or killers, as losers or profiteers. Some sacrificed their sons. Others sacrificed themselves.

What Miss Edna Boudreau sacrificed on Shirley's first day back at work was harder to describe, but it was a sacrifice nonetheless, and Shirley had the good sense to recognize it as such. She'd just taken her place before the console—being careful as she put on her headset, given how tender her scalp still was—when the door to Miss Edna's office opened and she stepped out, carrying a pitcher of lemonade and a plate of cookies, followed by Cassie Pickett, who held a tray with three glasses on it.

"We're glad you're back," Miss Edna said. "I've been filling in for you, and that stool of yours is so high, it gave me acrophobia." She set the lemonade and cookies on a table, then reached over and gently pulled the earphones away from

Shirley's ears and lifted off the headset. After laying it aside, she scrutinized her head, assessing the damage. "I burned my hair once, too," she said.

"How?"

"Stuck a match to it."

"Why?"

"Just decided I didn't like it. I was only seven or eight years old. I would've burned my whole self up if I could've. My daddy poured a bucket of cold water over my head."

"There's been days I *felt* like setting myself on fire," Cassie said, placing the tray on the table. "I ain't never done it, though."

"Well, Cassie," Miss Edna said, "you're still young. You've got time to do it yet. But I don't recommend it."

"Nor do I," Shirley said.

Miss Edna dragged a ladder-back chair out of her office and sat down, and Cassie perched on her stool, and the three of them ate cookies and drank lemonade. Once or twice, a button started blinking on one of the consoles, but Miss Edna waved her hand and said whoever it was could wait.

She held forth for a while on a subject that interested her a lot more than it interested them: the future of the local telephone company. She said that when the war ended, they'd get a new building, right down the street from the library. Plans had already been drawn up. The building would be completely modern, with offices for Fred Harney and her, assuming she hadn't decided to retire. The older consoles would be replaced with the most up-to-date equipment. It wouldn't be long, she said, before everybody in town had a phone, and if either of the younger women had been around back in the early days, they would know just how unthinkable that had once seemed.

"The day we opened up, on the second floor of that little building where Hanson's Gift Shop is now, there were exactly twenty-four telephones in the entire town. I took the first call at nine a. m., on October third, 1901. Mayor A. L. Gunnels phoned Leighton Payne at the *Weekly News* to complain that his views on the subject of whether or not to outlaw the hitching of animals to porch railings had been misrepresented. Of course, he wasn't really mad, it was just for show. Because everybody was so proud to have phone service, he had a photographer at the courthouse ready to take his picture, and another one was at the newspaper to photograph Mr. Payne. Nobody took my picture, but then, I wouldn't have taken it, either."

"I saw your picture in the school yearbook," Cassie said. "You had a pretty face."

"Cassie Pickett, if you went looking for my picture in an old yearbook, it's because you hoped I was just as big back then as I am now, and you know it." The girl's mousy features tensed, but Miss Edna chuckled. "I was every bit as big back then as I am now, but I'll tell you something, Cassie. It would be a mistake to think I never had any fun in my life. I did. It was about thirty-five years ago, and it was over in just a few minutes, but I had it. And there's another thing I've learned, Cassie, which you might do well to learn, too, and so might you, Shirley, if you don't know it already. Would you two young ladies like to hear what that was?"

Both of them nodded.

"Some minutes," Miss Edna said, "last longer than others." Then she laughed so hard her hips shook.

TWENTY-EIGHT

ROSETTA STEVENS was not a Stevens, but nobody knew it except Mr. Alvin and Miss Shirley, and neither of them would tell. Some might say that they didn't tell because they couldn't afford to, what with her knowing so much, deep down, about them. But what she did or didn't know had very little to do with it. They didn't tell because it never mattered what you put them on the inside of, they would find a way to become outsiders fast, and they recognized the outsider in her. She was outside whiteness because she was black, and she was outside blackness because she was herself.

She was thinking about outsidedness that morning right before Frank Holder and the other man came in. How folks love to draw lines and make boxes. You're inside this one, outside that one. You're this kind, that kind. The previous Sunday, Reverend Selmon had preached a sermon called "Dogs in the Church." According to him, the brethren could be divided on the basis of their resemblance to one kind of dog or another.

"Got the hunting dogs," he said, his jaw aglow. "Hunting dog's always sniffing around, and when he finds something that smells like game, everybody watch out!" He threw his head back and bayed. "Yes, Jesus," folks hollered. "Amen." Reverend Selmon pulled a handkerchief from his pocket and wiped the sweat from his forehead. "Yes indeed—Jesus, amen, that's right." He folded the handkerchief and put it away. "Now the hunting dog makes noise," he said, "and that can't be denied. And after a while, all that noise gets old. Bay, bay, bay, all night and all day. How in the world is anybody supposed to rest? But at least with the hunting dog, you know where you stand, because you know what the hunting dog's after. Hunting dog wants to hunt. Hunting dog says what's what.

"Then you got the lapdogs. What does the lapdog do? Why, the lapdog sits in your lap and licks your face. Yes indeed. Lapdog will lick you till he puts you to sleep, and the second you drop off, what happens? Why, the lapdog grabs your sandwich and runs. The lapdog laps, then leaves. He's a stealthy and dissembling type of creature. See any lapdogs, brothers and sisters, in the church here today?"

"Yes, Jesus! Sho' do!"

"Yes, brothers and sisters, and I do, too! But the lapdog's not the most bothersome cur in the church. Oh no. That honor is accorded the feist. For the feist is always *nipping* at your heels!"

If Frank Holder had belonged to the dog world, he would have been a mastiff, and Rosetta preferred the feist any day of the week. When Holder came through the door, stomping the mud off his work shoes, the floorboards creaked and canned goods rattled. The other man, in his late twenties, had no mud on his shoes, a pair of swanky wing tips. He wore a seersucker suit and a white straw boater and carried a leather satchel. He looked around the store as though he'd never seen anything quite like it. If Rosetta had held with wagering, her money would have gone on Jackson as his likely point of origin, though she supposed Memphis or Little Rock were possibilities, too.

Frank Holder never even looked at her. "Mr. Alvin around?"

"No sir."

"Say he ain't?"

"No sir."

"Where's he at?"

He'd gone over to Greenville again to see somebody about a big shipment of lard, but it was doubtful he'd want Frank Holder to know that. "He ain't said."

"He ain't said. Well hell, why would he? If I was him, I wouldn't say, neither." Frank Holder waved his hand around the room: at the shelves packed with canned goods, sugar, coffee and tea; at the refrigerator case, which was full of fresh meat and cheese; at the big stack of first-grade tires in the corner. "Ain't much you can't get here, Mr. Johnson," he said. "If you know what I mean."

"Yes sir," Johnson said. "I can see that."

"You want you a cold drink, maybe?"

"Well, I believe I could probably stand one."

Frank Holder walked over to the box and slid the lid open. He peered into the icy water. "Look like we got some Orange Crush in here and some RC colas, Barq's chocolate, strawberry and root beer. Any of them strike your fancy?"

"I'll take an Orange Crush."

Holder pulled the drink out, popped the top off in the opener and handed the bottle to Johnson. Then he got a root beer for himself. He walked over to the counter and threw a dime down. And he still didn't look at her.

Tucking the satchel under his arm, Johnson moved around the store, examining items, occasionally sipping Orange Crush. "Got a nice selection of goods here," he said. "There's enough sugar on these shelves to keep every whiskey still in Mississippi bubbling for a month. I bet a lot of merchants around the state would love to know who his suppliers are. Not to mention Senator Truman's preparedness committee."

"Yes sir," Holder said. "I reckon they would. Old Alvin would make a devil of a quartermaster, wouldn't he?"

The younger man laughed.

Holder laughed, too. To nobody in particular, he said, "That boy that drives the rolling store around?"

"Which boy?" Rosetta said. "Colored or white?"

Then he did look at her, and instantly she wished he hadn't.

"*Boy* means colored," he said. "If I'd been talking about Danny Timms, I would've said so. So I'm gone ask you again, is that *boy* that drives the rolling store around?"

"No sir," she said.

"No sir," he said. "All right. Where you reckon we could find him?"

"He's on his route, I imagine."

"I imagine so, too. One more time now. One, two, three. Reckon whereabouts on his route that *boy*'d be?"

She could tell the most elaborate lies to a white man without prior preparation. In this instance, nothing fancy was called for. "He probably be somewhere up close to the Fairway Crossroads about now. I believe he run from there to Forty-seven and head on back."

"You hear that, Mr. Johnson?" Frank Holder said. "He run from there to Forty-seven. And then he head on back."

Johnson laughed again. He finished his drink, placed the

bottle on the counter and looked around the store once more, as if to memorize every detail. Then he glanced at Holder, who said, "Ready to go?"

"I believe so," Johnson said.

Holder turned his root beer up and drained it, then stood it next to the other empty on the counter. "When Mr. Alvin gets back," he said, "tell him Mr. Frank Holder dropped by with a friend of his from Senator Bilbo's office. The senator just wanted to make sure the store was secure, since there's enough supplies in here to feed the U. S. Army."

She made no move to pick their bottles up until she heard Holder pull into the road; then she rose and grabbed them. She meant to stand the bottles in the wooden drink crates, nice and neat as always, but the sight of the little square holes, twenty-four per crate, each hole the same size, all of them there for the purpose of containing a single bottle, keeping that bottle separate from all the others, got the best of her, and the bottles dropped out of her hands, clattering against the worn floorboards.

TWENTY-NINE

I N FRONT OF L.C., a green cotton trailer rattled along, moving so slowly it might not reach town before Thanksgiving. He waited until he crossed the rusty bridge that spanned the Sunflower River, then pulled around. The driver of the tractor towing the trailer was a Negro who lived on the Vaiden place. L.C. waved, and Cecil waved back.

For a long time now, he'd been passing any slow-moving vehicle without waiting to see who was driving it, despite the lengthy lecture Alvin Timms had given him about proper comportment at the wheel. He said white folks, whether rightly or not, believed that if a colored person passed them, he was trying to get beyond his station. L.C. probably didn't know it, but lots of them thought that once a colored person got in front of them, he'd slam on his brakes, hoping to provoke a rear-end collision and collect damages from their insurance company. L.C. couldn't help smiling, and Alvin said, "It may be funny now, but it won't be for either one of us if it ever happens."

"Mr. Alvin?" L.C. said. "Let me ask you something. When was the last time you saw a nigger get in a wreck with a white person and the police say the white person at fault?"

"I ain't saying what I've seen," Alvin said. "I'm saying what folks think. But just for the sake of argument, L.C., when was the last time you saw a ghost?"

For once, L.C. couldn't think of an appropriate response, so he just kept his mouth shut.

He drove on down the main road another mile or so, then turned off onto a side road that ran back down to the riverbank, through land belonging to Mr. Angelo Moreli. Moreli was Italian, the son of an immigrant who'd come to this country around 1900, when big landowners like the Starks and the Stancills briefly tried to work white foreigners instead of Negroes. The experiment hadn't lasted long at all, because a few of the foreigners, like Moreli's father, figured out how to get a little land of their own, which meant there was less for the Starks and the Stancills.

Even though he'd been born here, Moreli spoke with a funny accent, saying, *I'm uh gonna go uh* rather than just *I'm gonna go.* He was a chubby fellow with dark hair and a pencil-thin mustache, and his eyes always had little creases around them, as if he were about to start laughing. For whatever reason, he generally treated the Negroes who worked for him a lot better than most.

There were twelve or fifteen folks picking cotton that afternoon, spread out from one end of the field to the other. Cooter Sam, who always did the Lucky Duck at the Saturday-night dances, was way out in front, picking two rows at the same time. He claimed he'd once weighed up four hundred pounds in a single day, and when you saw him picking, you had to figure he might've been telling the truth.

L.C. hit the horn. A few of the pickers looked up and went right back to work, because they didn't have any money, but the others dropped their sacks and trudged toward the turnrow.

A couple children bought Popsicles; one or two folks bought candy bars. An elderly lady whose skin had the texture of worn leather wanted a plug of chewing tobacco but didn't have enough money for the whole thing, so he sliced her off a good-sized chunk.

Cooter Sam bought a Dr Pepper. While L.C. made change, Sam asked when that worthless white man he worked for meant to let him start selling hard liquor.

"You *looks* like hard liquor," a young woman told Sam.

"Child, he just the kind of nigger bring a smile to the white folks' face," another woman said. "Work like a mule to make a dime and then crawl like a ant to give it right back."

Rather than respond to the insult, Cooter Sam trained his gaze on a distant plume of dust. "Somebody coming."

"Probably the dago."

"Ain't no dago."

"How *you* know?"

"Seen the dago go yonder." Sam gestured in the opposite direction. "Ain't seed him come back."

L.C. handed him a nickel and closed the cash box. The field hands started to straggle back into the field, all except Sam, who stood there drinking his Dr Pepper while keeping his eye on the road. A moment later, L.C. heard a vehicle pull up, the engine cut off and two doors slam shut. Sam's Adam's apple bobbed faster and faster, and then he wiped his mouth on his forearm and handed L.C. the empty bottle.

L.C. refused to look over his shoulder, though Cooter Sam's eyes indicated it was some sort of trouble, and then he saw Frank Holder walk around in front of the bus with a man he didn't recognize.

"I reckon them Eyetalians got some funny practices,"

Holder said. "I put a picker in the field, I expect him to pick. I don't expect him to stand around shooting the breeze."

"Yes sir," Cooter said. "How you, sir?"

"Not so good." Holder tucked his thumbs into the straps of his overalls. "You got a son?"

"No sir."

"I don't, neither. Used to, but he died defending this country. There's plenty more like him dying right now, good American boys, best we got. There's others that ain't gone die, because they're like me—so dad-durn mean that when a bullet gets near 'em, it turns around and heads back. Them boys'll march into Rome real soon, and when they get there, they gone want some fresh duds. So why don't you get right back out yonder? We can't sew them young men no new clothes if we ain't got no cotton."

L.C.'s pulse pounded. "Go on, Cooter," he said. "Mr. Holder probably want to do business, and I need to get back on my route."

Holder waited until Sam was a good distance away, then said, "You tell Mr. Alvin what I said about you mouthing mumbo jumbo?"

"Yes sir."

"And what'd he say?"

"He say to stop it. Sir."

"He did?"

"Yes sir."

"Well, that's real good. He's a gentleman and a scholar." He gestured with his thumb at the other man. "This here is Mr. Johnson. Works for Senator Bilbo, who I reckon you've heard of."

"He the one from Louisiana they call the Kingfish?"

"Naw, you got him confused with old Huey Long, who been dead about ten years." Holder turned to Johnson. "You remember what Bilbo said about Huey after he got shot?"

"That may be a story I've heard," Johnson said. "But I won't know till you tell it."

"He said wouldn't nobody need to shoot Huey if they'd carried him over here to Mississippi. Said he would of killed his own self just trying to get out of the state."

Johnson grinned. "Sounds like Theodore all right."

"You like that story, boy?" Holder asked L.C.

"Well, yes sir, it sound like a good story to me. But y'all right certain Mr. Bilbo ain't no kind of Kingfish?"

"Well, I'd sure say the senator's a pretty darn big fish," Johnson said. "Though he don't hold with kings nor princes." He placed a polished shoe on the bottom step. "I need to get on here and take a look around."

"Yes sir," L.C. said. "You gentlemen want me to get out?"

"No," Holder said, "we want you to set right there. Need to conserve your strength. I imagine a healthy-looking boy like you's itching to join the armed forces. No point in using up none of that energy climbing on and off a rolling store."

Johnson moved down the aisle, picking items up and looking them over. Holder remained standing at the foot of the steps. He was a big man. Not just tall and heavy, but thick and hard. L.C. never doubted for one minute that given the right conditions, he could kill you. But if you went ahead and played dead in his presence, he wouldn't go to the trouble.

"Mr. Holder?"

"Yeah?"

"You ever been down to Jackson, sir?"

Holder pulled a match from his pocket, studied it for a moment, then stuck it in his mouth. "What you think?"

"Why, I imagine you have, sir."

"Then how come you to ask me?"

"Thought maybe you'd seen that mummy."

"What mummy?"

"I heard they got one down there in the capitol building's supposed to be three or four thousand years old. Say it's about five feet long, wrapped up in white tape."

"I don't know nothing about no mummy."

"What I been wondering is, if they use white tape, do that mean for sure that mummy ain't a nigger?"

Johnson said, "This isn't a rolling store. It's a rolling treasure chest." He placed a can of motor oil back on the shelf. "Been doing lots of business, I reckon?"

"Yes sir. Business pretty brisk."

"Sell a lot of sugar, do you?"

"Yes sir, it's one of our fastest-moving items."

Johnson strolled back down the aisle and stopped beside him. "How many of them little bags of sugar back yonder you think you've sold today?"

That was a troublesome question, because L.C. had probably sold fifteen or twenty. A white woman whose name he didn't know had flagged him down, telling him Alvin said to let her have as many as she needed, and she needed plenty. He'd sold three or four bags to field hands, five or six to housewives and two to Reverend Selmon, who'd said that sugar mixed with a small amount of grain alcohol was a very effective remedy for back pain.

"Seem like I must have moved four or five of them sugars today, sir," he told Johnson.

"Seem like?"

"Yes sir."

"You can't say for sure?"

"No sir, not right off."

"Your boss hadn't told you that stuff's rationed?"

"Oh, yes sir. Mr. Alvin real strict about that."

"Strict, is he? Well then, I reckon you'll have four or five ration coupons for sugar on board here, won't you?"

"Yes sir."

"Let's see 'em."

He kept coupons in a cigar box underneath his seat. He hadn't bothered to open the box since sometime last week, when he'd stuffed it with a new batch. Alvin had said nobody off the local rationing board would ever bother him, but it was smart, just the same, to keep the coupons up-to-date.

He reached under the seat and pulled out the box. Before he could raise the lid, Johnson snatched it out of his hands.

While Johnson pawed through the coupons, Frank Holder looked away. L.C. had sold him tobacco illegally at least three times that he could remember, and he'd sold his wife sugar once or twice.

"A bunch of these coupons are from last month and the month before."

He said what Alvin had told him to say if anything like this ever happened. "I'm color-blind, Mr. Johnson. Sometimes I can't tell blue from green, and them coupons all look alike."

"That's how come they code 'em with different pictures. You can tell a tank from a battleship, can't you?"

"Well, sir, I could if I was looking at 'em. But my eyesight ain't real good to start with, and them pictures is awful small."

"You know there's a ten-thousand-dollar fine for willfully disobeying the rationing laws?"

"Yes sir. I done heard about that."

Johnson crammed a wad of coupons in his pocket and dropped the cigar box on the floor. He glanced at Holder, then looked at L.C. "How old are you?" he said.

The taste of the lies he'd told lingered, and it was bitter. The next one, if he told it, would taste even worse. So rather than claim, like a lot of Negroes who'd been born on plantations, that he didn't know how old he was, he looked the man straight in the eye and said, before he had time to think much about what he was doing, "Sir, that ain't none of your business."

Johnson blinked. He held L.C.'s attention for only a second or two, though, because Frank Holder's reaction was a lot more dramatic and much less expected. He began to make spitting noises. At first, L.C. thought he was trying to fight off a sneeze; then he remembered the day old Fulsome Carthage, the man who'd taught him to play guitar, had suffered a heart attack on the front porch. He'd slumped over, his eyes wide open, and was making noises like the ones coming from Holder now.

But Holder wasn't experiencing a heart attack, at least not in the traditional sense. He was weeping, crying in the stiff-lipped manner befitting a man his size, and as he climbed the steps and reached out to shove Johnson aside, L.C. began to feel as if he ought to say he was sorry, though he had no idea what he should be sorry for.

"You bastard," Holder said. "My boy was worth two hundred of you." The fist that slammed into L.C.'s jaw felt like a mechanical object.

He toppled out of the seat and lay on the floor, looking up at Johnson's startled face.

"I got a good mind to step on this impudent darky," Johnson said. In preparation, he lifted his foot off the floor, so that he was standing on one leg when Holder shoved him again, sending him crashing into a display case.

Still sobbing, Holder grabbed L.C.'s arm and pulled him to his feet. L.C. saw the tears in his eyes, big glistening drops. Frank Holder had the blues, bad and low-down, and he must have thought the only way to get rid of them was to give them to somebody else.

Toward that end, he rammed L.C.'s head into the dashboard. He pulled him back and rammed him again, then spun him around and punched him between the eyes, knocking him down the steps.

L.C. lay on the side of the road, trying to collect his wits enough to get up and run, but Holder was already on him. Once more the big man grabbed his arm and pulled him up. He drew his fist back to hit him, but before he could bring it forward, a voice said, "Now Frank, I'm uh gonna give uh you thirty-four seconds to get out of my sight uh."

Holder was so overwrought that he'd failed to hear the pickup, and neither had L.C. But both of them heard Angelo Moreli shuck a round into the chamber of his shotgun.

"You probably think uh now that's a strange figure. So I'm uh gonna tell you how I come up with it." The Italian stepped closer to Holder, leveling the barrel at the big man's chest. "My oldest son's uh fourteen. Next oldest, twelve. My daughter, she's uh eight. Total, thirty-four. That's the number I keep in my head. Before I do anything I may regret uh, I count uh to thirty-four. You real lucky you didn't piss me off about two years ago, or you'd uh already be dead."

Moreli had said everything in a perfectly pleasant tone, those laugh lines crinkling near his eyes. But if L.C. had been the one with the gun pointed at his chest, he would never have imagined that the Italian might be joking. Neither, apparently, did Frank Holder.

He dropped his fist and let go of L.C. He didn't bother to issue a threat about what he meant to do tonight or tomorrow, nor did he ever stop sobbing. He just turned and plodded over to his pickup, the spitting noises still issuing from his mouth.

He got into the pickup truck and cranked it. At that point, Johnson stuck his head out the window of the bus. "Hey," he said, "what about me?"

Holder, without even looking at him, pulled into the road and drove off.

Moreli stood there beside L.C., watching the pickup disappear, the flag flapping from its side planks. When the truck was completely out of sight, he rested the stock of the shotgun on the ground. "You don't got uh no olives in your store?"

THIRTY

HOLDER PARKED the pickup in front of his house and got out. His intention was to grab his shotgun, drive back to Moreli's place and kill him. Then he'd hunt down and kill the Negro boy. If he could find Johnson, he might shoot him, too, because the truth was he didn't like him either, any more than he liked Theodore G. Bilbo, who reminded him too much of his wife's daddy. He might have entertained the notion of shooting Bilbo as well, but he was probably in Washington.

He threw the door open so hard, it slammed into the wall.

Arva was sitting on the couch, a piece of paper lying across one knee. Her left hand clutched a wadded handkerchief, which usually meant she'd been crying again, but her eyes were dry, and she was smiling for the first time in months. She'd have a smile on her face, too, on Christmas Eve, when he would walk in and find her sitting in exactly the same place, with that same piece of paper lying on her knee once again, her body already growing stiff and cold.

"What is it?" he said.

"A lost letter—it didn't come till now." Her hand was steady as she passed it to him. But his, as he read it, was not.

Last night, the letter began, *a nigger in a trucking company saved the lives of me and another boy.*

THIRTY-ONE

WHOEVER DESIGNED the towers had made a royal mess of it. In addition to having tin roofs, they were accessible only by extension ladders that you pulled up after yourself, so you couldn't be overwhelmed by prisoners in an attempted escape. The towers were cramped to begin with, and the ladders and the enormous searchlight mounted on a gimbal placed severe restrictions on movement; aiming a rifle at somebody below would be no easy matter. He'd pointed that out to Munson after pulling his first watch, but the captain'd just told him it was doubtful he'd ever have reason to fire his weapon.

He hated tower duty. Sergeant Case rotated guards in and out each night in four-hour shifts, and Marty's almost always lasted from midnight until four. He usually couldn't fall asleep anyway until around eleven; after pulling one of those shifts, he never managed to doze off again before roll call.

Lack of sleep, though, was not his main worry. Unlike Kimball, who enjoyed playing with the searchlight while standing watch, Marty hated being in an exposed position at night. Even when you swept the beam across the compound, you couldn't tell that much about what was going on at ground level. Somebody could always slip from shadow to shadow, and you wouldn't even know anybody was there. But they'd know exactly where you were.

Crossing the rec area, he shivered. The temperature had begun dropping at night, the air carrying the sharp, crisp odor of burning leaves. He used to love it when the cool weather came on, the way a big fire in the front room left your nostrils feeling baked.

If he wanted to, he suspected, he could go over to his father's house and stretch out in front of that fireplace tonight and stay there as long as he wanted without anything too bad happening. Rather than risk disgrace by having his son stand court-martial, his father would go crawling to Eastland and work something out with the senator. They could get him declared essential labor, as no small number of planters' sons had been, and win his discharge, maybe even making up a story about an illness or a wound.

But Marty wouldn't take that route now, just as he hadn't taken it fifteen months ago, and while he'd been puzzled at first by his reluctance to do so, he now believed he understood why it had never been a real option. Evidently, some folks carried within themselves a sacrificial gene, and he supposed he'd gotten his from his mother. Meanwhile, the country itself was like a giant machine, one that ran on a high-octane blend of blood and bones. Guys like him and Dan Timms and his buddy Raymond Sample, whose body lay in a hole on an island of death, were just meant to be chewed up and spit out by the times.

The previous weekend, on Front Street, he'd bumped into his former baseball coach, and he'd been surprised to hear him say how good the town was looking, how many businesses had been revived, how many construction projects were being planned for the postwar years. "Look around you," the coach had said, waving his arm at the street, teeming that evening with cars and pickup trucks and people, too, both black and white. "The paste and glue factory's brought a lot of money into town. Jasper Sproles has been trying to keep it a secret, but he's planning to open up a second bank to compete with the Gaithers. He's already got *investors* lined up. And y'all doing your part out there at the camp. The farmers couldn't be happier with those German boys—everybody I talk to says one of them's worth any three niggers he ever saw. There's talk of asking the War Department to let 'em stay on if they want after Hitler gets whupped." He went on and on, throwing in heaps of praise for Marty and his fellow soldiers, all of whom, he said, ought to pat themselves on the back. For when this thing was over, not only would they have kicked the living shit out of the Krauts and the Japs but they would have restored the country to prosperity, too.

By the time the coach hustled off down the street to find his wife, Marty had no choice but to face a fact he'd somehow contrived to conceal from himself. Very few folks walked around thinking they could smell a rotting body, because no rotting bodies were nearby. The war might be hell for those who fought it, but barring the loss of a loved one everybody else was faring just fine. And only a truly churlish person would break up that party.

When he rounded the corner of the supply shed, the searchlight hit him in the face. He jumped as if electrocuted, then

threw his arm up in front of his eyes as Kimball's laugh rang out.

Standing there in the hot white light, his legs rocking beneath him, Marty slung the rifle off his shoulder. He snatched the bolt back, then pushed it forward and locked it down, chambering a round. He slid his foot forward and dropped into a crouch, whipping his forearm through the hasty sling.

"Jesus Christ, are you crazy?" The searchlight shot straight up, thrusting into the night sky. There was a clattering sound as a hard object fell from the tower; then Kimball hit the floorboards like a sack of cotton seed.

Once his legs had quit shaking, Marty flicked on the Enfield's safety and swung the rifle back onto his shoulder. Breathing deeply, he walked over to the base of the tower, where Kimball's rifle lay, the muzzle clogged with mud.

For several minutes, Kimball refused to climb down and wouldn't even lower the ladder, just kept whispering the word *crazy*.

"If your ass don't appear in the next thirty seconds," Marty finally said, "I'm leaving. I got smarter things to do than stand around."

"Wait," Kimball said. "I'll come down."

He lowered the ladder and descended, looking over his shoulder the whole time, ready to jump if he had to. When he reached the ground, Marty offered him his rifle. Kimball took it and backed away, still shaking his head.

"Before you fire that thing," Marty said as he stepped onto the ladder, "you might want to clean the muzzle. It's not nearly so accurate when it's full of dirt."

———

In the tower, he stayed on his feet, though he knew Kimball and Huggins and some of the others sat down with their backs against the railing and dozed whenever they felt like it. He kept his rifle at sling arms, rather than propping it against the railing like Kimball did, because he didn't want to have to fumble for it in the dark. He left the searchlight on but rarely moved it.

While standing watch, he thought a good bit about the implications of remaining upright. A couple of days after his company had hit the beaches near Gela, they overran a tiny village. The houses, some of which had been badly damaged by shell fire, were little more than stone huts, crammed with chickens, pigs, children and corpses. In the first dwelling he entered, he jerked open a closet door, to find a body standing stiffly behind a row of ragged dresses and coats, the man's bulbous eyes wide open, flies buzzing around his shattered jawbone, now visible after a piece of shrapnel had sheared off part of his face. He was just an old man, the grandfather of the children they'd found in the house, one of whom told a lieutenant who spoke Italian that the old man'd been dead three days. Apparently, they thought that as long as you remained on your feet, you were, in some sense, alive.

The lieutenant who explained the upright corpse to Marty did so in an offhanded manner, as if he'd seen stranger sights in his life, then said to move out, because there were other huts to examine, other villages to overrun. But Marty remained standing in front of the closet, unable to peel his eyes off the dead man.

The lieutenant sighed, stepped over and laid a hand on his shoulder. "Where you from, Private?"

"Sir?"

Evidently, the lieutenant didn't like the look on his face or the tone of his voice, because he repeated the question sharply. "I said *where are you from?*"

"Mississippi. Sir."

"Where in Mississippi?"

"Loring."

"That doesn't tell me much."

One of the flies lit on the old man's tongue, which was swollen and distended, a big piece of blood sausage.

"It's in the Delta. Sir. North of Jackson."

"What's the main form of wildlife down there?"

"Sir?"

"Wildlife. You know—creatures of field and forest."

"We got deer."

"You ever shoot one?"

"Yes sir."

"What happened to it?"

"It died."

"Well, that's what happened to Giuseppe Verdi there," the lieutenant observed. "He died because somebody fired a weapon in his direction. And he's just as dead standing up as he'd be lying down."

Marty didn't argue with the lieutenant, but somehow made his feet move and got through the door into the dusty lane, where he saw Raymond Sample step out of another hut, one in which an entire family had been killed when a shell smashed through the roof. He'd found the body of a little girl in there, both legs separated from her trunk. "You tell me," he said, "what the big difference is between them and us."

At the time, Marty took the question in the most obvious way and answered it in kind, saying, "They were on the wrong side." Now, however, he understood the question differently, and would have answered it differently if Raymond had been with him there in the tower. *Our hearts are still beating,* he would have said, *and theirs aren't.*

On that island, it was the only difference that mattered.

Around 0200, fog settled in, blanketing the camp, muffling sound and dampening the tower's floorboards and railings. Instantly, it got a lot colder, and before long he was fairly uncomfortable.

Having nothing better to do, he swung the searchlight over the compound, letting it pass quickly over the other tower. Through the swirling mist, he saw Brinley, who didn't seem to realize he'd been illuminated: he stood with his back to the light, perfectly still, his rifle nowhere to be seen. He was probably over there thinking about his dead aunt, and it was a safe bet that if he had his hands on anything, it was not his weapon.

Marty rotated the beam past the duty hut, the captain's quarters, the supply shed, the infirmary, the mess hall. He swept it over the long rows of tents where the prisoners lay sleeping, played it over his tent, too, in hopes of disrupting Kimball's dreams of California. He moved on to the latrines, then the showers—and it was there, near the entrance to the shower room used by the prisoners, that his eye detected motion.

Swinging backwards, the beam froze a figure in frosty gray light.

The prisoner made no attempt to hide, though he could easily have ducked around a corner. Instead, after a few seconds had elapsed, he stepped forward, his motions stiff and mechanical.

Marty swiveled the searchlight, keeping the prisoner in the center of the circle. The man took another step, and then another, each step distinct from the one that had preceded it and the one that would follow. You could almost hear his bones creaking.

Marty kept moving the light, until finally his hands began to shake. "Don't you take another step," he called, but the prisoner with the stained face came closer and closer. Marty might have swung the rifle off his shoulder for the second time that night, if not for his reluctance to turn loose of the searchlight. For whatever reason, it suddenly seemed important to achieve the clearest-possible view of the other man's face.

A short distance from the base of the tower, the prisoner stopped moving. For a few seconds, he stared straight ahead, as if he were looking at something on the far side of the fence, beyond the camp's perimeter. Then he slowly rotated his head.

You could say, if you wanted to, that the dense fog, electrified by the blazing searchlight, had the effect of distorting his features, that his eyes were not as far back in their sockets as they looked, that the stain on his neck and cheek was merely that and not the suppurating wound it appeared to be. You could note, if you so chose, that under his own power he had just crossed the rec area, a distance of some sixty or seventy yards, and that as he came ever closer, his chest rose and fell with each step he took. You could consult medical books, theological texts, works of philosophy or psychology, assemble a jury of preachers and rabbis, doctors and lawyers, prophets and linguists, and they could vote and publish their findings, but to Marty that wouldn't have mattered. He knew damn well what he was seeing, since he'd seen it before.

THIRTY-TWO

JASPER SPROLES loved showy cars, and his love sometimes led—as love sometimes will—to his falling prey to the unscrupulous. Back before he got rich, he'd bought a used Ford roadster from Ben Pope at Loring Auto, despite Alvin's warning that Ben was little more than a bandit dressed in a suit. The car, one of the fancy 1932 models with a customized V-12 under the hood, ran fine for almost a week. Then, over on the outskirts of Greenville, the engine caught fire. The mechanic who examined it discovered that somebody had filled the crankcase with transmission fluid to boost the oil pressure—one way, he said, to get a bad engine running long enough for the car to be sold. Jasper Sproles rode Trailways home. When he attempted to get his money back, the dealer claimed ignorance and reminded Jasper that, in any case, he'd bought the roadster "as is."

All three of Ben Pope's sons were among the first in Loring to receive draft notices. When their father appeared at the selective service office to plead, on various grounds, for their exemptions, Jasper grinned and said, "Uncle Sam needs 'em, Ben. And he'll take 'em as is."

Jasper had a fine car now, a Buick Century convertible, one of the last ones built before the War Production Board prohibited the manufacture of civilian automobiles. Alvin was eating breakfast and reading the Memphis paper when the car pulled into his driveway. He took his time chewing his toast, knowing that you didn't want anything caught in your throat when you dealt with Jasper Sproles.

It was raining again, but Jasper wasn't wearing a raincoat and didn't seem too worried about the prospect of getting wet. He climbed out of the Buick and walked across the yard, stepping in three or four puddles, bending his legs slightly, as was his habit, and moving a lot faster than it appeared. On the playground, Alvin had once heard his grammar-school teacher tell the principal, "That Sproles boy aims to walk when other folks run, but he still plans to beat them to their destination." She'd made the remark in a disparaging manner, as if she expected Jasper to come in last in every endeavor. But it had struck Alvin, even then, that being able to walk when other folks had to run was not such a bad thing. After crossing the finish line, they'd be winded and you wouldn't.

He dabbed his mouth with a napkin, drained his coffee cup, then went to the front door.

"You know I wouldn't be here," Jasper said before the screen had even been unlatched, "if there wasn't a big mess."

Alvin stepped aside to let him enter, but Jasper meant to talk first and engage in niceties later, or not at all. "The can of worms you done opened," he said, "is so damn stinky, a mud cat won't bite 'em."

"You want to come in, Jasper? Or you want to stand out

there on the porch, so that everybody passing by'll have his imagination ignited by the sight of you and me talking?"

"Piss on them," Jasper said, though he did step inside.

Alvin shut the door and motioned at the kitchen. "I got the pot on. Want you a little coffee?"

"Naw, I don't want no coffee. Did, I'd buy a cup. I can buy a cup of coffee."

"Yeah, I know you can, Jasper. You can buy lots of coffee. So what's your problem this rainy morning?"

Jasper looked into the living room, where several weeks' worth of newspapers lay scattered across the furniture. "You ain't gone ask me to sit down?"

"You want to sit down, Jasper?"

"Naw, I'd just as soon stand. But I don't want you to leave a single stone unturned when it comes to making me feel welcome, Alvin, because you've caused me a slew of problems, and I'm mad as a crippled rattler."

Sighing, Alvin walked into the living room, shoved some newspapers off the couch and sat down. Jasper had followed him out of the hallway but remained on his feet, studying the bookshelves that lined the walls. There were a few books, but most of the space was taken up by tall stacks of magazines— *Harper's, The Saturday Evening Post, Esquire, Collier's.*

"It's too goddamn dark in here," Jasper said.

"You want me to open the blinds?"

"No, I like it dark. What are you doing with all them magazines? I never figured you for a reader."

"Got to find my entertainment somewhere."

"That's the problem with you, Alvin. For all your underhanded ways, the only thing that really interests you's having a big time. You was always like that. Me, I ain't out to have fun. I'm out to conduct business. What good can them magazines do you? They tell you anything about dealing with a bootlegger?"

"No, and I wouldn't want 'em to. I *know* how to deal with a bootlegger—been doing it half my life. I want the magazines to tell me about some fellow living out in the Hamptons, wearing the latest all-wool pacesetter, taking a train into Manhattan on Saturday night to meet a chorus girl for a drink in the Village."

"Now that's just about as useful as a three-legged mare." Jasper threw his hat down on the coffee table and took a seat in an armchair. "You ever heard of an individual named Benny L. Johnson?"

"Can't say as I have. Not that the name's particularly unusual."

"Naw, the name ain't unusual, and that's one thing that bothers me—its ordinariness. My name's one you remember. Jasper Sproles. You ever run across anybody else called that?"

Alvin shook his head.

"Naw, and you won't. Not unless he's some chintzy place like them Hamptons you're so hepped up about." Jasper crossed his legs, then shifted around in the chair, trying to get comfortable. "The bastard works for Bilbo. And apparently he come up here the other day investigating you and your colored boy."

"Oh," Alvin said. "So he's the one."

"Yes, the very goddamn one. And he didn't like the reception he got in Loring County, so he wasted no time getting back to Jackson and on the blower to Washington. Then just yesterday, I got a phone call myself. Some son of a bitch comes on the line asking if it's me, and I say yes, and then he tells me to hold on, and another son of a bitch comes on the line and asks me the same damn question, and I tell *him* yes, too, and that son of a bitch says to hold on, and then the biggest son of a bitch of all's on there, name of Theodore G. Bilbo."

According to Jasper, the senator hadn't fooled around. He said the list of folks he'd have to work through if forced to follow official channels was so long, he'd get tired just reading it. "Got the secretary that's under the secretary to the secretary's secretary," the senator said. "I ain't a young man, nor a very healthy one, neither, and if I have to put myself out, my disposition's gone fray. I say that because, unlike some, I know Theodore G. Bilbo mighty well."

The senator didn't appreciate having his personal representative mistreated. Mr. Johnson had been sent to Loring County to ferret out misconduct, of which he'd discovered no moderate amount. In the process, he'd been attacked and beaten by a colored draft evader and then had his life threatened by some Italian who could be living here as some kind of spy. The senator deemed it outrageous that a man like Jasper, who'd secured a lucrative federal contract, would aid and abet those who either opposed or refused to support the United States government.

"He made it pretty clear," Jasper said, "that he wants that boy in uniform. Either there or in jail."

"How soon?"

"Sounded to me like yesterday may be too late."

"Well, I guess we've got Frank Holder to thank."

Jasper's jaw locked so hard, it must have ground a layer off his molars. "Yeah," he said, rapping the arm of his chair, "and the hell of it is, there ain't no easy way to settle that score. The poor bastard's son's already dead."

———

He eventually left, but not until he'd been prevailed upon to sample four or five different bourbons and eat a box of bonbons.

Before going, he told Alvin that L.C. would be receiving a notice within "the next few days"—the bonbons, rather than the bourbon, having pushed the timetable back—unless, of course, he chose to show up and volunteer. After Alvin said he'd talk to L.C. and his momma, Jasper warned him that any shady dealing he was involved in—"and let's face it, Alvin, you're a fellow that ghosts the darkest corners"—had better be curtailed, at least until Benny L. Johnson and his master turned their attention elsewhere.

Promising to take precautionary measures, Alvin then presented Jasper a case of brandy, which he himself carried through the rain to the Buick, because his guest's legs were wobbly and his hands had gone numb.

THIRTY-THREE

LATE THAT AFTERNOON, after spending a few hours back in bed and then taking a long bath, Alvin climbed into his pickup, intending to drive by the store and talk to Rosetta, if she happened to be alone.

A couple of cars and three or four trucks were parked out front, and several Negro kids were running around and hurling mud pies at one another. When Alvin pulled in, they stopped playing and, dropping their heads, shuffled into the grass along the road ditch. He sat there for a moment, letting the engine idle and watching the children whose fun his mere presence had disrupted. Every minute or two, one of them would cast a swift glance in his direction, then look back down.

He put the truck in gear and pulled into the road too fast, throwing up a storm of gravel. Looking in his rearview mirror, he could see the kids running back to the parking area and waving their arms.

He'd made love for the first time, when he was seventeen years old, to a woman named Ernestine Grider, whose husband had bled to death after a gin saw caught his arm and pulled him in. She was small, thin and angular, with dark hair that had started to turn gray at the roots. To call her face plain would have been kind but misleading. The night *The Wizard of Oz* opened in Loring and the Wicked Witch of the West appeared on-screen, more than one person in the darkened theater thought she looked just like Ernestine.

She'd taught Alvin and his brother at Sunday school. She spoke with a nasal twang and was reputed to be stern, so nobody wanted to be in her class. Yet from the first time he found himself in the same room with her, Alvin had not been able to look at her without feeling a certain warmth in his temples.

Once, on the steps of the post office, when he was thirteen or fourteen and had begun to miss church, she asked him if he'd kept up with his Bible reading, and though he knew she expected him to say yes, he couldn't bring himself to lie. When he said "No ma'am," the lines deepened around her mouth and in a very low voice, she said, "To tell you the truth, Alvin, I haven't, either, but I wouldn't want anybody to know it." She laid her hand on the back of his neck that day, and he almost said to her right then and there, on Front Street, what he would say at her kitchen table a few years later, after his father sent him over to pay for a mule.

"Mrs. Grider, I get a funny feeling when I see you."

He said that to her over the cup of coffee she'd inexplicably offered him as he stood on her front porch with his cap in his hands. After he said it, those deep lines reappeared. She reached over and touched him again, laying her hand atop his, and he looked down and saw how red and rough her knuckles were. "Alvin," she said, "the day'll come when you'll think twice before you make a statement like that to a woman like me. But we're not there yet, I guess. Which accrues to my advantage as well as your own."

It was quick, and it was messy, but he didn't have the sense to know it. Lying next to him in bed, with the covers pulled up to her neck, she said, "You're going to disappoint me real bad, Alvin, if you start thinking you love me and coming over here after tonight, because it would be the worst thing in the world you could do. It would be as bad, in its own way, as what we just did was good."

He did not disappoint her: he never went to her house again. But whenever he saw her on the street, he stopped to talk, asking how her farm was doing or, later on, after she remarried, how her husband, who'd come from Alabama, was liking Loring. In a manner of speaking, he supposed he'd come to love her, not least because she'd taught him an important lesson about the limits of engagement and the art of restraint.

What he'd learned back then from Ernestine Grider had come in useful in his dealings with Shirley. And *dealings,* he thought, driving down the road toward her house, as he so often had, at all hours of the day and night, was exactly the right word. An air of negotiation, of proposal and counterproposal, surrounded their every encounter. When a straightforward declaration of intent might have sufficed, they were both too wary to make it.

The pickup truck wasn't there, since it was Wednesday and Dan had probably taken it to town for Guard drill. What surprised him was the green Plymouth, which someone had parked next to the porch.

His mouth went dry. His first urge was to let the clutch out and stomp the accelerator, dig two deep ruts in the road and make as much noise as he could in hopes of ruining whatever pleasure she might be having. Then he looked at the car more closely and realized that he'd seen it before, standing on the street in front of the telephone company.

He parked the truck and got out. He could hear female voices and laughter inside the house. "And Miss Edna, my momma said she hadn't never, and my daddy said he hadn't never, neither. Uncle Luther comes driving into the yard, and first thing they notice is the windshield's gone. Second thing's Aunt Becky's feet, hanging from the open door. He'd done got mad at her again and kicked the windshield out, and she'd rode twenty miles, ready to jump every inch of the way." Another round of laughter.

From habit, he checked his clothes to make sure they were straight; then he climbed the steps and knocked on the front door.

Shirley opened it. For a few seconds, she made no move to unlatch the screen, but simply stood there looking at him through the thin wire mesh, and he thought she might not invite him in.

"Hello," she finally said.

"Got guests?"

She shrugged. Her hair had started growing back, in tightly matted clumps. "Dan has the pickup, and I needed a ride home, so Miss Edna and Cassie came over. You want to join us?"

"I probably got about as much business going to a prayer meeting," he said, "but just now my own company leaves plenty to be desired."

She had a fire going in the living room, but they were all in the kitchen, where Miss Edna Boudreau was peeling pumpkins and passing them on to Cassie Pickett, who cut them into wedges. Shirley said they'd decided to do some baking. The Boy Scouts were sponsoring a scrap-metal drive over the weekend, and the operators at the phone company had offered to provide pies and cakes as prizes.

Miss Edna, looking up long enough to assess his usefulness or lack thereof, noticed that he still had two hands and didn't appear to be blind. "Go over there to the corner, Alvin, and bring the rest of the pumpkins."

Afterwards, he was rewarded with a seat at the table. Shirley had made a pot of coffee, and they all drank some, the women continuing to work on the pumpkins and Alvin popping up every few minutes to carry the seeds and peelings to the garbage can out back.

Miss Edna, it developed, was not a bad storyteller, and she was more than willing to tell one on herself. Back in 1933, she said, before her father passed away, she had ridden with him down to Jackson in his Model A. They stopped at a red light in Yazoo City—"right there at the foot of Valley Hill"—and while they were waiting for it to change, she noticed a billfold lying in the street.

"I'm not here to tell you I was starving," she said, "nor am I about to claim that going hungry might not have done me good. But things were, as the saying goes, tight. So I told Daddy to hold on and I'd pick up that billfold. I opened my door and jumped out, and as soon as I reached for it, the billfold scooted across the street about two or three feet.

"There was a big old magnolia tree right next to the street, and if I'd been more alert, I might have noticed that the trunk was plenty big enough to hide behind. But I didn't have eyes for anything but that billfold. I decided my senses had betrayed me, that it hadn't really moved, and that the next time I reached for it, my hand would close around it.

"When the billfold took off again, I let myself get a little unbalanced. Now if that happened to you, Shirley, or to you, Cassie, it stands to reason you'd recover. Alvin wouldn't have seen the billfold to begin with, because this happened about nine in the morning, and he'd have been in bed. But I was there and I did see it, and when I tried to pounce on it, I went sprawling face-first into a mud hole. I looked up and saw some little smarty-pants running off down the sidewalk with that billfold bouncing along behind him on a string."

Shirley laughed, and Cassie did, too. Alvin tried to summon a grin, but it wouldn't answer the call.

"What's the matter?" Miss Edna said. "Did I offend you with that remark about the hours you keep?"

"No ma'am. I'm not one to take offense too easy."

"That's good," Miss Edna said. "If I had any reason to hoot with the night owl, I imagine I'd do it."

"I bet you'd hoot *real* loud, Miss Edna," Cassie said, and Miss Edna allowed that she most likely would.

Shirley stood over the stove, making pumpkin puree, her face damp from the steam. Cassie, in the meantime, mixed sugar, salt and flour in a big green bowl, and Miss Edna sat at the table, rolling crusts. While she worked, she talked to Alvin, asking him how his business was coming along and whether or not he thought he'd wind up in jail. If he ever did, he should contact her uncle Coleman down in Jackson, because he specialized in winning acquittal for folks that were guilty. "Mostly," she said, "he deals with the more dramatic criminals—murderers and bank robbers and some of the bigger bootleggers and pimps—but as a favor to me, he probably would agree to handling a petty graft case."

"Sounds like you got a fairly low opinion of me, Miss Edna."

After glancing at the stove, where Shirley and Cassie were tasting the puree, she leaned toward him over the crust she'd just rolled, as if she meant to tell a risqué joke. "Alvin," she whispered, "low and high don't figure in."

He dropped his voice and leaned forward, too. "They don't?"

"Not at all. It's just that I see you for what you are."

"And what's that, ma'am?"

Her mouth curled into an expression most men would call a lopsided grin, but he knew he was seeing something beautiful: Miss Edna Boudreau in remission from herself.

"Why, it wouldn't be so darned interesting if it had a single name," she said. "You're one thing today and another thing tomorrow. A snake sheds its skin. You just shed Alvin Timms."

Once the pies were in the oven, Miss Edna said she was sure folks would be pleased with their efforts but that she needed to get back to town because it was close to eight o'clock now and she went to bed at nine. On her way out, she told Alvin to let her know if he ever wanted her uncle's phone number.

For a while, he and Shirley sat on opposite sides of the table, neither of them willing to speak. Eventually, she said, "What's wrong?"

"Who says anything's wrong?"

"You wouldn't have come over if nothing was wrong. You know that just like I do."

"Time was, I'd come over because something was right."

"Yeah," she said. "But as you yourself said not too long ago, things used to be different."

There wasn't much point in arguing, so he didn't. "Senator Bilbo's office sent somebody up here from Jackson to check out me and L.C., and Jasper Sproles, too. I don't know exactly what happened, because L.C.'s not saying a word and Rosetta ain't saying much more. But Jasper informed me the boy's got to go in the army. Either that or he's going to jail, and me and Jasper may end up there with him. Ain't a thing in the world for me to do but go tell Rosetta. And I'd rather take a fiery poker in the rump."

Shirley got up, walked over to the sink and drew herself a glass of water. She stood with her back to him, drinking. She'd lost weight in recent weeks, and her dress fit her like a pup tent.

She set the glass down in the sink. "Well, if he has to go fight," she said, "I guess he has to go. Like so many other boys. Dan, for instance."

"They won't let colored boys fight," Alvin said. "If they'd let them fight, it wouldn't be so bad. But the government learned its lesson in the First War. They let colored folks fight then, and they came home wanting to be treated like white people. That's just not in the cards, not then and not now. What the army means to do is put 'em in uniforms and send 'em as close to the front as they can, where they'll have the pleasure of digging toilets or toting ammo. They'll be exposed to fire theirselves, but the army won't let 'em shoot back. They don't aim to put a gun in a colored boy's hands. He might take a notion to bring it home."

"Well, what are you doing with him?" Shirley said. "You make him drive a bus around the county, selling Popsicles and

MoonPies, and every Friday night he entertains you for the price of a little whiskey. You don't pay him one cent more than you have to, so he won't ever have enough to quit working for you. That's not much of a life, either, if you ask me. But it never crosses your mind that he might want something more. Because then you'd have to deal with all the implications, and that'd make you feel bad." She shook her head. "Jesus, you'll have to give him up, won't you? Just like you gave me up. You're running out of toys, Alvin. Before long, you won't have a damn thing to play with."

He realized then exactly how she saw him, how she explained his actions, past and present, to herself. A creature of convenience, he hadn't quite lost his sense of right and wrong, and was burdened by the need to grope for explanation and justification. It was this need, more than anything else, which kept people like Miss Edna and even someone as cunning as Jasper Sproles from recognizing him for the complete deformity he knew himself to be.

"Oh, Alvin," Shirley said as she finally stepped across the room and wrapped her arms around his neck, drawing him close, "I don't want to be a grown man's momma."

But having told him what she didn't want to do, she found herself standing there massaging his shoulders, trying to soothe him as if, in fact, he were her son.

"That feels good," he said. "Real good."

She could see his reflection in the window. He'd closed his eyes. He was sitting there, lost in the sensation produced by her hands. "You got anything here to drink?" he asked.

"Stronger than coffee, you mean?"

"Little bit stronger, maybe."

"Yeah." She took a bottle of whiskey out of the cabinet under the sink, and they walked into the living room and sat down on the couch.

"Kind of strange," he said, pouring two drinks, "for folks like us to be sitting around the table with the likes of Miss Edna."

That was a phrase he'd used before—*folks like us*—and one she'd never liked, so she asked him now what he meant by it. But before he could answer, she said, "And don't rear back with your hands behind your neck."

"Why?"

"I hate it."

"I'm comfortable like that."

"Well, maybe that's why I hate it."

"You don't like to see me comfortable?"

"I don't know," she said. "It just sometimes seems like there's a connection between you finding comfort and me not feeling any."

He laid his hands on his knees and sat there stiffly.

"You look like the father in one of those family scenes in *The Saturday Evening Post*. All you need is a turkey on the table and a napkin around your neck."

He laughed then, and she did, too. "You know any Scripture?" he asked.

"'Thou shalt not kill.'"

"Something more domestic."

"'Covet not they neighbor's wife.'"

The smile dissolved. "He wasn't really my neighbor. Not unless you give that word a pretty broad definition."

"I think whoever wrote that Scripture probably did define it broadly, don't you?"

"Yeah, I reckon."

"If Scripture's your guide, though," she said, turning her glass up and taking the first swallow of whiskey she'd had in a couple weeks, "it's strange that it keeps guiding you straight to my front door."

"Least it ain't guiding me to your back door."

"Like it was before?"

"Yeah." He studied the contents of his glass, then had a drink. "Like it was before."

They sat there for a while, sipping their whiskey, neither one of them speaking. Before too long, Dan would probably come home, and while she had no urge to be alone, she didn't want him to find her and Alvin sitting together on the couch. She'd just about made up her mind to say he needed to leave, when he pulled back his shirtsleeve and looked at his watch.

"Well, guess I better be going. Best time to talk to Rosetta's probably early in the morning. Her mood usually sours as the day wears on."

He finished his whiskey and set the glass back down on the coffee table, then leaned over and took Shirley in his arms. Her initial impulse—to pull back, to press her palms firmly against his chest and push him away, to order him out of her house and tell him not to show his face there again—was one she easily resisted.

"You never knew old lady McGregor, did you?" he whispered.

She didn't know who in the name of God he was talking about, and she didn't care. He smelled of sweat and whiskey and tobacco. The odor was thick, it had substance, and as she inhaled it, the moment seemed to thicken along with it. "Who?" she murmured.

"Ina May McGregor. She taught me and Jimmy Del back in fifth and sixth grade. Talking about definitions made me think of her. She was real big on making you memorize a word and then use it in a sentence to prove you knew what it meant. She'd give you twenty of those suckers a week, and we'd spend most of every Friday standing up there at the front of the room, every blessed one of us, using all twenty of them words, one right after another. And every time you come up empty, she'd make a black mark. Jimmy Del said he was getting to hate the whole English language, and I reckon I felt pretty much the same. At the time, it seemed to me like I wouldn't need to know a single one of them words, and now, damn near thirty years later, I still don't think I ever used more than three or four of them."

He said the one he had the most trouble with, the one he never did get and didn't know the meaning of today, was *lugubrious*. He kept thinking it had something to do with providing light, but Mrs. McGregor said he was thinking of *luciferous*, and then gave him a black mark.

"But as big as she was on definitions," he said, "even Ina May always told us that at any given time, a particular word might mean a good bit more, or a good bit less, than the dictionary said."

THIRTY-FOUR

HOBGOOD MADE them slog through muddy drills at the football field, then dismissed everybody but Dan. While the others straggled off toward the armory, the captain said, "Son, are you still bent on enlisting in December?"

"Yes sir. My birthday's the seventeenth."

"You know, you probably wouldn't have to do that, at least not right away, if you'd rather stay home another year or two and help your momma. You're the only surviving male on the farm, and the selective service board can make allowances."

"Yes sir, I understand that, but she already knows I mean to join up, and that's why she took the job at the phone company."

Hobgood gazed away at the goalposts, as if contemplating the chances of a field goal. "The day before your daddy . . . before he passed away, Danny, he come by the Highway Patrol office, and me and him sat and talked, like we did from time to time. He told me he hated like hell for you to see some of the things me and him saw, to do the kinds of things we did. Them things had to be done, and now they've got to be done again, but some of them are pretty hard to come back from. The last thing your daddy said was that he felt like he'd served the country enough for you and him both, and he'd do anything he could think of to keep you out of the army. And then, Danny, he said that word again. *Anything.*"

After hearing that, he needed somebody to talk to, and at this hour, Lizzie was probably the best bet.

The snack bar was only partially lit. He would've backed the truck away from the curb and driven home, but she was standing at the counter, wiping it down with a sponge, when she looked up, saw him and waved him in.

"How's soldiering?" she said. "You still got that fool mechanic from the Chevy shop playing corporal?"

He climbed onto a stool. "Yeah. But Captain Hobgood don't let him demonstrate weapons anymore."

"All Gerry Bunch needs to know about a weapon," she said, bearing down on the sponge, "is how to turn it on himself and pull the trigger."

"Sounds like you're not partial to him."

"You could put it that way."

"What'd he do? Leave the plug out of your oil pan?"

She quit wiping and stared across the street at the darkened Western Auto. "Forgetting to put something in," she said, "has never been his problem."

He was afraid to glimpse himself in the mirror behind the counter. His face probably looked as if he'd contracted roseola.

Lizzie threw the sponge in the sink, washed her hands, then dried them on a towel. "You want a piece of cake and a cup of coffee?" she asked.

He nodded.

"I wouldn't mind the same thing myself."

She brought out two pieces of pound cake, a pot of coffee and two cups, and they sat down across from each other in the booth at the rear. When he got back from the war, she explained, this place would look a whole lot different. Mr. Kelly had remodeling plans, getting rid of the counter and the booths and turning the place into a regular restaurant.

"And what's a regular restaurant supposed to look like?"

"I guess there's a bunch of little square tables with checkered cloths on them and a vase of petunias in the middle, and whoever waits on customers looks like she just came from church."

"What do you mean, whoever waits on them? Ain't that you?"

She stirred her coffee. "I've about had it," she said. "I been in here from eleven in the morning till eight or nine in the evening every day for sixteen years, except Sundays and holidays. I guess I'd stay on if nothing changed, but when it does, I don't want to be here. Because it's kind of like my home, you know, except I don't own it. Of course, I don't own a home, either, just rent."

He couldn't imagine Kelly's without her in it, and he said so. But she told him that there wasn't any point in thinking you couldn't imagine this or that. Someday soon folks were going to wake up and realize that the world wasn't the one they'd always known. Mr. Kelly, for instance, never had to compete with anybody for business, since the Loring Hotel was the only other place downtown that served food, and nobody in his right mind would step foot in that dining room. Now Kent Stark and a few others planned to open a full-service restaurant in the old post office building, and Kelly said that if he didn't adapt, they'd take all his customers in no time.

"I don't believe that," Dan said. "Folks are attached to this place."

"Maybe," she said, "but once you boys turn into soldiers, you'll leave here and go places you've never even heard of, and when you come back, it'll be with a whole different set of expectations. And some," she said, "won't even remember who they were before they left."

"I hope I can," Dan said. "Not that I think I'm anything special. I'd just like to know what I add up to when it's all said and done, and I don't reckon I can do that by forgetting everything up till now."

"I wish you'd stay just the way you are, Danny, because you're about the nicest boy that's ever walked in that door." Here she paused. "You know, I caught you looking down my blouse the last time you were in here, and you were stupid enough to think I didn't like it."

"But you did like it?"

"You're still in what my momma liked to call the yes-or-no stage of manly behavior."

"You find me manly?"

She grinned, revealing a silver filling. "Yes," she said, "and no."

"No?"

"You don't do that part first, hon. You start out with yes and work your way around to no."

"Sounds backwards to me."

"Well, it would, because you're a man, although a very young one, and men do tend to see everything backwards. But it's a lot more interesting if you start with yes. The truth is, you remind me of the fellow I married."

"Actually, that sounded like the no part."

She forked up a piece of cake and chewed it, then took a sip of her coffee. "You want to hear this?" she asked, setting the cup back down.

"Yeah."

"Then don't interrupt." She told him they'd met over in Arkansas, after he'd come back from the First War, just like Dan's daddy. They stayed married for almost six years and ran a commissary on a big plantation south of Pine Bluff. "Then one day, Lee up and disappeared. Didn't say a word, never wrote, never called or sent a telegram. Hadn't shown the slightest sign of dissatisfaction the whole time I'd known him."

"You reckon maybe somebody killed him?"

"No, because when he left, he took both pairs of pants he owned and both shirts, along with his winter coat and tackle box, the family Bible and a box of needles he had for vaccinating hogs."

"And you say he looked like me?"

"Not the least bit. He was a whole lot shorter and thinner. He told me that when he went to enlist back in '17, he had on four or five layers of clothes, and once he started peeling them off for the exam, one of the doctors said, 'Hey, this fellow's disappearing right before my eyes.' Just like he disappeared later before mine, I guess."

"So if me and him don't look anything alike, how come I remind you of him?"

She took another sip of her coffee, then reached over and took both his hands in hers. "When a woman does this," she said, "you better watch out. She wants something from you. That's the good news."

He was beginning to think he could probably do a lot more

with her, if he wanted to, than look down her blouse. She might be sitting there hoping he'd kiss her, or planning to ask him over to her house.

"You want to hear the bad news?" she asked him.

"Is this the no part?"

"More or less."

"I reckon now's as good a time as any."

"What she wants from you may not be what you want from her. Probably isn't, most of the time."

"That's a sure no, all right," he said. "No question about it."

When he saw the moisture creeping into her eyes, his first impulse was to flee. What stopped him was the knowledge that had their roles had been reversed, she never would've walked out and left him alone.

"That's why you remind me of Lee," she said. "I'm sitting here telling you I don't want what you want, and you're sitting there giving me what I do want. Lee did that, too, until he couldn't give it anymore. And even then he didn't pitch a fit or make a list of all the times I'd let him down, like most of the men I've known. He just took what he had to have and slipped on out the door."

They slipped out the door, too, but not until a quarter past ten, by which time they'd covered a lot of ground. He'd learned that her mother and her stepdaddy were both buried in a country graveyard near Dumus, Arkansas, and that she had a brother who worked at a sawmill in Crossett. If she left here, she said, she'd most likely live with him and his family for a while, try to find a job in a restaurant or maybe even a truck stop. Eventually, if she could manage it, she'd like to get a little house in the country, with enough land to raise a garden and have some chickens and maybe a couple hogs.

He told her about the strange conversation he'd had after drill with Ralph Hobgood, how the captain had stood there gazing at the goalposts and said his father'd claimed he'd do anything to keep him out of the army.

She spat out a single word: "Bastard." Then she took both his hands in hers again and squeezed them so hard they hurt. "Danny," she said, "the person who pointed a gun at your daddy's head was your daddy. The person who just pointed a gun at yours was Ralph Hobgood. If it was me, I'd shove that barrel in the opposite direction."

Standing on the street in front of the snack bar, he made a halfhearted attempt to get invited to her place. If she was scared to drive home this late, he said, he could drop her off and then come pick her up again in the morning.

She stroked his cheek. "That's as good a way as any to try to pull it off."

"Pull what off?"

"You know what," she said. "And believe me, Danny, I'm flattered. But it wouldn't solve a thing for either one of us. My pages have been scribbled all over, to the point where anything else just feels like more scrawling."

THIRTY-FIVE

AFTER A SLOW START, the Germans' farmwork had improved. It didn't hurt that, in accordance with the Geneva Convention, they received eighty cents per day, as long as they met the minimum daily quota of a hundred pounds apiece. Right now, Dan knew, they were being compensated in camp scrip, but Marty said the army had set up a savings plan so they could take partial payment in hard currency when the war ended, if they chose. Whatever the reason, they'd become zealous about picking cotton, especially the tall guy named Voss, who had such little ears.

They were in the habit of weighing up three times every day: once around ten-thirty, again at two, then a final time when they quit for the day. Dan's route brought him back near his fields in late morning, so he usually handled the first weigh-up, while Alvin drove over and took care of the second. Then, after Dan finished his route, he weighed their cotton one last time and hauled them back to Camp Loring.

A fair amount of horseplay occurred that morning as the POWs waited near the trailer in unusually high spirits. In mid-

October, for the second time in two months, the Allies had flown a raid over some town in Germany called Schweinfurt, where there was a big armament factory, and according to the sketchy news in the paper and on the radio, their losses had again been terrible. You could never be sure how much the prisoners knew, but reports of this disaster—already dubbed "Black Thursday"—might have reached them by now.

Voss hoisted his sack onto his shoulder and bounced up and down on the balls of his feet, humming what sounded like a polka, while Dan broke out the scales. Then the lanky German hung the sack, stood back and watched it being weighed.

"Seventy-six pounds, six ounces."

One of the other prisoners wagged his finger at Voss, who grinned and bent over and stood still as each of the others, except Schultz, strode up behind him and gently kicked him in the rear. After taking his punishment, Voss freed his sack, hurled it up into the trailer, then climbed in after it and dumped out the cotton.

One by one, the others followed, hanging their sacks from the scales, then stepping back to watch while Dan weighed them. Voss remained in the trailer. After Dan recorded the weights, each would hand his sack up to Voss, who'd empty it and then fling it over the side plank.

Schultz was the last to weigh up. As he stepped back so Dan could balance the scales, Voss climbed out of the trailer and jumped down, stirring up dust where he landed.

"Thirty-four pounds."

One of the other prisoners shook his head and said something to Voss in German, and Voss said something back as they strapped on their sacks.

For a moment or two, Schultz watched the others heading

off into the field. Then he turned back to the trailer and detached his sack from the scales.

"I'll get up there in the trailer," Dan told him, "and you pass me the sack."

"I climb," Schultz said. "Is okay."

Three good-sized pieces of two-by-four had been nailed to the front end planks. Schultz gripped the top one, planted his foot on the bottom one and swung himself into the trailer, reached over the side plank and grabbed the sack, then dumped the cotton and packed it down.

Dan was already walking back to the rolling store when the chunk of two-by-four came loose. He didn't see it happen, just heard the loud squawk of a nail tearing free from the wood and, a second later, the German's groan. Climbing out, he'd apparently fallen straight down onto the iron tongue. When Dan ran around to the front of the trailer, he was splayed across it, face contorted in pain as he struggled for breath.

"Jesus," Dan said.

Schultz's lips scarcely moved: "Side pain."

Dan gripped him under one arm and helped him sit up, then gently probed his rib cage. "Does that hurt?"

"Hurt. Yes."

"We better get you back to the camp. Can you walk if I help you?"

"Yes, I think."

Dan helped him to his feet and, with the German's arm looped around his shoulders, walked him over to the rolling store.

The other prisoners had quit picking. The one who'd wagged his finger at Voss started to lift the strap off his shoulder, but after looking over at Voss, he let his arm fall and stood watching while Dan started the engine and pulled into the road. Once the others disappeared from view, Schultz relaxed considerably, his shoulders no longer hunched in pain. For a mile or so, he sat quietly, observing the cotton fields passing in a blur. Then, as they neared the highway, he shifted his position, so Dan could see his face.

"Please?" he said. "One moment?"

"Yeah?"

"Not hurt," the German said.

"What?"

"Not hurt." To prove it, he patted his rib cage. "I lie."

Dan let off the accelerator. "Why?"

"I have desire to talk."

"To me?"

"To you, yes. But also with American officer. From prisoner camp. Very important."

"How come you didn't just say so?"

"Other prisoner must not to know. Please. I tell to *Kommandant*. Everything."

When he reached the highway, Dan turned the bus around and drove the prisoner to his own house, where he picked up the receiver and heard his mother's voice on the other end saying, "Danny? Danny? Is that you?"

Waiting for the captain to arrive, Dan offered the prisoner a glass of water, which he accepted with gratitude, ducking his head. He sat on the couch, drinking, his eyes roaming the walls, taking in all the pictures, including the one of Shirley in a porch swing, sitting between Alvin and Jimmy Del Timms. She'd hung it up a month or so after the funeral, and when Dan asked her why he'd never seen it before, she said it was because his father hadn't liked it.

He believed then that what his father hadn't liked was Alvin's proximity to Shirley, the way her head inclined toward him rather than toward the man who became her husband, and the position of Alvin's hand—in suspended motion, as if it had just been removed from her knee. Though he didn't discount that as a reason now, he'd begun to wonder if his father's aversion might not also have involved the uniform he wore.

Dan had never actually seen the uniform. The only time he'd asked to, his father claimed he'd burned it. He'd earned medals and citations, as well—Dan had learned as much by listening to him talking with Ralph Hobgood those afternoons on the porch—but nobody, as far as he knew, had ever been granted a glimpse of them. After his father's death, they'd never surfaced.

The POW nodded at the photo. "Your father?"

"Yeah."

"Which one?"

"The soldier. The other one's my uncle Alvin—the fellow that comes and weighs y'all's cotton sometimes."

"Brother is twin?"

Dan had never thought they resembled each other all that much. But in the photograph, he had to admit, the similarity was striking. "No. My father was a year older."

The prisoner stood and walked over to examine the picture more closely. "In First Division your father was?"

"I think so."

"Big Red One." He stuck his hands in his pockets. "Where is father now?"

"Dead."

Either Dan looked older than he was or the prisoner was bad at math, because he said, "Killed in last war?"

Dan didn't know what he'd say until it was said—and then, whether it was a lie. "No. In this one."

The POW returned to the couch and sat down, and they both fell silent, neither meeting the other's eye until fifteen minutes later, when the scout car pulled into the yard and Marty climbed out, followed by Captain Munson.

"Escape . . ." As the prisoner searched for a word, the skin on his cheekbones wrinkled, sending red ripples through the ugly stain. "Escape *meeting*," he finally said. "They have each day."

"When?" Munson asked.

"After night meal."

"Where?"

"In different place. This tent or that one."

Munson had withdrawn a pencil and a small notebook from his pocket, but he hadn't written a word. "How many are planning to go?"

"I don't know. Four, I think. Maybe more go."

"Where in the world do they plan to escape to?"

"Meksyk Gulf."

The captain shook his head, as if he'd never heard anything quite so ridiculous. "They want to go for a swim or what?"

The prisoner shrugged. "Wait for *Boot*."

"You're telling me they've already arranged their own transportation?"

"Voss say *Boot* to come. I don't know."

"It's close to three hundred miles from here to the Gulf. How do they plan to get there?"

"Steal auto."

"The countryside's crawling with military police and Civil Defense patrols. The first time they got stopped, they'd be asked for their papers."

The prisoner wet his lips, and for a moment or two he hesitated. "They make many *dokument*."

"What kind of documents?"

He glanced at Dan. "Driver license. Military name card."

Dan said, "It was *them* that stole my wallet?"

The prisoner dipped his head. "I steal. Sorry."

"You took this young man's driver's license," Munson said, "and his identification card?"

"Yes, I take."

"Why?"

"I, too, think to go. Now, no." He told them, in his fragmented English, how he'd stolen a bottle of ink from the duty hut, snatched a potato from the mess hall and used a nail to engrave printing plates made from cast-off linoleum—he pronounced it *lee-no-LAY-oom*—that he'd discovered behind the supply shed. He'd been hiding in the showers, making documents of his own, when Voss caught him. "They force me to make for them," he said. "Now they have."

Munson laid his pad and pencil on the coffee table. "Where in the name of God did you get the idea to forge documents using ink and potatoes?"

"In Polish school, how children make picture."

The entire time Munson was questioning the prisoner, Marty had been standing by the front door, his arms folded over his chest. Now he cleared his throat. "Sir?"

At first, Dan thought the captain meant to ignore him, and he hated seeing his friend embarrassed. But Munson finally responded. "You want to say something, Stark?"

"Yes sir." For once, Marty looked like a soldier. His uniform was freshly laundered, his bearing erect. "If those fellows are unsupervised out there in my buddy's cotton patch—well, shouldn't one of us get over there and keep an eye on 'em?"

"If you were one of those fellows," the captain said, "and accustomed to not seeing anybody except the occasional MPs driving by in a scout car, then suddenly an armed guard's scrutinizing your every move—what would that suggest to you?"

"I see what you're saying, sir."

"Stark," the captain replied, "you may make a soldier yet. In a year or two, the way things are going, you might be commanding me."

"I sincerely doubt it, sir."

"Well, you never can tell. Who would have thought that our guest here would be running a printing press under our noses?" He smoothed the creases from his shirtsleeves, then leaned back in his chair and cocked his head. To the prisoner, he said, "If you'd managed to escape, where did you plan to go?"

The prisoner's hands lay in his lap. For a moment or two, he gazed at them while gently massaging the base of his left thumb with his right index finger. His answer, when he gave it, was not the one the captain wanted, or at least not one he appeared to believe, but it made perfect sense to Dan.

"I don't know," the prisoner said. "Just leave here. Go anywhere."

THIRTY-SIX

AWAITING ROLL CALL, the prisoners congregated inside the gates. If any of them noticed that for the first time in months the towers were being manned before dusk, they didn't let on. They stood around laughing, bullshitting one another, happy that the hot weather was over.

Earlier that afternoon, Marty and Kimball had found forged documents stashed in the hollow metal legs of Voss's cot. The driver's license didn't look too bad, except that Schultz had put only one *p* in Mississippi and must have gotten confused when converting from the metric system: John Klein, according to the license, stood six foot six, and while that was probably close to Voss's actual height, his weight was given as eighty-five pounds.

The Mississippi State Guard card issued to John Klein could conceivably have satisfied a Civil Defense officer. If it failed to, another document, typed on the Royal in the duty hut, stated that Klein was "nationality of Switzerland" but had lived in the United States since 1936. For good measure, the document alleged that he was "loyal to American cause," and bore the official stamp of the United States Army.

They found a second driver's license in another prisoner's cot. Other documents, all variations on those issued to John Klein, turned up as well. In all, it appeared, at least four and possibly five men were planning to escape.

You could tell the captain was shaken—reporting this to Fourth Service Command would hardly make his stock rise with the brass—but at the same time he was impressed. "You weren't in intelligence, were you?" he'd asked Schultz earlier, as they left the tent with the forgeries in hand.

"Intelligent, no, I was not," Schultz said.

Case and Kimball laughed at that, but Munson didn't, and neither did Marty.

No documents pertaining to the prisoner's own background had turned up, but Marty no longer doubted that he was what he claimed to be—a Pole who'd served in the Wehrmacht. The remaining question had nothing to do with the prisoner's origin. It was a more fundamental question, one that defied boundaries of the type imposed by nations or advancing fronts: who *was* this guy? To answer that, you had to know not only where he'd been but also his ultimate destination.

The Pole was often wrapped in gauzy light. It had surrounded him the first time Marty saw him, that day Schultz—or Szulc—caught his shirt on tin siding, and again the night he emerged from the shadows and walked to the tower. They'd looked at each other for a good while then, but you couldn't say with certainty exactly how long, because time, in the ordinary sense, had stopped flowing.

Marty's drill sergeant back in basic had been a Jew from the East Coast, a man who, at the age of thirty-five, had left a teaching position at the University of Delaware to join the army, where he once more became a master of instruction. Most men's lives, he was fond of saying, broke down into a series of "incremental moments," and the tragedy of human existence was that virtually nobody could predict when those moments would occur. Generally, they passed before you knew you'd lived through them, assuming of course that you *did* live through them. Though not all incremental moments involved physical danger, a great many of them did.

"What I'm here to teach you," he'd said, "is how to survive an incremental moment. The first thing you've got to develop is a willingness to trust your senses. A dog smells fear. You guys have spent most of your lives learning not to be dogs. Now it's time to accept your own canine nature. You want to smell what others can't smell. You want to hear what they don't hear. You want the pores of your bodies to open up and let sensory data rush in, and you want to respond without thinking. If your senses tell you that a form—not a man, I repeat, a *form*—in your immediate vicinity poses a threat to you, you turn into one big fang, dripping saliva. Everything you see and hear and smell is *real*. The one statement you can never allow your brain to communicate to your arms and legs, your feet or your hands, is as follows: *This can't be happening*. It can be, and it will be, and if you fail to recognize that, you will not survive those incremental moments. If you do survive them, you'll most likely never again be able to experience reality in the very limited way that most men and women customarily do. You may come to mourn your inability to do so, and you may blame me for that, but all I can say is, I'd rather be a living dog, able to feel the grass beneath its paws, than a dead man with a bullet and a worm in his well-adjusted brain."

Marty's senses kept telling him that the Pole was more than just another prisoner, that the mark on his face was an identifying trait, that no moment spent in his presence was ordinary. He didn't know why this was so. He just knew that since first setting eyes on the man, he'd sensed a connection between them. He didn't know why it existed, but he was beginning to believe that he'd survived that day on the Niscemi road, despite failing to trust his senses and either pull the trigger or turn and run, so that he might have another chance. And that other chance had something to do with the Pole.

That afternoon Case had led the prisoner off to the infirmary, where they planned to keep him for the evening. While Kimball lingered by the scout car, Marty followed Munson. "Sir?" he said. "Could I speak with you?"

"What is it, Private?"

"Shouldn't we get that fellow out of here, send him somewhere else?"

The captain had placed the forgeries in an accordion file, which he clutched against his chest. "What would you have me do, Stark? Let you march him out into the cotton patch and shoot him?"

"No sir. That's what I'm scared those Germans'll do."

The Pole himself had suggested as much. That was why he'd decided to confess, he said. They wanted him dead, and before leaving, he believed, they meant to kill him. They hadn't trusted him since the day he came to camp. They hadn't even trusted him before that. "In my unit," he said, "two time German soldier shoot me. Both time miss. Officer once try. To English I escape. Happy capture."

Now Munson said, "You've done a one-eighty on our prisoner, haven't you, Stark?"

"I guess so, sir. I believe him anyway."

"You're real big on belief, aren't you?"

"Yes sir. I guess I am."

"Yet you don't strike me as the churchgoing type."

"No sir, I'm not, though I was raised to be. But there's different kinds of belief, sir. I believe this is the ground I'm standing on. I don't know it—I just act like I do." He realized he ought to stop talking, but for some reason he couldn't. "If I didn't act on my belief that this stuff beneath my feet was the ground, there's no telling what I might do. I imagine the same's true for you. Sir."

"You're one of the more complicated people I've come across, Stark. I even have a feeling that if I'd met you under a different set of circumstances, I probably would've enjoyed knowing you. But right now," he said, stepping closer and slapping his thigh with the file, "you're annoying the living hell out of me. I'll decide what to do with that fellow. I'll decide it in my own good time, after consulting my superiors, and until that time, I don't want to hear a word about him out of you. Is that clear, Stark?"

"Yes sir."

Munson turned and headed for his quarters.

"But sir?"

The captain didn't exactly stop, but he did slow his pace.

"Sir, I got a feeling the ground's gone open up."

The prisoners formed themselves into perfectly straight lines, and the sergeant called off all the names himself, one at a time, rather than sending the guards among the labor detachments to check them group by group. The new procedure was the first indication the prisoners received that something out of the ordinary might have happened.

Stationed along the fence, to the right of the gates, Marty got a good view of Voss. Half a head higher than anybody else, he stood in the third position, in the second row, legs together, shoulders back, his chest jutting forth. He stared straight ahead, but once or twice his tongue flicked out and mopped his lips.

Case continued alphabetically, and when he'd checked off the last name, he handed the clipboard to Huggins, who carried it into the captain's quarters. For a moment or two, nobody moved or said a word. Marty raised his eyes and gazed across the rec area at the south tower, where Brinley stood impassively, his fist wrapped around the muzzle of his rifle.

The door to the captain's quarters opened, and Munson stepped out, followed by Huggins. The captain wore his side arm and carried the accordion file. He strode across the yard, ignoring Case's brisk salute.

He handed the file to Huggins, then addressed the prisoners. "When you men were processed as POWs," he said, speaking loudly and clearly, for the benefit of those who understood English and would be expected to inform the rest, "you received from the Red Cross a document prepared by your government, titled 'Memorandum Addressed to German Soldiers.' It urged you to remain physically fit and stay informed of the rights guaranteed you by the Geneva Convention, and it also reminded you that it was your duty, as a soldier, to do everything within your power to escape.

"What it didn't tell you is something you had ample opportunity to observe for yourselves, when you made your train journeys from New Jersey or Maryland or wherever your processing center was to the place where you find yourselves right now. This is one big country. But just in case you didn't study a lot of foreign geography in school, let me provide a few points of comparison.

"The distance between New York City and Los Angeles is almost exactly three times the distance between Paris and Warsaw. The distance from the front gates over there to, let's say, the Gulf of Mexico isn't nearly so great, a mere four hundred and fifty kilometers. But the Gulf Coast might as well be on Jupiter, because the probability that any of you men could get there is zero.

"We've got military police on all the major roads, and Civil Defense patrols on all the minor ones. You men couldn't be expected to know too much about Mississippi, but this state's home to the meanest law-enforcement officers in the nation. Hunting season's a big deal down here, too, and I doubt the local sportsmen would mind a little target practice."

He stuck his hand out, and Huggins gave him back the file. The captain withdrew the forged documents, all of which had been clipped together. He waved the stack in the air. "Some of you men—not a lot, just a few—were apparently planning to take a vacation. I assure you that's all it would have been. A day away at most, but probably not even that. Some of you had phony driver's licenses, a few forged Mississippi State Guard cards, a couple of grammatically incorrect affidavits that attempt to explain why the bearer—whose English, if he speaks any, identifies him as a foreigner—ought to be regarded as a loyal American, exempt from active duty in the military for a variety of reasons, including my own personal favorite"—he riffled the documents until he located the one he wanted—"'total pain in bottom back.'" He stood there staring at the stack of forgeries and shaking his head, as if unable to imagine how anybody with any sense could concoct such an escapade.

The truth was that there weren't nearly as many MPs or Civil Defense officers out there as Munson said, and the locals weren't uniformly hostile to the Germans. The other afternoon, while Marty was on duty at the gate, one of the returning prisoners had climbed out of Bob Brown's pickup truck with a watermelon in his arms. When asked where the hell he'd gotten it, the German said, "Farmer give," so Marty let him carry it on in. Later, he learned that the prisoners didn't know exactly what a watermelon was. After some discussion, they split it open, scooped the pulp out and boiled it until they were left with sugar extract. Then they stripped the skin off and boiled the rind, along with the sugar, and made themselves a marmalade, which they spread on their bread at breakfast.

These were resourceful people, who would make something out of whatever you gave them. If he wanted, Munson could stand up there and shake his head, as though confronted by a bunch of wayward children, but they were neither wayward nor children. If the goals they'd set seemed unrealistic, their pursuit of them was nothing to scorn.

"Just as the Geneva Convention guarantees prisoners of war certain rights," the captain continued, "it also specifies what their captors can do to punish them in the event of an attempted escape. There's a wide range of options available. Prisoners can simply be issued a reprimand. They can be forced to perform extra fatigue duty during their free time. They can be ordered to work without pay, placed on restricted diet, or confined to the camp stockade for up to thirty days.

"The *Kommandant* of one of your camps, if confronted with a similar situation, would most likely begin with the harshest-possible response under international law—if, in fact, he felt himself limited by law. But I'm not going to do that. I'm going to begin with the most lenient response, which is to tell all of you, but especially the men in whose cots these illegal documents were discovered, that this is a warning. If we find any further evidence of an attempt to leave this camp, for any purpose other than authorized work details, the prisoners involved will be locked up in that little brick building behind the showers, which Sergeant Case informs me is infested with red ants big enough to eat a man's flesh and then carry off his bones."

The captain looked down at the stack of documents again, shaking his head at the display of groundless optimism.

Munson had almost reached his quarters when he heard the footsteps on the gravel. Rather than stop, he opened the door and stepped inside, then turned and looked out, his face still in shadow. "A lot of these farmers down here, they've got their backs to the wall, Stark," he said before the private could request permission to speak. "They're not like your father—they don't have enough money to make sure their crops get in on time, year after year. They need these fellows. If we start taking the Germans out of the fields whenever one of them makes a wrong move, they won't take long to realize that's a surefire way of not having to work, which in turn will hurt the local economy and make the farmers lose faith in us as a source of labor. The army doesn't want that—can't *have* it. So every one of these guys picks cotton tomorrow morning."

"What about—"

"I told you not to mention him again."

"You're not going to put him back in the field with them, are you, sir?"

Munson sighed. He laid the file down on the window ledge, then stepped out into the waning sunlight. "He's just one man, Stark, and he's on the wrong side."

THIRTY-SEVEN

THE TEMPERATURE had dipped into the thirties overnight and couldn't have been much higher than forty when Dan stopped the pickup on the side of the road and climbed out. Rosetta's chimney belched black smoke, and a piece of loose siding rattled in the wind. He knew she would've left the house around six-thirty, just like she did every morning but Sunday, to walk up the road to Alvin's store. When it started to get cold, she'd always put on two of everything—a second old blouse, a second old skirt and sometimes, under the skirts, a pair of khaki pants.

He hadn't gone very far across the field before he heard the noise, a lot of groaning and grunting and some kind of percussion, though it didn't quite sound like a drum. He never missed a step, just kept on walking, and coming closer, he realized L.C. was picking the guitar. He didn't strum it like a country picker, and there was nothing you could recognize as a chord or a melody. But these observations didn't interest him much, since he wasn't there for entertainment. He'd come to apologize to L.C. for thinking he'd stolen his wallet.

He'd barely set foot on the bottom step, when the music

stopped. He paused, the plank creaking beneath his weight. Before he could mount the next one, the door opened.

L.C. wore his work clothes, including the coat Rosetta had made him from discarded cotton sacks. He still had a few scabs on his face, and one front tooth was missing. Frank Holder had sure left his mark.

"Ain't time yet," L.C. said. "Your uncle done told me don't start the route now till round about eight. Say folks been getting in the field later and later."

"I ain't here about the route."

"What you want, then?"

"Can I come in?"

"Reckon you can do whatever you like. Last I heard, your uncle owned the house. Land, too." He turned and stepped inside, and Dan followed.

Colored people, he'd noticed, rarely used the word *live* when they talked about the place where they lay down at night. The verb they chose was almost always *stay*. "Hey. Where you stay?" As if living, in the true sense of the word, was impossible. But on the inside, Rosetta's house looked like a place where people lived just as well as they could. A Prince Albert can, mashed flat and nailed down, patched a hole in the floor, and old newspapers whistled where she'd crammed them into chinks. Her cot stood against one wall, a quilt that had once belonged to Dan's grandmother stretched tautly over the mattress, the outlines of corncobs visible beneath the quilt's ragged surface. L.C.'s cot, on the other side of the room, was neatly made, too. The guitar lay across it.

On the wall above the fireplace hung a sheet of butcher

paper, on which somebody had used crayons to draw a picture. In the center, the figure of a man was bent under the weight of an awful-looking cross. A bunch of other folks walked along beside him, waving their fists, their mouths open, their ugly expressions suggesting they were shouting. What was striking about the picture, beyond the artist's ability to make the forms look real, was that Jesus's face was way too dark, whereas the faces of the folks in the crowd were perfectly white, their features sketched in simple lines, with no shading added. "Who drew that?" he asked.

"Momma."

"She made Jesus colored."

"How you know he wasn't? You ever seen him?"

"No, can't say as I have. And don't want to anytime soon."

"Worse people's on the loose than Jesus."

"Yeah, I know, and I aim to keep my distance from them, too. Be all right if I set down?"

"Do it matter if it's all right or not?"

It did matter, at least to him, so he remained on his feet. L.C. watched him for a minute or two and then, as if he couldn't bear to maintain the same posture Dan was in, he sprawled backwards onto his cot, locking his hands behind his neck. "You looking at a latter-day nigger," he said.

"You plan on joining the Mormons?"

"Naw, just planning to act like I'm white. Time's coming when a lot of niggers, not just the frontwards, gone behave that way. You remember the fellow say man's the end result of the monkey? Well, what you seeing now's a evolved mule."

"You don't put faith in anything, do you, except your sense of humor?"

L.C. unlocked his hands, clasped his knees and rocked

forward. "Not a damn thing. But look to me like you can't even count on that."

Dan sat down on Rosetta's bed. To give his hands something to do, he patted the mattress. "My grandma used to own this quilt," he said.

"We didn't steal it. She give it to Momma. Right before she died."

"I didn't say you stole it."

"Well, right when you seen it, what you think then?"

Again, he felt like throwing himself on L.C., because in reality he was a goddamn thief, even though he'd taken no material possessions. Earlier he'd robbed Dan of the right to pity himself, and now of the will to say he was sorry. "You know why I came over here?"

"You wanted something."

"I wanted something?" Dan said. "What the hell could I hope to get from you?"

"I couldn't say. My mind don't work that way."

While Dan looked on in disbelief, L.C. lifted the guitar, set it down on the wrong knee and began to pluck the bass strings. "You know what I been studying on lately? After the Devil get through tempting Jesus and Jesus tell him to get lost, Saint Luke say the 'Devil departed from him for a season.' Now where you reckon he went?"

"I don't have no idea."

L.C. thumped the top of the guitar, then lifted both feet and brought them crashing down onto the floorboards.

good Lord tell the Devil
get thee behind me
go

Devil beg for shelter
say winter comin'
on so cold

old Satan bound to wander
got to see the Ritz
get him some rest
bellhop slam the door shut
say this place don't take
no Devil for a guest

The music sounded ragged, like L.C. was making it up as he went along. And it occurred to Dan as he sat there on Rosetta's bed, understanding he would not do what he'd meant to, that almost everybody he knew, including his mother and Marty Stark, L.C. and Rosetta, Captain Hobgood and Frank Holder, Lizzie and the prisoner with the ruined face, who claimed to be Polish, the Germans out there in the cotton field, so far away from their homes, maybe even Alvin—all of them were doing the same thing now every day of their lives, just trying to keep rhythm with times so irregular, searching hard for a melody and a few simple words that made any sense at all.

Both towers at Camp Loring were occupied that morning, and the guards manning them had replaced their rifles with Thompson submachine guns. Rather than clustering around the gates, grouped loosely in their work details, the prisoners remained in formation. Guards stood along the perimeter, their eyes scanning the ranks.

Dan waited on the side of the road with Frank Holder,

Bob Brown and several other farmers. Once or twice, he saw Holder cut his eyes over at L.C., who was sitting in the cab of the pickup truck, but each time Frank was quick to drop his head.

"What they expecting these fellows to do?" Bob Brown said. "Riot and take over the courthouse?"

"They caught some of 'em planning an escape," Dan told him.

"Where was they aiming to escape to?"

"Sounds like they meant to head for the Gulf Coast."

"Far as I'm concerned," Bob Brown said, "they're welcome to it."

A man called Roberts said, "What you got against the Gulf Coast?"

"Too damn close to New Orleans."

"So what's wrong with New Orleans?"

"They's too many mongrels down there," Brown said. "Can't tell what nobody is. Nigger and white's all mixed up together, and half of them don't speak no English. Send these Germans down there, they just might clean things up."

"Yeah," said Roberts, "they done a real good job sanitizing Poland. Maybe we ought to let 'em spray a little cleaning fluid on you." Then he walked off and stood near the fence by himself.

Bob Brown shook his head. "What's got into him this morning?"

If the others had any idea, they kept it to themselves and waited silently until the little sergeant walked over, unlocked the gates and stepped out.

His swagger was absent today. Serious and subdued, he spoke in a low voice, hugging the clipboard instead of brandishing it. "The army don't want to alarm you fellows," he said.

"We're glad to be hiring out these prisoners to pick your cotton, and happy that you've been so pleased by the results. Most of them are just good solid workers, not your UAW types. If they'd been at Flint a few years ago, up where I'm from, we wouldn't of had no strike. Your German generally does what the authorities tell him—and in this case, the only authority that matters is the United States Army. But a few of them probably had some Nazi thinking beat into their heads, a bunch of Adolfology, as my pop likes to put it, and it looks like they meant to go for an illegal stroll."

Consequently, the sergeant explained, some procedures were being altered. Nineteen of the details would leave camp that morning under guard, and only seven would go unguarded. Also, sometime around lunch, the guards would be rotated. And any contractor whose detail was unguarded at any time was responsible for notifying the camp immediately if any of the prisoners went missing. Finally, instead of remaining in permanent work details, men would be shuffled from group to group, so the farmers would no longer see the same bunch of prisoners from one day to the next.

The last statement drew a collective groan. "I'm used to my boys," one of the men said, and Bob Brown added that he'd begun to think of his group almost as if they were kin. His wife had been knitting gloves and socks for each of them, intending to pass the gifts out right before Christmas.

The sergeant said he could understand their dismay and that he would personally see to it that these young men received their presents. Then, after answering a couple more objections with assurances that everything would go along just fine, he walked back over to the gates and began calling names.

While waiting to hear which prisoners he'd be getting, Dan

saw Frank Holder walk toward the pickup, where L.C. was sitting. Holder's hands were clenched into fists, but he held them in an odd position, both of them pressed tightly against the small of his back, lacking only a pair of handcuffs to complete the picture. He stopped a foot or two from the truck, and for a good while L.C. stared at him through the glass. Then he rolled the window down three or four inches.

Dan couldn't hear what Holder was saying. Whatever it was, it took no more than a minute or two. When he finished, he just stood there with his hands held behind him. It was a long time before L.C. nodded and rolled the window back up, without ever saying a word. Then Holder shoved his hands into his pockets and started back toward the gates.

The prisoner with the marked face was the only member of Dan's original group who left camp with him that morning. According to the sergeant, one of the new men, whose soft, smooth skin made him look a lot younger than he must have been, had picked close to three hundred pounds one day for Ed Mitchell. All eight of them rode in back of the pickup, huddling into the collars of their camp-issued jackets. Kimball followed along behind in a scout car, after Marty left with Frank Holder's detail.

On the way to the field, Dan asked L.C. what Holder had said.

L.C. looked out the window. "Claim he sorry for beating up on me."

"Well, maybe he is."

"Then me and him got one thing in common," L.C. said. "I'm sorry about it myself."

"You know his son got killed, don't you?"

"Tell me what in the hell," L.C. said, "his son getting killed got to do with beating the shit out of me."

The cab of the pickup truck was small and only a couple feet separated them, but it might as well have been a thousand miles. Dan could've answered his question, but when he thought about explaining the connection that probably existed in Holder's mind between his son's death in North Africa and L.C.'s living presence in a rolling store on a road near Loring, Mississippi, he realized how pointless it would be, starting with the stuff about defending your country. While L.C. and Frank Holder both inhabited the same general location, anybody with even one good eye could see they lived in two different countries. He didn't know that he'd fight for the one L.C. had been assigned to, and wasn't sure if Holder would, either. "I guess it don't have nothing to do with it," he said.

Only scrap picking remained. The field had a ragged look, the cotton dangling from the stalks, buffeted that morning by the wind. The air smelled of wood smoke. It was the season when Dan's father had always worried, because the crop yield was never what he'd hoped for and cotton prices were always lower than he'd convinced himself to expect. But his father wouldn't have to worry this year, having left all his worries to somebody else.

Until now, Dan hadn't felt any anger at him. He believed he'd taken his life because his own brother had been sleeping with his wife off and on for God knows how many years, and he couldn't stand it anymore. Now, though, he wasn't so sure. Driving home the other night after his conversation with

Lizzie, he'd gotten mad at Ralph Hobgood for telling him what his father had said. But he'd woken up the next morning mad at Jimmy Del Timms, and he was still mad at him. Because it seemed to him that in trying to make one life count for two—if, in fact, that's what he'd had in mind—his father had been successful, though not in the way he'd intended.

After the Okie pilot crashed his plane on the levee, Marty Stark said the most intense moment of his life had come when he gazed into the eyes of a man who meant to kill him. "For just a second, before an officer hollered at him and he ran off down the road, he'd decided to blow my head off. And as I knelt there in that stinking water, I told myself, 'All right, this son of a bitch is fixing to do something that'll force him to carry me with him wherever he goes. Every time he looks at his son, if he has one, he'll see the man he murdered. Looks into a woman's eyes, he'll see mine, and when he shoves into her real hard and she whimpers, it'll be me that's whimpering too.' Taking another person's life don't just mean you killed them. It means they're *upon you*."

Dan now felt as if he were some combination of himself and his father, with double sets of virtues and vices, with his own sins to atone for as well as ones he'd never even had the pleasure of committing. He'd tried and failed to apologize to L.C. that morning, but he might just as well have told his mother he was sorry for blaming his father's death on her and Alvin. Maybe he needed to apologize to his uncle, too.

He parked the truck on the turnrow and climbed out. L.C. also got out, though there wasn't anything for him to do except wait beside the truck while Dan distributed sacks.

"There's not much cotton left out there," Dan told the prisoners. "Today and tomorrow ought to about finish it on this place." He couldn't tell how many of them had understood him, and it didn't really matter. After strapping on their sacks, they moved off, stooping over and picking smoothly, as if they'd grown up in these fields.

Kimball climbed lazily out of the scout car, leaving his rifle stuck in the boot, and walked over next to Dan. "Guess you heard about the big excitement," he said.

"Yeah." Dan kept his voice low, because the prisoners weren't that far away. "I'm surprised they put Schultz back out here. I figured they'd send him to a different camp."

"Your buddy tried to get 'em to." Kimball pulled a pack of chewing gum from his pocket, withdrew a stick, unwrapped it and laid it on his tongue. He put the pack back in his pocket without offering a stick to Dan or L.C., whose presence he hadn't even acknowledged. "Stark's an odd one," he said. "He always like that?"

"Like what?"

Kimball's jaws clicked while he worked at the gum. "So goddamn jumpy."

"He used to be about the calmest fellow around."

"That so?"

"Yeah. That is so. One year, we were five points down to Indianola, starting on our own three-yard line with four or five minutes left. Playing for the conference title. Well, we had three fourth-down plays on that drive. No time-outs, folks in the stands going crazy, coach standing stock-still on the sideline, praying—but Marty's just as cool as ice water. Called most of the plays right at the line and finally carried the ball in himself after breaking two or three tackles."

"He's not breaking any tackles lately, so I imagine that'll prove the high point of his earthly existence." Kimball stretched, then yawned. "I stood watch last night," he said, "and maybe I'll pull off the road somewhere and take a little nap. That be all right with you?"

"I don't give a shit. But won't you get in trouble if they catch you?"

Kimball laughed. "Nah, I'm trouble-free. Huggins has some pretty good connections, and if the army fucks with him or any of his pals, somebody'll fuck with the army."

He walked back over to the scout car and drove off. Dan stood there for another few moments, watching the prisoners as they picked toward the far end of the field. Then he looked at L.C. and said, "Well, let's go sell some neck bones and cracklings."

They drove by the house, where Dan's mother got behind the wheel and dropped him and L.C. off at Alvin's, and they stocked the rolling stores and headed out on their routes. The morning remained cold and gray, but the sun popped out in the afternoon, and they sold a fair number of sodas and even some ice cream.

Around a quarter to four, they off-loaded their Deepfreezes back at Alvin's, and Dan told L.C. that if he'd help him weigh up, he'd treat him to a hot dog and soda after they dropped the prisoners off. Shoving his hands into his pockets, L.C. said that would be okay.

They drove back down to the field, where the Germans waited on the turnrow, two or three of them sitting on their stuffed cotton sacks, the rest standing. Several yards away, Schultz squatted by himself, his sack only half-full.

L.C. helped the Germans hang their heavy canvas bags

from the scales, and Dan recorded the weights in his notebook. As always, Schultz was last.

"Forty-one pounds, dead even," Dan said.

The others had already climbed into Alvin's truck, so nobody except L.C. noticed when the prisoner stepped close to Dan and pressed two cards into the palm of his hand.

Dan looked down and discovered his State Guard ID and his driver's license.

"They don't find these," the prisoner said. "Now you have back. All right?"

"Sure," Dan said. "Thanks."

"All right, yes. You maybe need." Dipping his head slightly, the prisoner walked around to the back of the truck and climbed over the tailgate.

THIRTY-EIGHT

MARTY PULLED the bottle out from under the seat, screwed the top off and took another swallow. He'd been drinking off and on all afternoon, sitting on the turnrow in the scout car, his feet flat on the ground, the Enfield resting on his knee.

Lately, whenever he'd had a good bit to drink, he imagined himself alone with Shirley Timms. The setting varied every time, but their conversations always began with him confessing that as a kid he'd dreamed about calling her by her first name. While he fully intended to then profess a romantic interest, she always seized on his opening statement and told him to go right ahead and call her Shirley, and in that moment all his other needs evaporated. It was uncanny, the way it always happened. "Shirley," he'd say, and everything else would just fall away. He guessed this ought to worry him, and knew damn well that the psychiatrist who'd examined him a few months ago would've considered it evidence of some malaise. But the truth was, he couldn't get too worked up about it. If saying a woman's first name could satisfy you, why not be grateful for such a cheap and simple solution?

What he could get worked up about was the sight of the tall

prisoner they'd reassigned to Frank Holder. You could tell that lanky bastard's heart was full of mayhem. Once, he dropped his sack near the end of a row and stood there, hands on hips, staring at Marty and looking as if he couldn't control his breathing, his shoulders rising and falling like pistons.

Gesturing with the bottle, Marty said, "Hey, Voss—want a little nip?"

The German's mouth twisted into the semblance of a grin.

"I mean it. Just back off and I'll stand it at the end of your row, and when I get back over here where I can point my trusty peashooter right at your navel, you can have you a sip. Don't drool in the bottle, though, 'cause I still got an itchy finger from combat."

Voss turned his chin up, as if to give Marty a clear view of all the snot in his nostrils, and fired a ball of spit straight up into the air.

The wad hung for an instant at the top of its arc—long enough for Marty to flick off the safety and raise the rifle. He didn't hit it, but neither did he miss by much. At the report, Voss dived between the cotton stalks, doing his best to burrow with his elbows. Spread out in the field behind him, the others flattened themselves, too.

"On your feet, Adolf!" Marty laughed, but it sounded shrill even in his own ears. "Ain't you a lucky son of a bitch, playing out here where all the cotton and the corn and taters grow?"

THIRTY-NINE

THOUGH MUNSON had always enjoyed football and was a fair tailback himself, it was the last thing on his mind when he picked up the phone and placed his call. But it was all the person on the other end cared to discuss. If Munson hadn't put any money yet on the Army-Navy game, he said, he might want to, because word coming out of the Point was that Red Blaik had a big surprise to spring on the middies. Nobody would say exactly what it was, but Navy's winning streak was sure to stop at four.

"Thank you, sir," Munson said. "I'll put a dollar down, if I can find anybody around here to bet with. What I was calling you about, though, is the situation with our intended escape."

"Did you get them back in the fields today?"

"Yes sir."

"Any problems?"

"They should be back at camp in a little while. As far as I know, everything's gone smoothly."

"Good. You've done a fine job there, Munson, and it won't go unnoticed. We're working to get you out of there, I believe I mentioned?"

"Yes sir."

"Just be patient. You'll get to hit the beach before it's over—I can almost guarantee it."

"Thank you, sir. But what I wanted to ask is whether or not there's been any decision about transferring this guy who tipped us off. We kept him in the infirmary last night, because of course he'd faked that accident, but—"

"You *did* send him back to work today, right?"

"Yes sir."

"Fine. If you let them start thinking they can claim they're hurt or sick or whatnot, they won't hit a lick. And like I told you, we don't want to lose the confidence of our labor contractors. You've done a good job, Munson. On all fronts."

"Thank you, sir. But my question now is what to do with him tonight. Because since I put him back in the field today, I can't really send him back to the infirmary."

"Of course not. You'd look dumb as shit—like you'd buy any bag of trash he's selling."

"Yes sir. But if I put him back in with his tentmates tonight—"

"So don't. Use your brain, Captain. Today you broke up the regular work details, right?"

"That's correct, sir."

"And the fellows trying to escape were in his tent, weren't they?"

"Two of them were, but a couple were in another tent. And those are just the ones we're sure of."

"So tonight you adopt the same tactics. Change everybody's tent assignments. Break up the cliques. Put your mystery man in with a new bunch of guys—or leave him where he was and put a new bunch in with him. End of story, right?"

"Yes sir. I hope so anyway."

"Of course it will be."

"Sir, I don't suppose we've ever located any papers on the prisoner?"

"No, and we may not for a while. Some of these guys we're using as file clerks can hardly read, let alone file. Even so, your prisoner's nobody important, because if he were, his papers would've have been handled by somebody with an actual IQ. Now tell me something, Munson."

"What's that, sir?"

"Did you ever, even in your worst nightmares, think the Naval Academy would defeat us four years in a row?"

FORTY

RIFLE HANGING OFF his shoulder, Marty stood just inside the tent, slurping bourbon-laced coffee from a GI mug. The tent was badly lit, a single lightbulb dangling from the socket ring that held the sheet-iron tubing in place.

"Come on there," he said, "hurry up."

The men who were leaving stuffed their belongings into their packs, while the one who would stay sat on his cot, both hands resting on his knees, and studied the potbellied stove that stood in the center of the tent, providing what warmth there was.

Voss had been surly ever since Munson announced tent assignments were being changed. Earlier, in the mess hall, he'd banged his fist on the table, knocking pinto beans all over the floor. Now he moved about the tent in a cold, silent fury, grabbing one item after another and shoving them into the canvas pack. The last thing he produced was the big yellow can stashed beneath his cot. Because it had surfaced during the search for forged documents, Marty already knew what was in it: German butter, probably two or three years old by now and rancid as hell. Normally, Marty wouldn't have given a damn if Voss wanted to lug the can around with him, but the bastard had spit at him that afternoon. He'd enjoyed seeing Voss throw himself on the ground, and he'd laughed when the German finally stood up and began to brush the dirt off his knees and elbows.

"Hey, Adolf."

Voss turned to look at him.

"Our butter's not good enough for you? Why you got to tote that shit around?" He nodded toward Voss's cot. "Just leave it over yonder."

The can must have weighed five pounds, but Voss flicked it back and forth, from one huge hand to the other, then held it out with a flourish and said something in German.

Marty understood: *If you want it, come take it.* Suddenly, the tent seemed crowded.

He drained his mug and dropped it on the ground, then unslung his rife. He meant to tell Voss one more time to put the can down and step away from the cot. Once the German complied, Marty would open the door to the stove, shove the can inside and shut the door. Before long they'd hear the container pop open, and if it was loud enough, a few of them might flinch. A moment later, they'd smell the burning butter.

But before he issued his order, Schultz said, "He won't give."

"What?"

"Won't give. To him this can mean something. He fight for it."

They all stood there looking at the Pole: Voss with the can of butter in his hand, Marty with his rifle, the other men with various keepsakes—a pair of leather slippers, a tiny square pillow hardly big enough for a man to rest his head on, a roll of toilet paper so brown from age and dust that it looked as if it had already been used, and such a large assortment of dolls and stuffed animals that you might have thought you'd entered a nursery.

FORTY-ONE

FROM HABIT, Szulc lay on his stomach, his head pressed into the cot, his arms at his sides as he shrank, once again, into himself. He knew from long experience that a man could reduce the size of his body. In the desert, even if pausing for only an hour, they'd always dug slit trenches, just deep enough that a tightly compressed body would lie below ground level; he'd seen men two meters tall withdraw into a depression hardly large enough to hold a child.

Different bodies produce different sounds. On the far side of the stove, on the cot that had been Voss's, lay a big Bavarian with a deviated septum. He did not snore so much as whistle, making music in his sleep. A pair of feet protruded from the cot next to his, small and white, and they remained in constant motion, the ankles grinding against each other.

The awareness that his body could produce a sound he hadn't willed was appalling. He'd heard bodies gurgle, or suck, or expel great bursts of tainted air. They sometimes rattled, or jingled like a box filled with coins. Bodies could honk and shriek, hit a note and sustain it. On Bloody Sunday of the Dead, when they'd repulsed the initial British advance on Tobruk, he'd held a tone so long himself that Hauptmann Fischer slapped him and then, having failed to still his voice, shoved him to the ground and forced him to fill his mouth with sand.

"That horrible stain on your face," Fischer asked, lying on top of him to keep him from rising, "where did you get it?"

He spat out the sand. "At birth."

"Does it hurt?"

"Not physically."

"A psychic wound? How modern."

Fischer's breath tickled the back of his neck. As he hugged the ground and listened to the British shells exploding, he performed a calculation: the number of hours in the average day—four, he estimated—spent with dirt or sand against his face, times 365 would equal 1,460 hours, which divided by twenty-four came to sixty days and twenty hours.

Almost the same as being buried for two months. Except that, in a strictly medical sense, he was not yet dead.

FORTY-TWO

MARTY ROSE a few minutes before midnight, stumbled into somebody's footlocker, then stepped outside the tent in his underwear. The night was clear and cold, a big moon shining just beyond the south tower. No sign of Kimball up there, which probably meant he was taking his evening nap.

Stepping into the shadows, he opened his fly and let loose. His urine stank of coffee and whiskey, and burned him badly. He shook himself off, went back inside and got dressed. Then he lifted his mattress, pulled out the half-pint bottle and stuck it in his pocket, grabbed his rifle and a big flashlight and left, fully armed, to stand his watch.

If you had asked him, as Munson did, what made him detour down the dirt path between the long rows of prisoners' tents rather than take the direct route to the south tower, he couldn't have told you, though he would've said he'd never done it before. If you'd questioned him further and demanded to know why he'd stopped outside the last tent on the left—one of three tents that stood empty, waiting for a new group of prisoners scheduled to arrive any day—he couldn't have answered that question, either, except to say that he had no idea.

In turn, you wouldn't have known that shortly after setting off again, taking five or perhaps even six strides toward the tower, he turned and retraced his footsteps. Neither did he know why he'd done that.

He could have said that as he stood before the empty tent, he pulled the bottle from his pocket, tucked the flashlight under his arm, screwed the cap off the bottle and took a swig. The whiskey seared his throat and nostrils, making him cough. That had made him think about Raymond Sample—which itself was inexplicable, since Sample, a Mormon from Heber City, Utah, had never taken a drink in his life. Marty screwed the cap back on, stuck the bottle in his pocket, then reached for the tent flap and pulled it open.

Dark and cold, the tent reminded him of a cave his father had taken the family to see during a vacation in the mountains. A guide had explained the difference between stalactites—calcareous icicles that hung from the ceiling—and stalagmites—similar material that instead rose from the floor. Both types of deposit were bone white, ice-cold, and unpleasant to touch. The guide had shined his flashlight around the enormous underground vault, revealing hundreds, if not thousands, of forms.

But when Marty thumbed the button on his flashlight, the beam revealed only one form, suspended from the socket ring at the top of the tent.

The angry stain on the face was streaked with blue. The tongue, protruding a couple inches, exhibited a bluish tinge, too. A deep gash in the forehead had bled a little, but not much. Both eyes were open, the left one rotated slightly upward, as if something on the tent ceiling demanded immediate attention.

On the floor, beneath the dangling feet, their toes splayed out like claws, were two items: a dirty rag and a ceramic GI mug that, when Munson examined it a few moments later, stank of cheap whiskey.

FORTY-THREE

THE ODORS of that midnight would remain with Munson always: the scent of whiskey, the acrid smell of smoldering leaves and a hint of roasted garlic, though he had no idea where that came from.

"You saw nobody, either when you left your tent or on your way over here?"

"Not a soul."

He didn't bother to correct him—*not a soul, sir*—because he was beyond the urge to provide correction, as Stark was beyond the point at which he might accept it.

"And you didn't hear anything?"

"Not a sound."

He turned to Case, who stood beside the door with a handkerchief clamped to his mouth. "Sergeant, are you going to be sick?"

"No sir."

"Then put that handkerchief away."

"Yes sir." Case folded it primly and tucked it in his pocket.

"Who'd we have in the towers?"

"Kimball and Huggins, sir."

"Neither of them reported seeing or hearing anything?"

Stark cleared his throat. "They couldn't see or hear anything. Soon as they get tired of playing with the spotlight, they sit down and go to sleep."

"Case, go get both of them. Post guards around the perimeter, and put somebody who's awake up in those towers right now."

He waited until Case left, then walked over and poured himself a cup of coffee. Then he remembered the mug, which was standing on top of his desk, right beside the manual on courts-martial. He walked back over to the desk and gestured at the mug. "Any idea where this came from?"

"It's mine. Or at least I was using it."

"How'd it end up in that tent?"

"I imagine somebody carried it in there."

"Any idea who?"

"Whoever hung that Polish fellow."

"How do you suppose they got it in the first place?"

"I left it in the poor bastard's tent."

"When?"

"Earlier tonight. When I went in there to move Voss and them others."

"So why does it smell like whiskey?"

"Because that's what it had in it."

Munson lifted the gray mug, turned it over and looked at the bottom. "If I were guessing, I'd say this is what made that gash in his head. Wouldn't you?"

"I don't give a shit what made the gash in his head."

"Why's that?"

"The gash in his head ain't what killed him. It was the rope around his neck did that."

"What makes you so certain?"

"Because the head wound barely bled. They hung him first and hit him later."

Munson then made a remark he would regret for the rest of his life: "You sound like an expert."

He never actually saw Stark rise. He was in the chair one minute, his hands at rest in his lap, and on his feet the next. Like one of those western shoot-outs, where you never saw the gunslinger draw. "Yes, I am a fucking expert," he said. "Want me to tell you something—Captain, sir?"

"No, Private Stark," Munson said, "I don't want you to tell me anything. I just want you to sit back and—"

"Me and my friend Bubba Garrett did it," Stark said, "when we were in seventh grade. Bubba's daddy used to own the meatpacking plant, that big old red building across from the compress, but when it failed, they moved to Biloxi, and I ain't seen him in years. He may be dead now, for all I know. Anyhow, we got us some navel oranges one day, put 'em in his daddy's freezer and left 'em till they froze solid as rocks. Then we took 'em out back and used 'em like baseballs. And the sound a body makes when you fire a slug into it from four or five feet away—well, sir, it's the same sound them oranges made when the bat hit 'em. Halfway between *splat* and *thunk* . . . *Splunk*."

Munson looked down at the mug in his hands and thought of his father. A big difference between him and his father, who had taught junior-high science, was that his father had never looked at anything—whether it was an object, like the ceramic mug, or a living creature, such as a beetle or a sunflower—without asking himself a whole series of questions, most of which had to do with origins. How had the thing *achieved*—that was always the word he used—its existence? Existence was always a bit of a miracle, as far as his father was concerned. And he'd viewed the demise of anything, even an object like the mug, much less a human life, as tragic.

When Munson looked at the mug, he saw something that had been designed to contain coffee but which had recently been put to the wrong use. He didn't worry about how it had achieved its existence, and the only reason he wouldn't just send it back to the camp kitchen and forget about it was that it had become a piece of evidence. He had no idea how Marty Stark viewed a mug, or a beetle or sunflower, or a corpse dangling from a rope, but to him, each of them must've seemed qualitatively different.

Munson wished his father were alive and could somehow be summoned to this room, because he believed he would've known what to say to Marty Stark. There was a set of words, if they could only be found, that could cool Stark's fever and still his mind; he also knew that he was not the man to speak them.

But he did his best. What the moment seemed to require was someone as different from himself as a man could possibly be, so he asked himself what the last thing he'd naturally do under these circumstances might be. And once he'd arrived at the answer, he set the mug down, stepped around his desk and put both arms around Stark. "It's all right, Marty," he whispered. "It's all right."

"No sir," Stark said, "it's not."

FORTY-FOUR

THINGS WERE NOT all right the next morning at formation, though to Munson's dismay he'd been ordered to behave as if they were. His request for ten more guards had been denied— no extra men available—but the provost marshal, en route from base camp, would convene an investigating board once the prisoners returned from their work details.

Among the group of men Munson now stood facing was at least one murderer—in all likelihood, three or four. "Though in a strictly military sense," the voice on the phone had said, "whoever killed that prisoner did exactly what they'd been trained to do. The prisoner was a traitor, pure and simple, and the killers exacted summary justice. I've said it before, and I'll say it again: We could learn a thing or two about professionalism from those men."

You could also learn a thing or two from the voice on the phone about the country you lived in. Because now, rather than keeping the prisoners under lock and key until the murderers were discovered, he was about to send them back to the fields to pick cotton. If principle wasn't indispensable, apparently commerce was.

He waited while Case called names, and when the sergeant yelled "Schultz," he let his eyes roam the ranks. The men stood at attention, most of them staring straight ahead, more than a few looking half-asleep. After what seemed like two or three minutes, Case made a mark on his roster and hollered "Schussler," continued through "Zintsch," then stuck the pen in his shirt pocket, walked over and handed his clipboard to Munson.

Who stood there looking down at the names, at the checkmarks beside them, the single blank spot. He'd never been given to righteous indignation, but that morning he felt it. The problem was where to direct it. He'd already bawled out Kimball and Huggins, both of whom claimed, of course, they'd been on their feet for the duration of their duty. When he told them to get their worthless asses out of his sight, he understood that it would be no time at all before Huggins made a phone call.

He couldn't place the entire blame on them, though, because whoever killed the Pole, if that's what he was, would have found a way to do it sooner or later. He couldn't blame Stark, and didn't want to. He couldn't really blame himself, since he'd been following orders. And from that day several years ago when he'd received the letter granting him admission to West Point, he hadn't once blamed the army for anything.

He'd spent four years marching to class beneath the gray arches, drilling for hours on the Plain, standing one inspection after another, somebody constantly jaw-to-jaw with him, yelling and criticizing, and he doubted a single day had passed without his hearing the word *grave* or *gravity*: "These are grave actions. . . . Don't underestimate the gravity of the situation." Yet for all the gravitas, he'd never quite conquered the feeling that what he was engaged in was play, much like what he'd done with his best friends, at age eight or nine, in the backyards of Wynoka, Minnesota. Back then, he'd marched along, stiff and stylized to the point of parody, occasionally hurling himself into a pile of leaves while someone hid in the bushes and made spitting noises, imitating the sound of a German machine gun.

He still felt as if he were a boy. But unlike his childhood friends, a great many of the prisoners arrayed before him, if not all of them, had been killers the day they arrived at Camp Loring and weren't playing any games, though it now seemed that both he and the army had behaved as if they were.

"You men are about to finish picking cotton," he said, starting to move along the ranks, walking slowly, careful to take deep breaths so his voice would have that sturdy timbre the army liked. "By most accounts, you've done a good job. I've even learned that some of the farmers around here are planning to make Christmas packages for you. I hope that over in your country somebody'll be making packages for our men in the German camps. Somehow, I doubt that'll be the case, but who knows?

"We have another holiday before Christmas, and it'll be coming up pretty soon. You may have heard of it. We call it Thanksgiving. People eat turkey and thank God for their good fortune. You'll be getting turkey, too. You'll get that and you'll get mashed potatoes and two kinds of dressing, stewed beets and carrots, with some cranberry sauce on the side."

He had no idea where his speech would take him, but he found solace in the sound of his own voice, which up until that moment he'd always been suspicious of, fearful it might break. The only thing he feared now was the silence that would ensue if he quit talking.

"After the Thanksgiving meal," he said, "you'll get a good night's sleep, believe me. Then the next morning you'll get up and go to the latrine, where you may notice that your urine's bright red from all the beets you've shoveled down your throats. When you see that red liquid draining out of your own bodies, I hope you'll ask yourselves what it feels like to know your life's in the process of expiring. Then I want you to imagine you suffered that realization somewhere far away from home, in a dark, cold place, with a rope around your neck."

He'd reached the end of the front row. The last man in line, a slim brown-eyed guy who looked oddly feminine, refused to meet his gaze. At first, Munson thought the man had looked away out of guilt—that he'd taken part in the murder or knew who had—but then he heard the noises that had drawn the prisoner's glance: boards creaking, the grating sound of metal on metal.

Then he turned around and looked for Case. "Sergeant? Who's in the south tower?"

The little burger place in Greenville stood between the tobacco store and the barbershop. Barely big enough to contain the grill and a few seats at the counter, it reeked of smoke and onions. Marty's father had taken him there when he was eight or nine, ordered him a cheeseburger with fries and told the man behind the counter he'd be back in a little while. It wasn't until Marty bit into the cheeseburger that he remembered being there a few years earlier, and that his father had left him then, as well. Now, as he crouched out of sight in the tower and lined his clips up on the floor, then jerked the bolt back on the Thompson to chamber the first round, it seemed to him that on the second trip to Greenville he'd understood his father had gone off somewhere to meet a woman. But he might be confusing that day with a later one. In fact, his father took him to the burger place many times and always disappeared. At some point, surely, there must have been a moment when he suddenly realized what his father was up to. But how could you say when, exactly, awareness occurred?

How could you say precisely when somebody quit being alive and started being dead? It didn't, he knew, necessarily have shit to do with when your heart stopped beating. Raymond Sample hadn't died the moment those bullets from the Schmeisser destroyed his face. He'd been dead at least since finding the little girl whose body had been ripped in half. You could even argue that he'd died somewhere in Utah, when he grew up to become the kind of person who couldn't hear another human being crying out in pain and not run off into the darkness to help him.

The Pole hadn't died in the tent—that just happened to be the place where he took his last breath. Brinley, who was up in the north tower right now, had probably died in the South Pacific. Jimmy Del Timms had died somewhere in Europe back in 1918 and then impersonated the living for the better part of twenty-five years. Dan was probably already dead, too, though there was no way he could know it.

Peeking over the ledge, he surveyed the scene. The Germans were assembled in perfectly straight ranks, most of them staring dead ahead; Voss, by virtue of being the tallest, was easy enough to spot. Munson and Case, Kimball and Huggins and the other guards formed a loose perimeter, in ragged contrast to the disciplined mass in the middle. The country might win the war, and he hoped it would, but that would require different men than these and a different man than him. For once, whether by accident or by design, the army had made the proper move and sent them all where they could do the least damage.

"The Thompson," his drill sergeant had said, "is known as a blow-back weapon. You jam the clip in the magazine, snatch the bolt back to chamber the round, then squeeze that trigger. And as long as you keep the pressure on, each round fired blows the bolt back and chambers another round. This weapon offers zero accuracy but can create maximum mayhem. Basically, men, the Thompson's perfect for somebody who can't shoot straight and can't think straight, somebody who's got himself cornered and can't see a way out."

Raymond, always good at injecting a little humor, pretended to be intrigued by the terminology. "Sarge," he said, "if you use a blow-back weapon in one of them incremental moments you're always talking about, would you say you was having a blow-back moment?"

"Sample," the sergeant said, "that would be as good a term as any."

Frank Holder had removed the American flag from the side planks of his truck. The flag was cheap, made of thin cloth, and you could see clean through the stars and the stripes. He might've left it on there if the flag had been made of thicker, heavier material, not so chintzy-looking.

Holder himself was feeling even heavier than he was—almost as if he were made out of lead. His motions had grown leaden. When he walked, he barely had the sense that he was moving. He'd dragged many a heavy cotton sack along dirt rows in his life, and lately felt like he was always pulling that weight along behind him. He guessed that's how folks end up. Everything you'd ever done that you wished you hadn't, or hadn't done and wished you had, everything you'd ever lost or wanted and never got—all of it attached itself and dragged you down, more of it all the time, until you flat gave out.

He couldn't sleep much and had given up trying. What he did, for several hours every night, was walk the roads near his house, pacing along with his hands clasped behind his back or, if they started getting cold, jammed into his coat pockets. He'd walk toward that place in the road ahead where everything came together in a big ball of darkness. He never quite got to that spot, because light kept creeping in, but he knew he'd get there eventually.

Last night, he had walked the roads from shortly after the moment when Arva fell asleep until the sun began to color the eastern horizon. Even so, he wasn't hungry—he never had much appetite anymore—so he decided to skip breakfast and drive out to Camp Loring.

Since it was way too early and none of the other farmers would show anytime soon, he pulled over about a hundred yards short of the gates and sat there in his pickup, surrounded by silence. The morning was as quiet as any he'd ever seen. Finally, for the first time in twenty-four hours, he closed his eyes. He kept them closed until a loud noise startled him, and then, without pausing to consider what he was doing or why, he opened the door, climbed out and knelt by the side of the road.

In Wynoka, Minnesota, when Munson was growing up, a doctor bought the house next door. A small-town general practitioner, he was a friendly and responsive man who set broken bones, stitched up cuts and gashes, delivered a few hundred babies and otherwise attended to all his patients' needs. Always on call, he was frequently awakened at night and often had trouble getting back to sleep. And if he ran out of firewood in the middle of a sleepless night, he'd go outside and chop some—still unaccustomed to town life, having grown up on a farm out in the country. The first time he did it, Munson's mother leaped out of bed and crashed into the wall, certain that somebody had gone wild with a shotgun. The second time, she raised the window and screamed at him. He waited about half an hour, then began chopping again in a tentative, almost experimental way—a single lick here, two more licks there—as if coaxing the log to split apart.

The first bursts that issued from the tower reminded Munson of those halfhearted taps with the ax. Two or three rounds were followed a few seconds later by two or three more. Nothing for a moment, then a slightly longer burst.

By that time, most of the prisoners were facedown on the ground. A few men at the rear had broken ranks and run for shelter at the mess hall or the showers.

Munson froze, still waiting for Case to answer his question, but only until a long burst threw up dirt across the rec area; then he dived behind a galvanized garbage can at the corner of the latrine. A second later, the wind was knocked out of his lungs as someone—Case, it turned out—flopped down on top of him.

"Jesus Christ," the sergeant gasped. "That crazy bastard." Then his face began to change color, tending toward purple, but he said nothing more.

Munson only gradually realized that he'd locked his hands

around the man's throat. Letting go, he said, "Goddamn it, Case, who's up there?"

"Thark," he gurgled.

"You put *Stark* in the tower?"

Then a burst came from the opposite direction.

"Who's in the other one?"

Case pressed his face against the wall. "Brinley."

When one of the Germans hollered, Munson peeked out and saw two prisoners leap up and race toward the mess hall, immediately drawing fire from both sides of the compound. As the men hurled themselves inside, a window shattered, tin siding buckled and, a moment later, someone began moaning.

Munson tried to recall what he knew about the Thompson. It fired roughly six hundred rounds per minute, and the clips in the camp held fifty rounds apiece. A five-second burst would empty the clip. His best guess was that Stark had already fired thirty to forty rounds, Brinley no more than fifteen or twenty.

"How many clips did they draw this morning?"

Case gnawed his lip. "I don't know."

"What?"

"They just went in there and got whatever they wanted."

Munson shoved him in the chest. "You didn't sign the ammo out?"

"I never expected no trouble."

Brinley fired a long burst that emptied his clip, then Stark opened fire again. One second, Munson's ear said. Eight to ten rounds.

"Look at those Germans," Case said, shaking his head. "That's what I call *trained.*"

As indeed they were. Facedown in their perfectly formed ranks, they hugged the ground, motionless and silent, as though realizing that the quickest way to die was to force themselves upright.

Munson was awash in uncertainty that morning, but there were a few things he did know.

He knew, for instance, that no matter how long he remained in the army—and he'd stay until the war ended—his military career was finished. He knew that if by some chance, many years from now, he happened to spot one of the men he'd served with, in a train station or a bus depot, he would do his best to avoid contact, that if need be he'd hide in the washroom. He knew that from this moment forward, there would be things he could never tell his wife or daughter, and that if they asked about his experiences at Camp Loring, he'd change the subject. He knew, too, that many of his classmates at West Point, and no small number of officers, had marveled at his accuracy on the pistol range. More than once he'd emptied an entire clip of .45-caliber ammo right into a silhouette's midriff at a distance of twenty-five yards. Nobody could figure out how he'd acquired his skill, since his father had never owned a gun and he hadn't fired one himself until the day he stepped foot on the range.

"Captain?" Case said as Munson unsnapped the strap on the holster and withdrew his sidearm. "*Sir?*"

In the tower, Marty Stark stood straight and tall, as if for once in his life he meant to cooperate fully.

FORTY-FIVE

A GRAVEL ROAD bisected the cemetery. On the west side lay the graves of Loring's founders, as well as those of their sons and daughters and grandchildren and even a few great-grandchildren. The east side had been added some hundred years later, and over there, in a small plot across the ditch from the paste and glue factory, was Jimmy Del Timms.

Dan hadn't worn a hat, and his overcoat wasn't much use against the cold rain that blew in during the graveside service. He didn't see the point of watching them lower the box, so he turned and walked back to the pickup, leaving Shirley and Alvin to crowd in under the funeral parlor's tent, along with pretty much everybody else in town, including Marie Lindsey, whom he hadn't seen since the night he made her mad outside the snack bar.

He climbed into the truck and sat looking through the rain at his father's headstone. He'd been buried nine months ago. It had been raining then, too, another cold, damp day, but there hadn't been much of a crowd: just Shirley and Alvin, Ralph and Mrs. Hobgood and three or four other folks who'd kept liking Jimmy Del Timms even after he started acting funny.

Dan couldn't help but wonder who'd attend his funeral, if he got shot up and they found enough of his body to ship it home. He knew Lizzie would be there, if she hadn't left town yet, and Alvin and Shirley and Ralph. Something told him that Marie herself might show up, that she wasn't really mean, that in fact many of her flaws, if not all of them, were the result of being seventeen. A fair number of his own, he believed, resulted from the same affliction.

The crowd beneath the tent began to break up, the mourners straggling back toward their cars and trucks, making their way through the moss-covered markers, careful not to step on graves. Alvin hung back for a few minutes, standing off to one side with Jasper Sproles, who looked anxious to get indoors.

When Shirley opened the truck door, Dan jumped out and let her slide into the middle of the seat, then climbed back in beside her.

"Well, that's that," she said, pulling a handkerchief from her purse and blotting her face with it. "God, his poor mother."

Back at the church, Mrs. Stark had been wedged into a sitting position between Marty's father and one of his uncles. You could see that if she were left on her own, she'd just curl up and cry. Mr. Stark himself betrayed no emotion, but the uncle kept sniffling and rubbing his eyes.

The worst part of it, most folks agreed, was that the family might never know exactly what had happened. Marty's father had received a phone call from Camp Loring, asking him to meet a military escort at the funeral home. When he got there, some provost marshal nobody had ever seen before informed him his son had been killed, along with another guard and a prisoner. Several POWs had been wounded, too, and the whole event was "under investigation." The officer was curt, according to the funeral director. When Mr. Stark began to bluster that inside five minutes he'd have Senator Eastland on the phone, the provost told him that the army had already been in touch. Then he stood and walked out, followed by the MPs who'd delivered Marty's body.

To Dan, the curious thing was that a lot of the same people who said they felt so sorry for the Starks had begun to make up lies about Marty. Folks said he'd graduated from high school only by stealing exams from teachers' desks and that Mr. Stark had paid off the principal to keep the whole thing quiet. He used to drink before football games, they claimed, and without the alcohol, he didn't have the courage to take a lick. Somebody said that when he was a lifeguard at the swimming pool, he'd pulled a little girl's drawers down. It was as if, in order to believe in their own essential virtue, they needed for Marty to have been bad all along.

"Dan," Shirley said as they sat there in the pickup, "I don't want you to join the army. I've never come right out and said so before, but I don't want you to. That means somebody else's son will, and I know it's selfish to think like that, but I don't give a damn. I'll do anything you ask, give up anything that I already haven't, though I don't know what that could be. Just please, let's talk to Alvin and ask him to help us work something out."

Jasper Sproles had managed to get under the only tree left standing in that part of the cemetery, and he looked like he was cowering as Alvin stood gesturing with his hands, even pointing a finger right at Jasper's chest.

"That's not what he's over there talking to Mr. Sproles about, is it?"

Hard lines formed on her face, and for the first time he glimpsed the old woman she would become. "I don't know what they're talking about. These days, I know a lot less about Alvin's business than you probably think."

The picture in the living room had been on his mind lately, and he kept thinking about how the Polish prisoner had taken the two men for twins. He'd also been trying to recall a single instance in which Jimmy Del Timms had called him "son." It seemed now that he'd always used some version of his name—rarely Daniel, mostly Danno or Danny Boy—or else, when discussing him with others, he'd say, *That boy of mine.*

"Momma . . . I want to ask you something."

She clamped her knees around the gearshift, closing her hands over the knob. "Sounds like a question I may not want to answer."

"It may be one you can't answer."

"Then go ahead, and we'll see if I can."

It appeared that underneath the tree, Sproles was agreeing to whatever request had been made of him. Nodding his head vigorously, he held both hands up as if to fend Alvin off.

"Who's that man over there?" Dan asked.

"What?"

"That man under the tree, talking to Mr. Sproles. What word would you use to say what he is to me?"

At first, he thought she couldn't help but misunderstand the question, because he'd posed it so inelegantly. But he could tell, soon enough, that she knew exactly what he was asking.

"A minute ago, you called me *Momma*," she said, "and it's ridiculous how happy I was to hear it. I used to hate that word because it always seemed to rule out so much else. I didn't like *wife* or *momma* or *sister-in-law*. But when you said *Momma* just now, it didn't change a thing in the world about who I am or what I am. It was the *right* word, at the *right* moment, and that's the only thing that matters."

Alvin offered Sproles his hand, but instead, Jasper pulled his coat sleeve back and pointed at his watch.

"Well, the word for what *that man,* as you put it, is to you is the same one you've always used. The word for what he is, or was, to me probably exists in some language, but it's not a language I can speak. So I just call him by his name. That's the best I can do."

His chest felt constricted, like the time he'd come down with pleurisy, and for a moment he couldn't breathe.

"Now, since I answered your question," his mother said, "I'd like you to answer mine. Can we go ahead and do whatever we have to, to keep you out of the army?"

"I've got to go," he said. "But please don't ask me why, because that's something—right now—I just don't know."

FORTY-SIX

O N THE FRIDAY before Thanksgiving, Dan helped Alvin load eight five-gallon cans into the back of the pickup. His uncle pulled a paint-stained tarp out from under his porch and they spread it over the cans, then weighted the corners with bricks.

The cans contained refund gas, injected—Alvin warned him—with red dye so any law officer or Civil Defense agent could identify it as strictly for agricultural use. If anybody stopped him and looked at the cans, he should say he'd left Mississippi at a moment's notice to see his brother in the Great Lakes Naval Hospital, and that he hadn't had time to unload this gas he'd purchased for his uncle's farm. Carrying refund gas down the road in a pickup, Alvin said, wasn't a crime; short of dropping a string into the tank, nobody could tell he'd filled up with it, and he doubted they'd go to that trouble.

Dan himself wasn't so sure, and since Alvin had plenty of fuel coupons and had given him more than enough money to travel on, he asked why it wouldn't be easier to buy what gas he needed en route. But Alvin shook his head. "A dog that won't gnaw its bone," he said, "will one day wake up hungry."

Dan had brought a thermos of coffee from home, and he shoved it under the seat, along with a sack of sandwiches Shirley had fixed. Then Alvin handed him something that looked like a claw made of light metal.

"What the hell's that?"

"You use it to scrape your windshield. Fellow gave it to me when I went up to Ohio that time to get them old buses with your daddy. Careful with it, or you'll scar the glass to where you can't see a damn thing."

"Think we'll run into ice and snow?"

"Could be. It'll be cold's the only thing I can tell you for sure."

Dan got in and started the engine, letting it warm up. Rather than tip his hat and walk off into the store, Alvin waited by the truck until Dan finally nodded good-bye, then tapped on the window, motioning for him to roll down the glass.

With the two of them face-to-face, Dan noticed that his uncle's mustache was streaked with gray. Creases had formed around his eyes and mouth, and his neck was developing that pebbled texture you saw on older people. The tuft of chest hair poking out of his collar was almost white.

"If you get into a bind," Alvin told him, "call me. Tell me exactly where you are, and I'll come try to buy you out."

"And if that don't work?"

"Well," Alvin said, and now he did tip his hat, "then I reckon we'll be in the same place at least."

L.C. was waiting on Rosetta's porch, and it didn't look like he was taking much with him. His guitar, wrapped up in an old cottonseed sack, lay propped against a cardboard valise not much bigger than a hatbox. Tucked under one of his arms was a great big Bible.

"Rosetta ain't home?" Dan said.

"Gone down to the store."

"She know what you mean to do?"

"Your uncle come over and talked to her, then I did, then he come over and talked again. Then we give her a day off and start all over. Somewhere in the middle's where it got settled."

"Sounds like she put up a pretty good fight."

"Yeah, but she finally say it's better to freeze to death than get shot."

"Where you going, it's possible to do both."

"Where you liable to be going, too."

"I can't say you're wrong there," Dan said. "You ready to get on the road?"

"Let's hit it."

Dan picked up the valise, carried it over to the truck and slipped it underneath the tarp as L.C. shoved the big Bible and the guitar in beside it.

"When we hit the cold weather, won't that guitar crack?"

"That thing done already been cracked two, three times," L.C. said. "One night, I busted it over some nigger's head, then picked it up and glued the pieces back together. Seem like it sound better now."

Pulling onto the road, Dan glanced over to see if L.C.'d display any sadness at leaving a place he'd lived for nearly ten years, but he just leaned back, shut his eyes. And within a couple minutes, he was sleeping soundly.

———

Traffic lights halted them several times that morning, and the farther they got from Loring, the longer the looks they began to draw. In your home county, being seen in a pickup truck with a colored person was one thing; two or three counties away, though, it was another thing altogether. While waiting for a light to change in Tunica, Dan spotted a policeman sitting down the street in his cruiser, giving them the eye, but when they drove through the intersection, the cruiser didn't move.

Somewhere L.C. had a card stating that Lexington Charles Stevens had complied with the Selective Service Act, registering for conscription with the local draft board in Loring, Mississippi. If anybody confiscated the card and checked the number, it would prove to be bogus—and then, Alvin said, he was strictly on his own. Jasper Sproles would feign ignorance, while allowing that he did remember going to the office one morning and finding a window open, even though he was ninety-nine percent certain he'd latched it the previous evening.

In which case, Alvin observed, L.C. would be a thief as well as a draft evader, thus presenting somebody with an interesting dilemma: to send him to prison, where he could be worked to death, or to the war, where he could be shot to death? If it came to that, Alvin bet they'd opt for prison, since there was always a chance the war wouldn't kill him. But L.C. told him there was a third possibility—and knowing white folks, that was probably the one they'd choose. They'd send him overseas and, if he survived, ship him back home and put him in prison anyway, and then, right before they'd worked him to death, shoot him.

Alvin had laughed last night as he related this conversation to Dan and Shirley. Then he said he sure hoped L.C. could make a living playing music, since nobody would need to shoot him if he had a regular job. He'd simply die of boredom.

They crossed the river in Memphis, which L.C. apparently hadn't counted on. After he gazed at the murky water, a mile or more across and topped with whitecaps, he looked suspicious. "You sure you know the way?"

"I got a map right under the seat."

"Well, I don't," L.C. said, "but I seen one before, and look to me like Chicago's on the other side the river."

"Yeah, but look a little closer and you'll see there ain't no road that runs straight up the east bank." Once they rolled down off the bridge into Arkansas, he reached under the seat and handed the map to L.C. "I got the route marked. We'll cross the river again in St. Louis." He glanced over. "You ever heard tell of Reelfoot Lake?"

"Naw."

"Well, back in the last century, an earthquake made a great big hole and the Mississippi filled it in. History books say the river ran backwards for three straight days. That damn lake's still there, and it looks pretty wide. I reckon that's why you can't drive straight up."

"Aw," L.C. said, staring at the map, "I heard about *that* thing. What you say done it?"

"Earthquake. Seismic activity."

"That wasn't no seismic nothing."

"So what was it—evil spirits at work?"

"Naw, that ain't it, neither. For one thing, evil spirits don't work. They just lay around, don't run all over town hustling business. Business come to them sooner or later. But all this meanness going on lately, folks gutting theyselves like it's hog-killing time, spilling blood enough to fill up a lake its own self—what you think that's evidence of? Good spirits at work?"

If he didn't answer, Dan figured, L.C. would eventually shut his eyes and start humming, then make up some words to fit the moment. While that could be annoying, right then it was just fine, so he kept on driving. And sure enough, in a mile or two, L.C.'s foot began to pat the floorboard.

> *blood on the highway*
> *blood on the hillside too*
> *poor boy got to kill you*
> *what else he got to do*

Somewhere in northeast Arkansas, Dan pulled off the highway onto a gravel road, then parked behind a run-down country church. They ate lunch, took turns slipping off into the bushes, then refilled the tank. They left the empty cans behind, like Alvin had told them, when they drove off.

Night caught them twenty miles south of St. Louis, in a cold white mist that looked like it might turn to sleet or snow. Dan pulled onto the shoulder so they could finish the remaining sandwiches and the last few sips of coffee. His eyes were starting to burn, his legs were stiff and his back ached.

"Want me to drive some?" L.C. asked.

"You feel like it?"

"Might as well."

"Think you can handle St. Louis?"

"Good as as you can."

When Dan climbed out, the cold cut right through him,

and it was thrilling. He stood there for a moment or two, watching the cars and trucks go by, most of them traveling north. For all the time he'd spent behind the wheel of one vehicle or another, he'd never had the sense of actually *going* anyplace. But now the opportunity for movement was upon him. In a month or so, he'd be bound for basic, where he'd meet men from all over the country. After that, there was no telling where they might end up. In a year, he could be someplace in the Pacific that he didn't even know existed, or in Paris or even Berlin. He might see the town where his father had lain in prison, and find himself fighting over the same piece of ground.

None of that seemed daunting. It seemed more like a just reward for living these past months with a stiff upper lip, doing what needed to be done without complaining too much.

He walked around to the passenger side and climbed in; then L.C. pulled onto the road. As always, he drove too fast, but before long they found themselves behind a military convoy, which slowed him down considerably. He darted into the left lane, but the view ahead was not promising: a long line of jeeps, six-by-sixes, scout cars and tankers—traveling about twenty-five miles an hour—for as far as they could see.

"Shit," he said, pulling back in behind the last vehicle.

"Just be patient," Dan told him. "Chicago'll still be there in the morning." He leaned back, intending to sleep for five or ten minutes, then wake up and see St. Louis.

Instead, he opened his eyes to a landscape whose only buildings seemed to be grain elevators. Light snow was falling. A red light was flashing in the rearview mirror, and L.C. was saying, "Oh Jesus."

———

The Illinois deputy sheriff was short and smooth-faced, and you could tell, as soon as he reached L.C.'s door, that he was a serious and thoughtful man. No chaw of tobacco swelled his jaw. In his pocket he would carry no half pint bottle.

"Let me see your driver's license," he said.

L.C. reached into his coat for the license and handed it to him.

The deputy shined his flashlight on the card. "You're a long way from home. Mind telling me what brings you up our way?"

Dan leaned over so the deputy could see his face. "My brother's in a naval hospital," he said. "Momma sent me to see him." He gestured at L.C. "He . . . my friend here, he came along to help me drive."

"Must be a good friend," the deputy said pleasantly. "Glad to see they're making that kind of progress down south. Which naval hospital's your brother in?"

"That one up there at Great Lakes Naval Station."

"He's in good hands, then," the deputy said. "Now correct me if I'm wrong, but you young men are not actively engaged in any type of war-related activity at the moment, are you?"

"No sir."

"I didn't think so. It's your brother that's in war-related activity, right?"

"Yes sir."

"And he's in the hospital at Great Lakes."

"Yes sir."

The deputy still had L.C.'s license in his hand. He stepped back away from the pickup, shining his light at one of the front wheels. "The reason I asked about war-related activity is that I noticed—driving along behind you young men at a rate of speed far in excess of the posted limit—that the tires on this pickup look to be brand-new. And they are. To my eye, they look like first-grades, and I'm sure you know those are reserved for military use."

He grasped the handle on L.C.'s door and pulled it open. "Why don't both of you step out now and help me see what's underneath that tarp back there."

Dan climbed out, but L.C. sat there staring through the windshield. For a second, Dan wondered if he was planning to leap out and throw himself at the deputy, or just take off across the field. Instead, he finally swung his legs out from under the dashboard and walked carefully to the back of the truck. While the deputy shined his light in the bed, they removed the bricks and lifted off the tarp.

The deputy surveyed the items: the guitar, the suitcase, the Bible, the remaining gas cans. "Carrying some extra clothes to your brother?" he said.

"No sir," Dan said. "My friend just brought a change along for himself."

"In case he decided to stay up here with us?"

"No sir. He just thought maybe we'd have trouble with the truck and he'd have to work on it, and he can't stand being dirty."

The deputy flicked the beam at L.C. "That right?"

"Yes sir."

"Can't fault you for that," the deputy said, redirecting the beam. "And sure as hell can't fault you for traveling with the Good Book. Looks like one of you's musically inclined, as well. I like a good song."

He turned his attention to the gas cans, playing his light over the caps on each of them, instantly noticing the red stains. He leaned over, twisted off a cap, shined the beam at the opening and looked into the container. "That's refund gas," he said.

"Yes sir," Dan said. "Me and my uncle run a farm."

"I understand Mississippi's big farm country. This is, too. But around here, we've had a problem with people buying that refund gas and then filling their trucks and cars with it." He used the flashlight to gesture at L.C. "Step up front there if you will and raise the hood."

After L.C. did as he'd been told, the deputy leaned over the engine and screwed the nut off the carburetor, then removed the top and shined his light inside. "I'm deeply disappointed in you boys," he announced. "In addition to depriving the military of much-needed rubber, you're ensuring that somewhere a tractor's been idled."

Suddenly, the light was in Dan's eyes. The deputy trained the beam there forever, blinding him, making him want to throw his hands up in front of his face.

"You look like you're old enough to be in the army."

"I will be. In just a few weeks."

The deputy played the light over him inch by inch. "Let me see some identification."

Dan didn't know why he was shaking. It was cold, but no more so than it had been earlier. Fumbling, he pulled out his wallet, removed his driver's license and handed it to the deputy.

He held the card under the light. "Yes, I see you're about to turn eighteen. I'm sure you'll make a fine soldier." He handed Dan's card back but kept L.C.'s. "Of course, if the date on your friend's license is accurate, he's already eighteen." He swung the light around and shined it on L.C.'s face, just as he'd shined it on

Dan's. "I imagine you've got your selective service card with you?"

"Yes sir."

"I'd like to have a look at it."

Dan didn't know if L.C. could see him through the glare or not, but when he answered, he seemed to be speaking to Dan and not the deputy. "It's back yonder. In the truck bed. Tucked into my Bible."

While they were in Illinois, not Mississippi, all Dan's instincts told him that any deputy sheriff would take more satisfaction from shining his light in a colored person's face than in a white person's. He wouldn't choose to sacrifice that pleasure, even for safety's sake.

And indeed, when Dan said, "I'll get it," the deputy said, "You do that," and continued to direct the hot white beam on L.C., his back turned to the truck. He was still in that position when the brick struck his skull.

FORTY-SEVEN

TENTACLES OF GRAIN ELEVATORS, stockyards and feed mills reached out from Chicago's South Side. As Dan and L.C. got farther in, driving through midday snow flurries, a widening maze of overhead tracks blocked what little light there was. Brownstones rose up on either side of the street, the second-floor windows even with the tracks. Everything was stained with coal dust.

"What you aim to do up here?" Dan asked.

L.C. was watching people hurrying along the sidewalk with their heads down, most of them bundled up in scarves and gloves and heavy overcoats. "Try to get a job."

"What kind of job?"

"Whatever they is. Fellow I know over on the dago's place, he got a brother supposed to be here."

"You know his address?"

"Not yet."

Dan drove on, following Alvin's instructions. The tooth L.C. had broken for him the previous night was starting to ache a good bit, and his nose felt like it was broken, too. L.C. had gotten the better of the fight, though Dan had managed to reopen one of the cuts he'd suffered at the hands of Frank Holder.

They'd pulled the deputy back into his car so he wouldn't freeze to death. Then L.C. tied his wrists together with strips he'd cut off the tarp, and Dan drove the cruiser behind a corn-crib alongside the road. They stayed on backroads for thirty or forty miles, trying to put some distance between themselves and the event. And then, when Dan saw a secluded spot near an abandoned farmhouse, he swerved in, jumped out and ran around in front of the truck. He was about to open the passenger door when it kicked open on its own, and L.C. screamed, "Don't you even try it." Dan was already raising his fist, crying something about being turned into a common criminal by somebody too gutless to go fight like everybody else. L.C. quickly slipped aside and cracked him over the ear, and the next thing Dan knew, they were rolling across the frozen ground, spitting and kicking. At some point, he called L.C. a nigger, and L.C. called him one, too, and said he'd root for both the Germans and the Japs until he knew which ones they'd sent Dan to fight.

Long before they ran out of physical energy, they both were low on spirit. When they finally collapsed against the truck, each of them bloody and heaving, Dan said, "Well, goddamn it, L.C., I know it ain't easy being colored, but this is still the best place around."

"What—this fucking field we in?"

"This country. America."

"It might could be," L.C. said. "But I ain't gone say till I done seen all the others."

A few minutes later, they helped each other up, scooped up a little snow to wash off their faces and got back on the road. In the first good-sized town they came to, they stole an Illinois plate off a parked truck and slipped theirs under the seat. In the next town, Dan went into an all-night diner and ordered sandwiches and more coffee, L.C. waiting outside with the engine running.

Dan let him out on Fifty-fifth Street, in an area swarming with sailors. They emerged from restaurants and beer parlors, heading into a stiff wind that blew in off the lake, a fair number of them drunk, their arms thrown over one another's shoulders, some of them singing, a few looking like they could barely walk.

L.C. reached into the back of the truck, lifted out his guitar and suitcase, then stuck his head inside once more. "Don't matter what you do with that Bible," he said, "but don't let my momma know I ain't got it. And study that map and find you a different way back. Deputy woke up this morning with the blues *and* a headache, and that's a nasty combination."

He started to close the door then, already shivering in the ice-cold wind in his threadbare coat. Dan figured he'd never see him again. "L.C.?" he said.

The dark, impassive face finally broke into a grin. In that instant, Dan's mind formed an image, labeled it *L.C.* and filed it away.

"Just can't say it, huh?" L.C. said. "Me neither. Ain't that something. Done knowed one another ten years."

He shut the door and moved off into the crowd.

FORTY-EIGHT

HEADING SOUTH, he took a route through Indiana, reaching Indianapolis well after dark. He found a diner there and went in and sat down in a booth at the back. The waitress who took his order, a cute redhead who bore a certain resemblance to his mother, asked where he was from. When he told her, she smiled and said she thought so, that for Christmas last year she'd visited her sister out in Long Beach, California, where she'd gone out with a boy from Mississippi. He was a sailor, she told him, a tall, skinny guy who was just about to ship out, the worst dancer she'd ever seen, but a good sport. She couldn't remember his name, she admitted, but she did recall the name of the place he came from: Indianola. It had stuck with her, probably, because it was so similar to Indianapolis. Dan said he knew the town well, that he might even have played ball against her friend. That was something, she said a little later, when she brought him the bill. She'd met two different guys from a part of the country she'd never seen, and to think they might've been on the same football field just a few years before. He agreed it really was something—and laid a dollar tip on the table.

He got back in the truck and drove on awhile longer, then pulled onto a side road and slept for a couple hours before setting out again. The radio didn't pick up much in southern Indiana, but he didn't care. The little towns he passed through were fascinating. One of them, no more than five or six houses and a gas station that looked like it might be out of business, nevertheless displayed a huge sign near its lone intersection:

EXLEY, INDIANA
HOME OF THE 1913 INDIANA STATE
BASKETBALL CHAMPIONS

He wondered where those men were now in November 1943. There sure weren't enough houses for all of them. Some might be out in the countryside, farmers like their fathers before them, men in their mid- to late forties sleeping peacefully beside their wives, with sons and daughters Dan's age or even older. Some might have moved away, to nearby towns, to big cities like Indianapolis or Chicago, maybe even as far away as California. Most likely, some of them had fought in the First War. It was possible, too, that one or more had died a long way from home. But it gave him a warm feeling, as he drove south that night, headed back to his own hometown, where, in less than a year, he'd seen both his father and his best friend buried, to know that the people of Exley, Indiana, had not forgotten their champions.

Acknowledgments

During the writing of this novel, the following sources were invaluable: Stephen E. Ambrose, *Citizen Soldiers;* Carlo D'Este, *Bitter Victory;* Ladislas Farago, *Patton;* Paul Fussell, *Doing Battle;* Judith M. Gansberg, *Stalag U. S. A.;* Jeffery E. Geiger, *German Prisoners of War at Camp Cooke, California;* Victor Davis Hanson, *The Soul of Battle;* Marie M. Hemphill, *Fevers, Floods and Faith;* John Keegan, *The First World War* and *The Second World War;* David M. Kennedy, *Freedom from Fear;* Robert Kotlowicz, *Before Their Time;* Arnold Krammer, *Nazi Prisoners of War in America;* Colonel Reiner Kriebel and the U. S. Army Intelligence Service, *Inside the Afrika Korps,* edited by Bruce L. Gudmundsson; Harold P. Leinbaugh and John D. Campbell, *The Men of Company K;* David Maraniss, *When Pride Still Mattered;* George S. Patton, *War as I Knew It;* Hortense Powdermaker, *After Freedom;* Merrill R. Pritchett and William L. Shea, "The Afrika Korps in Arkansas," *The Arkansas Historical Quarterly,* vol. 37, no. 1; Ron Robin, *The Barbed Wire College;* Ben Shephard, *A War of Nerves;* Richard S. Warner, "Barbed Wire and Nazilagers: PW Camps in Oklahoma," *The Chronicles of Oklahoma,* vol. 64, no. 1; and Richard Wittingham, *Martial Justice.*

I would also like to thank the following people who provided support and guidance: Linnea Alexander, George Booker, David

Acknowledgments

Borofka, Luis Costa, Scott Ellsworth, David Engle, Lillian Faderman, Victor Hanson, Brad Huff, Phyllis Irwin, Paul Mousseau, Michael Ortiz, Trudy Pace, Amber Qureshi, Annette Trefzer, Dick Warner, Jack Wise and John Yarbrough.

Thanks to Patricia Henley for the drive through Indiana, to Sloan Harris for being the greatest agent alive, and to Ewa, Magda and Tosha for living all these years with a writer.

Lastly, special thanks to my friend and editor, Gary Fisketjon, an artist in his own right.

"Perceptive, finely wrought . . . captures post-Reconstruction Mississippi, caught between the promise of progress and a lament for the antebellum order." —Vogue

VISIBLE SPIRITS

In 1902, in a small community deep in the Mississippi Delta, nearly a generation after the end of slavery, events obscured by time but impossible to forgive or forget echo in the lives of blacks and whites alike. As bound together by history as they are separated by mutual distrust, the citizens of Loring face present tensions as they look toward an uncertain future.

Into this charged atmosphere rides Tandy Payne—prodigal son of a prominent planter, brother of the current mayor, and dissolute gambler—looking to reclaim the family estate. When he takes advantage of a perceived slight from the town's black postmistress, the ensuing clash with his principled brother results in a harrowing confrontation. Fueled by dark and brutal memories, their familial dispute quickly spreads through the countryside. Steve Yarbrough confronts character with morality and reason with blood in this moving novel that explores the farthest boundaries of human nature.

Fiction/0-375-72577-6